The Invaders

John Rowe Townsend

The Invaders

Oxford University Press

Oxford New York Melbourne

Oxford University Press, Walton Street, Oxford OX2 6DP
Oxford New York Toronto
Delhi Bombay Calcutta Madras Karachi
Petaling Jaya Singapore Hong Kong Tokyo
Nairobi Dar es Salaam Cape Town
Melbourne Auckland

and associated companies in
Berlin Ibadan

Oxford is a trade mark of Oxford University Press

Copyright © John Rowe Townsend 1992
First published 1992

ISBN 0 19 271681 6

A CIP catalogue record for this book is available
from the British Library

Printed in Great Britain

AUTHOR'S NOTE

This is a self-contained story. You do not need to have read another book before coming to it. All the same, it has a forerunner: a novel of mine called *The Islanders*, which has the same setting two generations earlier.

The geography of Halcyon resembles that of Tristan da Cunha, in the South Atlantic Ocean, but the people and events in both books are fictional.

J.R.T.

PEOPLE IN THE STORY

The islanders

Tilda Wilde, an island girl
Annie Wilde, Tilda's mother
George Wilde, Tilda's father
Molly Wilde, Tilda's grandmother
Robert Attwood, an island boy
May Attwood, Robert's mother
Polly Attwood, Robert's small sister
Old Noah and **Old Ted Attwood,** Robert's great-uncles
Adam Goodall, the Reader, or head man
Ellen Goodall, Adam's wife
Alice and Ben Jonas, an island couple
Jamie Campbell, an unmarried islander
Tom Reeves, another single man
Sophy Kane, an island girl
Old Isaac Reeves, who plays the fiddle

and also (island families)
Johnny, Lizzie and Nancy Oakes; Dick, Marge and Colin Kane;
Jack and Bella Reeves, with Lucy and four younger children.

The incomer

Cyril Jonas, from the Mainland.

The colonists

Brigadier H. J. W. Culpepper, the Commissioner
Daphne Culpepper, his wife
Sonia Culpepper, his daughter
Philip Saunders, the Civil Administrator
Lieutenant Peter Willett, engineer officer
Lieutenant Andrew Rawson, radio officer
Sergeant Herbert Young, the senior N.C.O.
Corporal Reg Wainwright, storekeeper
Private Gerry Baines, wireless mechanic

The Santa Cruzians

Major-General Rodriguez, appointed as Governor
Captain Esteban Montero-Garcia, his aide-de-camp
Sergeant Jimenez, liaison with the islanders
Corporals Felipe Lopez and **Emilio Santos**
Privates Lorenzo Juarez and **Ramon Ortega.**

First Wave

*T*HE *island is a tiny dot in a vast expanse of ocean. Its name is Halcyon. It is the tip of a volcanic mountain, rooted in the sea-bed far below and breaking the surface to rise to a sharp, cloud-circled peak. For centuries the volcano was dormant, though sometimes it stirred in its sleep.*

The island is steeply sloped; but at one edge of it is a level shelf of grassy land, and on this strip is a village, the home of a hundred hardy souls. They are the descendants of shipwrecked sailors, of refugees from lands that have come to grief, or of wanderers who sought to leave the world behind them.

Until a few years ago, Halcyon had no harbour; the islanders launched their patched and mended boats from the beaches and rowed them out through boiling surf between black vicious rocks to fish in the stormy seas around. They raised sheep, and planted potatoes, and ate sea birds and their eggs. Women and men alike were tough and resourceful; children knew more of work than of play. The islanders survived. A few of them learned to read.

Far away there was a Mother Country, to which the islanders were loyal. They spoke its language. But they did not think about it much, and it did not think about them. The age of steam had made Halcyon more remote than ever, as the sailing ships that once called for water were driven from the seas and the shipping routes passed the island by.

There was one link with the world outside. Three or four times a year, at erratic intervals, the battered coaster Amanda *lay at anchor off Halcyon for a few hours and, when the weather allowed, bartered tea and tobacco and old clothes and hardware for freshly-killed lamb and newly-caught fish. Now and again, not often,* Amanda *carried a passenger to Halcyon; and one day a passenger landed with something new to the islanders: a radio, or, as it was then called, a wireless set. Suddenly the outside world could be heard talking; and what it said did not bode well for Halcyon. Though the islanders did not know it, their peace and isolation were almost at an end.*

Chapter 1

THE day Robert Attwood took his oar and became a
man was the day the *Amanda* landed Cyril Jonas on
Halcyon. Tilda Wilde and her mother Annie saw it happen.
Coming home from the potato patch, they passed close by
the Lookout, a high point above the village from which the
bay came into view. And there lay *Amanda*, rusty and
shabby, tossing at anchor in the Halcyon swell, with thin
strands of smoke torn by the wind from her funnel and
shredded across the sky.

Huddled together against the wind, and stamping their
feet with cold, Annie and Tilda stood for a while to watch.
Far below them, they could see on the beach the little
figures of the men as they launched the boats. Two of the
crews were going out. Robert was in the first boat. The
men manhandled it into the water, pushed it off and leaped
aboard, then took up oars and pointed the bow into the
breakers. As it hit the first wave, the boat bucked. A rush
of flying spray hid it for a moment; then it was heading out
in the lull between waves, its six oars moving in expert
unison. Another breaker rolled in, and then another; the
boat rose high upon each of them in turn and was thrown
briefly backward before the thrust of oars urged it forward
again. Twenty yards to its lee was a sharp black rock that
would hole it at once if wind and current swept it out of
control.

It was a rough day. If *Amanda* hadn't come, the boats
would not have put to sea. But it was weeks since the
steamer's last appearance, and would be weeks before her
next. And Captain Fisher was an impatient man; he
wouldn't hang around for the weather to improve. If the
island boats didn't go out, he'd be on his way. So they were
taking the risk. Risk was a way of life on Halcyon.

It was an anxious moment for watchers. But neither boat hit the rock. When they were past the surf the worst of the danger was over, and Annie and Tilda could relax.

'Not the day I'd choose for a lad to take his oar,' said Annie. 'But there was nothing else for it, was there, with his Great-uncle Ted getting feeble? It was high time old Ted gave up. The young ones need to have their chance. And *Shearwater*'s the best boat.'

'Robert's rowed in it before,' said Tilda. 'More than once.'

'That's true. But it wasn't his oar then, it was Ted's. Makes all the difference.' She turned to her daughter. 'Robert's come of age, Tilly. It's a great day.'

Tilda said nothing.

'I remember when your dad took his oar,' said Annie. 'Proud as Punch, he was. It was like he'd grown six inches overnight. "I'm a man now, Annie," he says. "We'll start building a house. Then we can get wed." And he gave me such a look, I've never forgot.'

'I know, I know,' said Tilda.

'And he wasn't no older than Robert, not to speak of. A few months, maybe. Nearly eighteen. And within a year of him taking his oar . . . '

'You was married,' said Tilda.

'And never regretted it. Your dad's a good man.'

Tilda was silent again. She knew her dad was a good man. But there was nothing to say about it.

'Your Robert's a fine lad, too.'

'He's not *my* Robert,' said Tilda.

'Not yet, but he will be.'

'So you say.'

'You *know* he will. Your dad worked it out with Robert's dad before he died. Twenty sheep from our side, and the half-acre plot at West End their side, and with Robert taking his oar you'll be well away. And we got enough wood between us for a house. We could start building any time.'

'I'm not in a hurry,' said Tilda. 'Nor is Robert's mum.'

'I know. Very attached to that boy, May Attwood is, specially since she lost her husband. She'd rather keep Robert at home. But there, life goes on. And it's not up to us women, is it? We got to make the best of it, and if you get a good man you're in luck. Your dad wouldn't let you go to a bad 'un, Tilly, you know he wouldn't.'

She looked up affectionately at Tilda, who was taller than she was. Annie was a little thin woman with faded fair hair. Tilda took after her father's side of the family, especially her Grandma Molly. She was strong and solid and brown-skinned, not pretty but handsome, with thick dark hair and a big nose and mouth.

'And your dad'll let you take your time,' Annie said. 'You needn't wed Robert till you're ready. But best not wait too long. Sixteen, and well grown—you're a woman, Tilda, and you may as well get used to it.'

Tilda was tired of talking about Robert. She'd known for three years past that she was intended for him. He was a decent enough lad, and she didn't really mind having to marry him. But it wasn't an exciting thought. She changed the subject.

'*Petrel*'s out there, too,' she said.

'Yes. Both boats'll be needed, I reckon. And in spite of the weather, it's good luck that *Amanda*'s here the day Robert celebrates his oar. I been looking forward to the party tomorrow, haven't you? There'll be tea and cakes, for sure. And jam, and biscuits too, I shouldn't wonder. And dancing for the young ones. If I know May Attwood, she'll give a slap-up do for that lad.'

The first boat had reached *Amanda*'s side by now, and a rope ladder had been let down to it. Someone was climbing up. At this distance, Tilda couldn't really see who it was, but she knew it would be Adam Goodall. Adam was the island's head man, known as the Reader because in former times the head man had been in charge of the island's guide to conduct, the Book. Adam was twenty-four, and some thought him too young to be Reader—'not much more than a lad'—but he was thoughtful and steady. He'd been chosen as Reader in succession to his grandfather, another Adam Goodall, who'd been Reader for fifty years and a much-revered figure. It was the Reader's right and duty to go on board first.

Another figure followed up the ladder, and another and another. The second boat reached *Amanda*, and the process was repeated. Both boats bobbed up and down against the ship's side. For a while nothing more could be seen.

'They'll be bargaining,' said Annie. 'And signing papers and all that.' Her mind was still on the party. 'We'll get chocolate biscuits, maybe,' she said. 'And tinned fruit, too, I dare say. Makes your mouth water to think about it.'

Ropes were let down, and baskets and boxes hauled from the boats to *Amanda*'s decks. Then, after a pause, the goods for Halcyon were lowered from the ship. There were packing-cases and boxes and mysterious bulky parcels; then what looked like the mailbag. Finally, the crew members clambered back down the ladder and settled themselves in the boats, which were visibly lower in the water. The last person to descend seemed slow and hesitant.

'Let's go down and watch them land,' said Tilda. And, a moment later, '*How* many was there in *Shearwater*?'

'Six, same as usual. A full crew.'

'Well, there's seven now.'

'You sure, Tilda?'

''Course I'm sure. I can count, can't I?'

'Well, your eyes is sharper than mine. But fancy that! Maybe it's Cap'n Fisher, coming ashore for once.'

'He won't come ashore a day like this. I reckon we got a visitor, Mum. We got a visitor!'

Tilda was excited. It was a long time since there'd last been a visitor. Anyone arriving on Halcyon had to stay at the least until *Amanda* next came. No one could tell for sure when that might be. And Halcyon had no such thing as a hotel.

Tilda was hurrying away down the hillside. Annie

6

followed her into the village. People were pouring from their cottages and down the track to the beach.

The boats came in fast, for speed was safest. *Petrel* was first, catching a great wave and shooting in with a rush to ground on the beach. Men leaped out to drag the boat ashore, helped by any villagers within reach. Everyone got wet, but everyone was used to that. Then, a couple of minutes later, came *Shearwater*. And all eyes were on the stranger it carried; even the folk who'd already begun unloading the other boat stopped to stare.

The new arrival was a youth, about the age of Tilda and Robert. He wore a navy-blue suit. No islander had a suit. He was thin, dark-haired, pale-faced; his face at the moment a greenish-white. He stood, uncertain and apprehensive, in the middle of the boat from which the crew had already jumped.

Adam Goodall, already ashore, called to one of the men dragging the boat in, 'Give him a lift, Johnny.' And, piggy-backed on an islander's broad shoulders, the incomer was delivered, to stand, shaky and dizzy, on the Halcyon beach.

Adam shook his hand heartily and said, 'Welcome to Halcyon.' And, turning to the still-staring villagers, 'This is Cyril. He's come from the Mainland Colony. But he's one of us. Cyril Jonas.'

Cyril stood in the midst of a ring of people, a couple of large suitcases and a wooden box beside him. Among the sturdy island folk—the men in great woollen sweaters or sheepskin jackets, the women in thick heavy clothing down to their ankles—he looked slight and spindly. His face was narrow but with the promise of good looks; his eyes greenish, his sleek dark hair combed straight back from his forehead and lying flat in spite of the wind. On his upper lip were the straggly beginnings of a moustache.

Islanders had no need for social graces in their daily lives, and the people who'd gathered around didn't restrain their curiosity. They stared. Cyril's eyes moved warily round the group, then returned to Adam's. He shivered.

Adam took off his jacket and put it round the boy's shoulders.

'Tell them why you're here, lad,' he said. 'If you're not feeling too seasick.'

'I'm all right now,' said Cyril. He groped for a comb and ran it through the shiny hair. 'It's my uncle and auntie. I've lived with them since my mum and dad were killed. They're getting divorced now. They don't want me, neither of them.' He added wryly, 'I didn't *ask* to come here. They sent me back. They said I could live with my dad's cousin Ben and his wife.' He spoke the same language as the islanders, but not in the same way.

'Talks funny, doesn't he?' whispered Annie into Tilda's ear.

'That's the Mainland accent,' said Jamie Campbell, standing beside them.

Red-haired Jamie was one of the few islanders who had travelled abroad. He had been a seaman for five years and had also lived in the Mother Country's colony on the mainland, fifteen hundred miles away. Now nearly thirty, he was regarded as Halcyon's chief authority on the outside world. Some thought he should have been Reader instead of Adam. Jamie thought so himself. He was a strong and combative personality, a single man who lived at present with the Oakes family but was building a cottage for himself with his own hands. When it was finished, it was supposed he'd be looking for a wife.

Cyril's words had been blown away on the wind, and only those nearest to him had been able to hear. Islanders asked other islanders what he'd said. Then a buzz of talk broke out. Somebody asked, 'Who *was* your mum and dad?' Somebody else said, 'And your grandad and grandma?'

Pushing angrily to the front, Alice Jonas, bony and middle-aged, said, 'Ben and me never heard from no mainland Jonases.' She didn't sound friendly.

'If he's a Jonas . . . ' somebody began, 'it'll be *up* to the Jonases . . . '

'I'm not taking anyone in,' declared Alice, 'till I know more about them. And Ben'll say the same. We've only this lad's word for it. He might not be a Jonas at all.'

Adam said, 'We're not going to look into such matters here. There'll have to be a Meeting. Tonight, after supper, every adult on the island. That includes you, young Robert, now you're of age. You'll all hear the bell. I'll see you in the Meeting-House. Meanwhile, this lad goes home with me. Come on, Cyril. Dick, will you and Johnny give us a hand with his gear?'

Cyril stood uncertainly by as Dick Kane picked up the suitcases.

'*And* the box,' said Adam to Johnny Oakes.

'Hold on!' said Cyril, suddenly animated. 'Careful how you handle that! It's my set!'

'Your *what*?' said Johnny.

'My set. My wireless set.'

Jamie Campbell laughed.

'A wireless set! He's brought a wireless set!'

The other two men looked baffled.

'You know what a wireless set is, don't you?' Jamie asked.

'Plays music and that, doesn't it?' said Johnny. He didn't sound too sure. 'Like a gramophone, but . . . well, different.'

'Brings you stuff from a long way off,' said Dick. 'And not just music. Talking, too. I had a letter last year from my cousin Elsie on the mainland, saying they'd got one. Cost a lot of money.'

Jamie turned to Cyril. 'That's Halcyon for you,' he said. 'Way behind the times. But . . . ' And he burst out laughing again.

'What's so funny about it?' Cyril demanded.

'Well, a wireless set's no use to you here, laddie. For a start, we've no electricity.'

'They told me that before I came,' said Cyril. 'But I brought batteries. And Captain Fisher'll bring me more next time the ship comes. I can manage.'

Jamie still had a grin on his face. Cyril was irritated.

'I can't see the joke!' he said.

'You will, laddie, you will. When I came back here myself, I brought a wireless. It's in the outhouse now. Useless, unless you like listening to hisses and crackles. You can forget about programmes. We're fifteen hundred miles from a transmitter here. Your set won't pick up anything, unless maybe a ship.'

Cyril was angry now. A flush showed in his pale cheeks.

'A lot *you* know about it!' he said. 'This is a *real* set! Six-valve short-wave, made by an expert. Fifteen hundred miles is nothing to it.'

'Don't upset the lad, Jamie,' said Adam. 'Everything'll be strange to him.' And, to Cyril, 'You'll be hungry, I dare say. Come and meet Ellen—that's my wife—and have some food!'

'I'll take the set with me, if you don't mind!' said Cyril, still cross. He picked up the heavy box with some difficulty and followed Adam, clutching it to his chest.

'Attached to your set, Cyril, aren't you?' said Adam, dropping back to walk beside him.

'Yes, I am!' said Cyril. 'It's a pal to me. It's company. Has been for a long time. My uncle and auntie never did want me, really.' He looked around him at the bare, windswept landscape. 'This must be the last place God made.'

'We'll sort something out for you,' Adam said, reassuringly. 'And you'll get to like Halcyon, I promise you. *We* all do. I've lived here all my life, and never wished to be anywhere else.'

'Well, if you've never *known* anywhere else . . . ' Cyril said.

Cyril had been labouring under the weight of the box. Adam said nothing, but took it from him and strode effortlessly ahead. Cyril panted behind.

Back on the beach, more people had arrived. Groups of

islanders, usually taciturn, were talkative now. They were all discussing family relationships. If you went far enough back, you would find that most people on the island were related to most others. Second, third, fourth and fifth cousins abounded. Just now, everyone was concerned with the Jonases.

Alice Jonas was at the centre of it all. She and her husband Ben were the only remaining bearers of that surname.

'But that don't mean it's us that have to have this lad!' she insisted. 'It's not fair. We never even knew he existed.'

'Listen to me, Alice!' said Lizzie Oakes. 'If children gets orphaned—and it does happen, we all know it happens, with men lost in storms and women in childbed—their nearest kin has to take them in. That's how it's always been on Halcyon. Always has been and always will be.'

'But never folks that no one knows about,' Alice said. 'Strangers. *Incomers*! And no warning to anyone that this lad was coming! For all we know, he's an impostor. Only pretending.'

'Why should anyone pretend they're a Jonas, Alice?' asked Jamie Campbell sweetly. '*I* don't want to be a Jonas.'

Annie Wilde said peaceably, 'It's a matter for the Reader. Adam'll decide who's responsible, and if they need help they'll get it. He'll be talking to the boy now, finding out who's who and what's what. We can trust Adam. Now let's all go home to dinner.'

Robert had been helping other crew members to unload *Shearwater*, then drag it up the beach and turn it over. Now he came up to Annie and Tilda. He was a well-built lad, exactly Tilda's height, with round boyish face and cropped brown hair, which his mother cut from time to time with her kitchen scissors. Sometimes it seemed to Tilda he was years younger than she was, though if you went by the calendar he was six months older. He was peaceable, good with his hands and helpful; and though his mother May embarrassed him by treating him as still a child, he was patient with her and never made a disloyal remark. Yes, thought Tilda, he was a good lad and would be a good man, like her father. And yet . . .

Today Robert was pleased with himself, as he was entitled to be.

'I did all right, didn't I?' he said. 'It was real rough, you know, the sea. Not a day for beginners. *Petrel* had a bad time—just missed Sowbite Rock, coming back. But *we* was fine, no worries at all. Adam said I handled my oar well, and Adam don't throw praise around.'

'Three cheers!' said Tilda ironically; and then, when Robert looked hurt, she was sorry. She hadn't meant to put him down, but she'd found herself doing it. That happened rather often.

'Tilda!' said Annie sharply. 'You should *respect* Robert, now he's a man!' And, to Robert, 'Take no notice of her. She's like that sometimes. Uppish. I think she wishes she could go in the boats herself!'

'I do, too!' said Tilda.

'Well, you can put such ideas out of your head,' her mother told her.

On Halcyon, women's work was well defined. Women looked after the house and children, spun and knitted the wool from the island sheep, and worked on the vegetable patches. They didn't go in the boats.

Robert, intending loyalty to Tilda, said, 'She don't mean it, Mrs Wilde.'

'I do,' said Tilda.

Robert looked at her uncertainly and decided to let the matter drop.

'You're coming to dinner with us, Robert,' said Annie. 'I fixed it with your mum. She has her hands full, getting ready for the party.'

'You didn't tell *me* about that,' said Tilda.

'I thought it'd be a nice surprise for you,' said Annie.

'Oh.'

They'd been plodding up the track from the beach, and were now in the village. The houses were close together on the grassy plain, below the mountainside. They were single dwellings of one storey, long and narrow, their roofs thatched with tussock grass and held down by heavy stones against the Halcyon gales. They lay like a fleet at anchor, their gable ends pointing into the prevailing wind.

Inside, Annie and Tilda's house was dark and warm. A good fire gave enough light to see by; the lamp would not be lit until nightfall, for oil was precious. George Wilde—Annie's husband and Tilda's father—sat in one of the two rickety chairs, and his mother, Grandma Molly, in the other. George hadn't been on the beach to see the boats come in; he'd been at the other side of the island, gathering driftwood and bringing it home in the handcart. Grandma Molly lived in a house of her own, but often came to sit or have meals with George and Annie.

George, who was carving a picture on a piece of whalebone, nodded at Robert, but didn't say anything to anyone. He was a stolid, quiet man who only spoke when he had something to say; and this wasn't often. Molly—a vigorous old woman with a weatherworn, humorous face and the reputation of being eccentric—was more of a talker, but on this occasion she didn't get a chance. Annie was still excited over the arrival of *Amanda* and above all about Cyril. Dishing out stew from the big pot that waited on the fire, she described him in detail and went on to the question of his relationship with Alice and Ben, the island's surviving Jonases.

'They got no children of their own,' she concluded. 'You'd think they might like having someone to cheer them up, and look after them in their old age.'

'Maybe he won't fancy living with them,' observed Tilda. '*I* wouldn't.'

George had been quietly gearing up to speak. Now he made what was for him a speech. Everyone listened respectfully to the man of the house.

'Taking in a nearly grown lad,' he pronounced, 'ain't the same as bringing up a baby. There's risk in it.'

'That's true,' said Annie.

Grandma Molly had been spooning up her stew and

giving no sign that she was listening. Now she spoke, sharply and decisively.

'There's some risks,' she said, 'that have to be took. And if an island lad's come back to Halcyon, somebody's got to take him in. And if nobody else'll do it, I will.'

George was startled into further speech.

'Don't be daft, Mother,' he said. 'It's none of your business. You're not a Jonas. And you're not taking anyone in.'

'Don't you tell *me* what I'm doing and not doing!' said Molly.

'But you haven't even *seen* the lad. You might not like the look of him,' said Annie.

'And you're an old woman,' said George. 'Seventy! You may be all right now, but you'll be getting feeble soon. By the time the lad grows up you'll be dead.'

'Then he won't be burdened with me!' said Molly triumphantly. 'But as for getting feeble, my dad lasted till nearly ninety and never used a stick. I got years in me yet!'

'Headstrong. She always was headstrong,' said George to Annie. 'There's times in my life I've been ashamed to call her Mother.'

'Wait and see what happens at the Meeting,' suggested Annie peaceably; and George and Molly fell silent. Tilda and Robert finished their stew and Annie handed each of them a wizened apple, saved from last year's scanty crop. Now, at winter's end, it was a treat.

'Why don't you two go out a walk together?' she said. 'Talking's not much fun for young folk.'

'You mean you want to talk without us hearing,' said Tilda. 'You'll be arguing with Grandma, won't you? But it won't do no good. She don't take notice of nobody, do you, Grandma?'

'You mind your manners, young woman,' said Annie.

'Tilda's her grandma's girl,' said George. 'That's where she gets her stubbornness from. And, just a minute, Robert, you took your oar today, didn't you?'

'Yes, Mr Wilde.'

'Not "Mr Wilde". Now you're a man you call me George.'

Robert blushed with pleasure.

'And you can take Tilda down the Dell,' George added.

The Dell was a sheltered spot in which a few stunted fruit trees grew; and it was the place where courting couples went. Not that anything unseemly ever happened there. Halcyon morals were strict; and if the moral code was occasionally breached, such breaches didn't take place in the Dell. Walking out in the Dell was a recognized stage on the road to marriage.

Robert blushed again.

'Thank you . . . George,' he said.

'I ain't sure I want to go down the Dell,' said Tilda.

'You heard what your dad said,' Annie told her. 'You go down the Dell with Robert. And don't worry, Robert will behave himself, won't you, Robert?'

'Yes, Mrs Wilde . . . Annie.' Robert blushed once more.

Tilda was still reluctant.

'Go on,' said Grandma Molly to Tilda. 'Give the lad a chance. You're only young once. Be good. But not *too* good.'

'*Mother!*' protested both Tilda's parents, scandalized.

When you were in the Dell you were out of the wind, but you could still hear it, along with the roar of the breakers and the cries of the endlessly wheeling sea birds. You had to speak loudly to make yourself heard. Tilda wasn't in conversational mood, and when Robert took her hand she disengaged herself. Robert was nervously silent for some time; then he said, close to her ear, 'Tilda, you heard what your dad said. I'm a man now.'

'I know. I been told it a dozen times today.'

Robert was silent for a few minutes longer. He took her hand again and held it firmly so that she couldn't get it away without a struggle. Leaning towards her, he said with nervous boldness, 'I ain't never kissed you yet.'

15

'No, you ain't,' Tilda agreed.

'And we're intended for each other, aren't we?'

'I suppose so.'

'Well, don't you think we ought to?'

'Why?'

'Well, couples that's intended for each other *do*. I mean, they're *expected* to.'

'I can't see that it's anybody else's business. Anyway, *who* expects them?'

'I bet your grandma does,' said Robert.

Robert said this without thinking. His was not a cunning nature, but if it had been he couldn't have made a better-judged remark. Tilda had more regard for her Grandma Molly than for anyone else on Halcyon. She considered the matter carefully and decided that Molly would have expected just that. Molly's own younger days were rumoured to have been—by Halcyon standards—colourful.

'All right,' she agreed.

Confronted with her assent, Robert seemed uncertain what to do. He put his arms round Tilda, enclosing her body and a good deal of clothing. Not being comfortable, he adjusted his grip, twice. His face approached hers and encountered an obstacle, in the form of her nose. He withdrew and carried out a sideways adjustment. Contact was made. Tilda's mouth was firmly closed. Robert pursed his lips and administered a brief, wind-dried kiss. He drew back an inch or two, still holding Tilda to him. He didn't quite know what sensation he'd expected, but felt it should be more than this. He tried again, keeping his mouth on hers for twenty seconds or so.

'Have you finished?' she asked when he took it away.

'I reckon so.'

'Let me go, then. I'm getting chilly, standing here.'

Robert released her. They walked on. After some initial disappointment Robert began to feel pleased with himself again. It was a day of triumph. He had taken his oar and acquitted himself well. He'd been given permission to call George Wilde by his first name and to take Tilda down the

Dell. He'd kissed her and she hadn't objected. Sometimes in the past he'd wondered whether Tilda really accepted him, but this put the seal on it. Unconsciously he swaggered a little. A further idea struck him.

'Let's wrestle,' he suggested.

Wrestling was an accepted form of courtship on Halcyon. In a climate that, for most of the year, made sitting or lying side by side in the open air impossible, it was a way of keeping warm and making physical contact at the same time. It could be varied according to your degree of intimacy. Boys and girls wrestled together, fiercely or amiably or sometimes laughingly. You could convey quite a lot by wrestling that you couldn't put into words.

Tilda didn't mind. Robert had more muscle, but she was quicker on her feet and strong enough to put up a fight. They swayed back and forth, Robert trying to throw her on her back and so claim victory. But he couldn't quite make it. They heeled over together and struggled on the ground: pressed against each other, front to front, and without the self-consciousness of the kiss.

Tilda became aware of the hardness of Robert's body; maybe he *was* a man, not merely the awkward boy she'd known for so long. An unexpected physical warmth ran through her. For a moment she yearned towards him; felt a surge of attraction. She pulled his face to hers and kissed him decisively, finding as she did so that she knew how to do it. It was a different experience from that of a few minutes before.

They drew apart, both a little shaken, and got slowly to their feet. Tilda said, 'You didn't throw me, you know.'

Robert said, 'I could have done.'

They went on their way. Tilda's feelings returned to normal. She didn't know what had come over her. She was rather ashamed of herself. A Halcyon girl wasn't supposed to be as forward as that. But she was intended for Robert; she couldn't deny it now. When he took her hand again, she didn't draw it away.

Chapter 2

*T*HE Calling Bell, rung vigorously by young Joe Goodall, sounded through the village. It was the original ship's bell from the sailing ship *Delivery*, in which the founding fathers of Halcyon had come to the island a hundred and fifty years earlier. Now it hung outside the Meeting-House and called the islanders to their weekly Prayer Day service, as well as announcing from time to time a meeting at which some important matter was to be discussed.

Today the matter for decision was what was to be done about Cyril Jonas. News was a scarce commodity on Halcyon, and by now Cyril's arrival had been discussed in every house in the village. Aged uncles and aunts who remembered three and more generations back came into their own, as island traditions and relationships were analysed. Several old people who claimed to be too infirm to attend the Prayer Day services had managed to hobble to the Meeting-House for this occasion.

Robert, taking his place among the adults for the first time, sat modestly on one of the upturned boxes at the back. The more senior islanders sat on crowded benches in front. Excitement was running high when Adam Goodall arrived with his small, neat wife Ellen and with Cyril. Adam stood at the lectern with Cyril beside him. Cyril was still wearing the suit and the city shoes, and had combed his hair immaculately back from his forehead. His face seemed uncannily white. To the islanders he was an exotic sight.

'You all know why we're here,' Adam began. 'We have with us a member of a fine old Halcyon family, the Jonases, dating right back to the first settlement of the island. Some of you old stagers will remember William Jonas, who was the Reader before my grandfather. We haven't had the pleasure of knowing Cyril until now, but here on Halcyon we are loyal to our own, and I want you to greet him with a real warm welcome.'

Adam began to clap, and the islanders applauded with him, though Alice Jonas notably didn't take part and her husband Ben, having joined in hesitantly at first, caught her eye and stopped.

'Now, Cyril, maybe you'd like to say a word,' said Adam.

'Hullo,' said Cyril. He seemed inclined to leave it at that, but when Adam looked at him expectantly he continued, 'Thank you very much.' And, after further hesitation, 'It's nice to be here . . . I suppose.'

'It's not quite what you expected, I know,' Adam said.

Cyril grimaced.

'My auntie talked as if it was one of those island paradises you see in the travel advertisements,' he said. 'You know, blue skies and golden sands and palm trees and all that. But this . . . '

Adam said, rather rapidly, 'I've told you, you'll like it when you get used to it.' Then, addressing the islanders at large, 'What we have to decide, together with Cyril himself, is who he's going to live with.'

'If he's a Jonas, he lives with the Jonases,' said somebody instantly.

Alice Jonas stood up and began angrily, 'Who says . . . ?'

Adam hushed her.

'First thing we have to do,' he said, 'is establish just what the relationship is. And I must begin by telling you I've seen Cyril's birth certificate and other documents, and there's no doubt about it, he's the son of Samuel Jonas, who lived in the Mainland Colony and died three years ago.'

'That's my cousin Sam,' said Ben Jonas.

'No so fast!' said his wife, digging him in the ribs. 'Don't admit anything!'

'It ain't no secret!' said Ben, braving her wrath in the interest of accuracy. 'My Uncle Alf went off to the Mainland as a young feller and never came back. But I heard years later that he'd got wed and had a son called Sam. There couldn't be two of them, could there? This lad must be *Sam's* lad.'

'That's right,' said Cyril. 'My grandad was called Alfred. Alf Jonas. Nice old chap he was.'

'I never knew none of 'em,' said Alice Jonas sourly. 'Didn't know I was marrying a man with *relations*.'

'We all have relations,' said Adam mildly. Then, to old Noah Attwood, 'Maybe you could give us the rest of the picture.'

Noah, who was believed to be nearly ninety, couldn't read or write, but prided himself on his detailed grasp of island genealogies. He stepped to the front, happy to be in the limelight.

''Course I can,' he declared. 'Alf Jonas was Wilf Jonas's brother, and they was both of them nephews to old William Jonas, that was Reader before Adam's grandad.' He paused, then finished triumphantly, 'It's as plain as a pikestaff! Young Cyril here is a first cousin once removed to Ben!'

Alice Jonas looked as if she'd have liked to contest this finding, but Ben was nodding agreement.

'First cousin once removed, that's it,' he said. 'I'm his nearest relative, no doubt about it.'

'Maybe *you* are, but *I'm* not!' proclaimed Alice. '*I* don't want no lads his age forced on to me at my time of life! And anyone what goes off to the mainland and don't come back stops being an islander. Stands to reason, don't it? That branch of the family ain't islanders at all. Cyril ain't got no claim.'

'Well, I don't know,' began Ben. 'Blood's thicker than water, they say . . .'

Alice quelled him with a look.

'It's all very well for you!' she said. 'It isn't you that'd have to look after him, it's me. And I'm not going to!'

There were murmurs of disapproval all over the Meeting-House. Alice was not popular. Noah Attwood, who hadn't returned to his seat, said, 'It's been the custom here, from times what nobody can remember to the contrary, even me. If there's a child what's left without parents, the nearest relatives take it in.'

There were sounds of general agreement. Alice, on the defensive, said, 'It'd be an extra mouth for me and Ben to feed.' She looked at Cyril with some contempt. 'And what can *he* do to help? You can see from the look of him, he's never worked in his life. He'll never take an oar. He don't look as if he could so much as lift a spade.'

Cyril said, 'I got money. Whoever I stayed with, they'd get paid.'

There were blank looks at the mention of money. Adam said gently, 'Money's no use to you here, Cyril. We don't use money on Halcyon. We don't need it.'

'*No money!*' said Cyril, astonished at the idea of life without money.

Adam went on, 'But anyone with an extra mouth to feed gets help from us all.'

'It's not only that,' Alice said. 'It's the trouble. And not being private in your own home.'

Grandma Molly, at the end of the front row, had been simmering with indignation at Alice's successive remarks. Now her anger boiled over. She stood up and jabbed a furious finger in Alice's direction.

'You make me sick!' she pronounced. 'What sort of a welcome is that for a young lad, being told he's not wanted? If I was you, Alice Jonas, I'd be ashamed of myself!'

'It isn't you that's being asked to take the lad in,' said Alice. 'And he ain't no relative of mine, he's only Ben's. Maybe if it was *you* what was being expected to share your home with somebody you've never heard of, you'd sing a different song.'

'If you won't take him,' declared Molly, 'I will. And glad to. In fact I'd have him anyway. Poor lad, it wouldn't be much fun for him, living with *you*!'

Cyril was looking confused.

'Maybe I shouldn't live with anyone,' he said. 'If there's somewhere where I could manage by myself, I could do that.'

'You'd starve within a week, laddie,' said Jamie Campbell.

'Half a minute, Molly,' said Adam. 'Are you serious?'

''Course I'm serious. I say what I mean, don't I? And I mean what I say. If Alice don't want that lad, I'll have him.'

'Maybe you should give yourself time to think about it.'

'I don't need no time. I made up my mind while I was listening. I got room for him, and I'm lonely since my Dan died. I'll be glad to have him.'

'I'd better put it to the meeting,' Adam said. 'Would everyone be happy if Cyril here went to live with Molly?'

There were general sounds of assent.

'And what about you, Cyril?' Adam asked. 'Is that all right for you?'

'Oh, it's all right with me,' said Cyril. 'Take life as it comes, that's my motto.'

'Well, then,' Adam said. 'I think we can look on that as settled, and I'll close the meeting. A happy outcome. Thank you, Molly.'

Islanders began to file out of the hall. Several of the men stopped to shake Cyril's hand and wish him well; the women gave him shy smiles but went past him in silence. It wasn't seemly to stop and talk to a male stranger.

At the Meeting-House door, a little group of teenage girls and boys were waiting to get a closer sight of Cyril. The boys were inclined to be scornful of his physique. Some of them had said as much already. But the girls were excited. They'd agreed among themselves that Cyril was better-looking and more sophisticated than the island boys.

Grandma Molly marched Cyril past them.

'Time to be on our way!' she said. 'You'll meet the young folks tomorrow. There'll be dancing after Robert's party. Just now you're with me, so look sharp! No hanging about! Don't worry about your things, they'll be brought up in the morning.'

22

Molly was stumping away into the darkness. Cyril followed and caught her up. As if answering an unspoken question, Molly said, 'You and me's going to get along fine. We needn't have no problems. But there's one thing we need to be sure about from the beginning, and that is, who's to be boss. And it's me.'

The white walls of cottages loomed out of the night, clearly outlined from time to time as a three-quarter moon scudded from cloud to cloud. There was the endless sound of breakers far below. From the mountainside, a wild dog's howl was carried on the wind; two or three village dogs barked in answer. In some of the windows lamps flickered.

Grandma Molly's was the last and highest cottage of the settlement. Its door opened straight into a living-room, faintly lit by the glow from a banked-up peat fire. Molly lit an oil-lamp, then stirred the fire.

'I got cocoa,' she said. 'You want some?'

'No, thanks,' said Cyril cheerfully. 'Never touch the stuff.' He waited to be offered something else, but no offer came. Molly picked up the lamp and led the way to an adjoining room with an earth floor, spread with straw. 'This is where you'll sleep,' she said.

There was a strong animal smell.

Cyril sniffed.

'The goat's been in here, nights,' Molly said. 'I let her sleep inside when the weather's bad. But it's getting a bit better now. She'll be all right in the outhouse.'

'You mean the weather's been worse than this?'

'It's good today, for the time of year.'

'And how'm I going to sleep in here? I don't see any furniture. Not even a bed.'

'Well, you *could* sleep on the straw. If you was caught overnight on the mountain you'd be glad of it. But don't look like that, lad. I got a bed for you. You can clean the room out tomorrow.'

The bed was in the living-room, where it served as a sofa.

It was an old box-bed with a sagging striped mattress. Cyril helped Molly carry it through. When they'd finished, he said, 'I didn't realize you were so . . . ' He paused, on the brink of saying 'poor', and began again, 'You haven't *got* much, have you?'

'What do you mean?' Molly said indignantly. 'This is one of the best houses on Halcyon. They don't all have a boarded living-room floor, I can tell you. And I got real wallpaper, not just pasted-up newspapers like most of them. And two armchairs and a table, *and* a tablecloth for best. You're living in luxury here.'

Cyril managed a rueful grin.

Molly said, 'If you don't want no cocoa, you may as well go to bed. I'll give you a lamp. But we don't waste oil here. Get yourself to bed quick and put it out. And, Cyril—'

'Yes?'

'There might be a few fleas in that mattress. We got them in every house on Halcyon. Don't let them worry you. They're not bad, this time of year. They'll be worse in summer, but you'll be used to them by then. We hardly notice them ourselves.'

Chapter 3

Cyril slept poorly on his first night on Halcyon. The wind whistled under the eaves, veering occasionally to buffet the window. After several days at sea, he hadn't quite got his land legs, and his bed's lack of motion amid the tumult didn't feel right. The bed was lumpy and uncomfortable anyway, and he soon became convinced that fleas were biting him already. Towards dawn he heard the bleating of the goat, close at hand, and thought it had got into the room, though it hadn't. At last he fell deeply asleep, to wake in full daylight with his exposed shoulders feeling the cold.

Shivering, he got up and inspected himself. At least he didn't seem to be flea-bitten. He drew on his trousers, then knocked on the door between his room and the living-room. No reply. He pushed the door open and found the room empty, the fire still banked up. He sat in one of the two battered armchairs and meditated. Cyril had spoken truthfully when he said he took life as it came; but lately life had been coming at him rather hard.

He'd been deceived. His grandfather had talked about old days on Halcyon as if it were some kind of paradise, a beautiful place where all were friendly and everyone worked for the common good. But the old man's memories had been blurred and softened by time. True, now he came to think about it, his grandfather hadn't said anything about those supposed golden sands and palm trees; they'd been added by his aunt when she wanted to get rid of him. No one had given him an inkling that Halcyon would be bleak, desolate, windswept. And here he was, without even suitable clothing.

He would leave next time the ship came. His money,

useless on the island, would pay for his passage. What would he do at the other end? He couldn't go back to Aunt Janet; didn't even know where she was. He wouldn't want to live with her and her new man anyway; he was no more fond of them than they were of him. He might be able to find a room and a clerking job . . . Uncharacteristically, Cyril felt sorry for himself.

His gloomy thoughts were interrupted when Grandma Molly came in.

'I been up for hours,' she told him.

'You could have woken me.'

'I could've, but I didn't. Thought I'd let you lie, just your first day. You can't go on like that, though. Want some porridge?'

Cyril had never cared for porridge, but by now he was hungry. He hadn't eaten much of the fish and potatoes offered to him in Adam's house the day before. He emptied a bowl of porridge rapidly, and would have eaten more if it had been offered.

'The boats is laid up again today,' Molly informed him. 'Gales is bad out there. That makes six days in a row. If it goes on, we'll be hungry . . . You ever milked a goat?'

'No.'

'Want to try?'

Cyril almost said 'Not particularly,' but restrained himself.

Molly said, 'Might as well learn to make yourself useful. Time we was milking her now. Pick up that stool and bucket.'

The goat was in the outhouse. Cyril asked, 'What's her name?'

'She don't need a name. Everybody knows my goat.'

'Oh.'

'Now, sit down and get on with it. You know what to do, don't you?'

Cyril squeezed the big, warm teats. The goat was restless, not liking unfamiliar hands. She reared. Cyril hadn't realized what a large, powerful beast a nanny-goat was. Molly calmed her down. Cyril squeezed again and went on squeezing. Not much milk came out. A trio of small children appeared in the doorway and watched, first with interest and then with amusement. Cyril sweated. The goat was still restless.

Molly herself was grinning.

'That'll do for now,' she said, and edged him aside. Under her expert hands, milk drummed rapidly into the bucket.

'You'll learn,' she said drily. 'You can try again tonight. She'll have to get used to you.'

Cyril pulled a face. Molly said, 'Put this in the house. Then pick up the other two buckets and fill them at the washpool. Just follow the track.'

Cyril took the buckets and set off down the track. The wind blew as it had done the night before. The heavy iron buckets ballasted him; without them he felt he'd have been blown away. Low clouds moved rapidly against a background of chilly grey. The village lay in a scatter just below him; beyond were cliffs and sea; round to the right the harsh, dark outline of the mountainside, falling sheer to the water.

The track picked its way between cottages and then crossed a quarter-mile of grassland to the stream. The stream had been roughly dammed to make a pool which was plainly the washpool. Nobody was about. Cyril filled his buckets, but could then hardly pick them up. He tipped out some of the water and staggered away with what was left. After fifty yards he put the burden down, breathing hard, and surveyed the red marks made on his hands by the bucket-handles.

At this point Robert overtook him. Robert was carrying Cyril's suitcases.

'Them buckets is too much for you,' he said. 'Let me take 'em. You carry the suitcases.'

Cyril, embarrassed, said 'Thanks.'

Robert peered into the buckets. 'They're half empty,' he observed. 'Let's fill 'em proper.'

Cyril reddened. Robert strode back along the track towards the stream, filled the buckets almost to the brim, and strode ahead of Cyril to Grandma Molly's cottage.

'Adam said we was to see what clothes he's brought with him,' Robert told Molly, 'and then to send him along, so as to see if we should lend him some.'

'Let's have a look, then,' said Molly.

'Don't ask my permission, will you?' Cyril said.

'We wasn't going to.'

Cyril wondered whether to object to the inspection, and decided against it. He stood by as Molly and Robert spread the contents of his suitcases around the room. Their eyes opened wide when they saw that he had a dozen shirts, three or four pairs of smart shoes and one of patent-leather dancing pumps. He also had two well-pressed suits, a striped blazer, a gabardine raincoat, several vivid neckties, a brightly-coloured swimsuit, a little stack of pocket-handkerchiefs, a set of brushes, hair cream, and a manicure set.

Grandma Molly and Robert looked at each other first with curiosity and then with near-incredulity as these wonders were brought to light. When, finally, they came to a sun-hat and a pair of sun-glasses, the pair of them collapsed on Molly's bed, their sides heaving with laughter.

'I never seen such stuff in all my life,' said Molly. 'When you going to wear clothes like these? You going to cut peat in them shoes? Or dig the potato-patch in that fancy jacket and trousis? Or sunbathe, out in the wind?'

'I was misled,' said Cyril crossly. 'They didn't tell me it was a place like this.'

Molly recovered and said seriously, 'There's nothing here that'll be any use to you on Halcyon.'

Robert said, 'Adam'll find you some proper clothes. And he wants you to pick up your wireless.'

Cyril's spirits were raised by the thought of being reunited with his wireless set.

'Like to help me set it up?' he asked as they walked side by side down the track.

'Yes, I would!' said Robert at once. He'd heard about the wireless set and was eager to see it. The very idea of wireless was to him mysterious and intriguing. He had practical skills and clever fingers. He would love to get to grips with this strange machine.

Adam and Ellen Goodall greeted Cyril warmly.

'Well, how have you got on with the old lady?' Adam asked.

'We got on fine,' said Cyril cautiously. 'She knows what she wants, doesn't she?'

'She does indeed. Now, let's see what we can find for you.' Adam rummaged in a pile of old clothes in a corner, and produced an old Army tunic, a heavy sweater, various thick but ragged vests, a set of oilskins, and a pair of boots that he thought would fit Cyril if padded with layers of socks. Cyril looked at the pile with dismay; everyone else looked expectantly at Cyril. He saw what was expected of him, stripped to his underpants, and, overcoming a certain amount of suspicion—what was it Molly had said about fleas?—put on a selection of the garments offered.

'There!' said Ellen. 'They suit you fine. Now you look like an islander!' She produced a cracked hand-mirror, in which Cyril could get a somewhat inadequate view of his own appearance. Twenty-four hours earlier, he'd have been shocked at the very thought of dressing like that, but now he wasn't sure. The bulky clothing made him look less skinny, less of a freak in this setting.

Ellen, noticing his uncertainty, said, 'You'll be able to wear your own clothes for the dance tonight.'

'And in the meantime,' said Adam, 'I've got a job for you. The mail came in yesterday. You can read, Cyril, I'm sure.'

' 'Course I can read!' said Cyril indignantly.

'Most folk on the island can't. We haven't had a teacher since the last missionary left, and that was thirty years ago. They need their letters read out to them. I can read myself, a bit, but I'm not very quick at it. You can sort out the mail, if you will, Cyril. Take it round and read it if they ask you to. That way you'll get to know people.'

'All right,' Cyril said.

'And Robert'll help you deliver. Show you where they all live.'

'Some time,' said Cyril, 'I want to get an aerial up for my wireless. I thought if I could fix a pole to somebody's chimney-stack, it might give me enough height.'

'I don't know anything about wireless,' Adam said. 'But you can't go fixing things on roofs in today's wind. You'll have to wait till it drops.'

It took most of the day to deliver the mail. Not that there was a vast amount of it. For most of the islanders, three months' accumulation of mail didn't add up to a great deal. For some there was none at all. But the process was confusing, since Halcyon had only eight surnames divided among twenty-five households, and the cottages were scattered higgledy-piggledy with no streets or numbers.

Robert showed Cyril where everyone lived, and by evening he had in his mind a clear map of the village. He took some pleasure in handing to a frozen-faced Alice Jonas a letter in his aunt's handwriting from the Mainland Colony; he knew as well as she did that it would contain the news of his imminent arrival. Cyril wasn't sorry he was not to stay with Alice. The letters that Cyril read aloud to the recipients were mostly from relatives in the Mother Country or the Mainland Colony, and gave information about births, marriages and deaths. It was clear that over the years a good many islanders had emigrated. They kept in touch, and so did their children. Many a letter declared that the sender remained an islander at heart.

'But they don't come back,' said Robert.

'Do *you* want to leave?' Cyril asked him.

'No. I'm all right here. I got an oar in a good boat, and

when I'm wed I'll have forty sheep and three potato patches. Well, me and Tilda will.'

'Tilda? The hefty girl with the big nose?'

Realizing that this description might not please Robert, Cyril added hastily, 'And the nice smile?'

Robert wasn't inclined to take offence.

'Yes, that's Tilda,' he said. 'She's a fine strong lass.'

'And you're thinking of *marriage*?'

'Well, I *would* be. But my dad died last year, and my mum wants me to wait.' Robert frowned.

'You're a bit young, aren't you, anyway?'

'I won't be all that young by wedding time. It takes time to build a house. Me and Tilda aren't in a hurry exactly—I mean, she isn't *pressing* to be wed—but I wouldn't mind getting on with it.'

Robert left Cyril to return the empty mailbags, and went home to his mother's cottage. As he approached the door, his ten-year-old sister Polly came to meet him. Unlike most island children, who tended to be rather silent and to behave like small grown-ups, Polly was lively and talkative. In Robert's opinion, she was cheekier to her older brother than any girl had any right to be; but he was fond of her.

Today, Polly pulled a long face.

'You're in trouble, Robert Attwood,' she told him.

'With Mum? Why? If you mean I've not been helping her get ready for the party, she told me yesterday to keep from under her feet.'

'It's not that. It's what Margery Kane saw.'

'Marge Kane's an old busybody. What *did* she see?'

'She saw you in the Dell with Tilda.'

'What if she did? There's nothing wrong with that. Tilda's dad knew about it.'

'She saw you *wrestling*.'

Robert scowled. 'And she had to go telling Mum. But I don't know why Mum minds. She knows me and Tilda's intended.'

'Marge Kane says you was *on the ground*. 'Twasn't decent, she says. And you and Tilda being intended won't stop Mum being upset. Things is different since Dad died and she's on her own.'

'I better face it,' said Robert resignedly.

And it was worse than he expected. May Attwood was reproachful. How could Robert think of behaving so as to get himself talked about in the village? And to upset her on this day above all, when she was so proud of him and taking so much trouble, and she'd been working her fingers to the bone to give him the best party she could! She'd had two sheep killed that she couldn't afford, and used all her stock of flour and sugar and tea that she'd been saving since last year, specially for this occasion. He was the mainstay of the family now, and he mustn't forget it. He and Tilda had years ahead of them; plenty of young folk on the island didn't marry until they were twenty-one or two. Meanwhile, it wasn't fair to Tilda to carry on like that. A girl could lose her reputation . . .

It went on for some time. Polly tried to intervene on Robert's behalf, and was sent packing for impudence. Robert felt battered by his mother's words and confused by his love for her, his feelings of guilt and obligation, and at the same time a sense that he hadn't actually done anything wrong. For a while he suffered May's outpouring in silence. Then, tormented beyond endurance, he burst out, 'Stop it, I can't stand it. I wish I *was* wed to Tilda and away from here!'

The moment he'd said the words, he regretted them. There was no way of taking them back. But they stopped his mother in her tracks. She broke down in noisy sobs and put her arms round him.

'Don't leave me, lad!' she implored him. 'You're all I've got, you and Polly. You're what my life's *for*.'

Robert tried awkwardly to comfort her. He assured her that he didn't mean what he said, that he wasn't on the point of departure, that there was plenty of time, that he and Tilda weren't going to misbehave. He and his mother stood clasped together for some minutes. Then she suddenly straightened herself, wiped her face on a corner of her pinafore, and said, 'Come on, we got a lot of work to do yet for the party.'

By the time the guests assembled, May Attwood was smiling.

It was mutton that made it a feast. Islanders ate meat a dozen times a year if they were lucky. Normally their diet was dominated by fish and boiled potatoes. Today the two sheep had been roasted, on spits turned by Robert's Great-uncles Noah and Ted, and the resulting meat triumphantly served up in the Meeting-House. There were baked potatoes, accompanied by swede and turnip; there was cranberry pudding to follow, made with cranberries from the marshland beyond the vegetable patches, and then a large cake with hoarded currants and raisins in it. As a final treat, the adults had tea and the children milk.

There were sighs of happy repletion as Adam got up to make a brief speech admitting Robert to the new status of adulthood. Robert himself, still emotionally battered from the confrontation with his mother, had sat silent through the meal and made a speech in reply consisting of the words 'Thank you, Adam.' This was enough to bring him generous applause. Then began the work of clearing away and getting ready for the dance, to which the whole village was invited.

Ellen Goodall, who'd helped her husband to kit Cyril out with island clothing, had advised him on what he should wear for this occasion.

'They'll stare at you anyway,' she said. 'You might as well give them something to stare at.' So Cyril put on his sharpest suit, his brightest shirt, and a tie with a pattern of exploding orange and purple suns; and on arriving at the Meeting-House he slipped on his gleaming patent-leather pumps.

The contrast was as striking as anyone could have

wished. Islanders wore their patched, sometimes thread-bare and invariably old-fashioned Prayer-Day clothes. Most of the men had jackets, though few could boast a collar or tie. Women and girls wore such finery as they had: long bulky dresses of cotton or sometimes satin, acquired over the years or handed down in families; taken-in or let-out and lovingly mended.

Cyril's impression of having travelled back in time was reinforced by the island style of dancing. Music was provided by sixty-year-old Isaac Reeves on a fiddle. He sawed away valiantly, with sweat pouring from his forehead, as the adult islanders pounded around the hall in a succession of reels, jigs and traditional dances.

Cyril, having been assured that modern-style dancing would follow, didn't attempt to take part in these. And at length Isaac gave up exhausted; an ancient gramophone with a huge curved horn was brought out, to deliver scratchy versions of quicksteps and waltzes. Older is-landers lost interest and stood around the walls chatting, but two or three younger couples ventured on to the floor and went somewhat gracelessly through the motions.

It was Cyril's chance to shine. He was an excellent dancer and knew it. He went confidently over to the little knot of unmarried girls who stood all together in a corner of the hall, and approached Sophy Kane, whom he'd docketed already as the prettiest. He was surprised when she blushed and refused. So did three of the other girls. They were well aware that all eyes in the Meeting-House were focused on Cyril, and were too embarrassed to stand up with him.

Polly Attwood, Robert's small sister, saved the day by pushing forward to take Cyril's offered hand; and though she wasn't very good, they got around the hall somehow. After that, the girls danced willingly if inexpertly, and Cyril enjoyed himself as he foxtrotted, waltzed and quickstepped with three of them in turn. He didn't ask Tilda. Tilda was relieved and disappointed at the same time. She didn't know many of the steps, but she felt her foot tapping; she was light on her feet, and would surely learn quickly if she could dance with Cyril. Robert, shy and somewhat clumsy, would never be a dancer.

Cyril sang along tunefully with the fourth and last record—a number called 'Tea for Two'—and thereby greatly impressed his current partner, Nancy Oakes. The gramophone ground scratchily to a halt, and Isaac, refreshed by a rest and a large mug of tea, took up the fiddle again. The mass pounding of the floor was resumed.

Proceedings concluded with the most traditional Halcyon dance of all, the Potato Dance. Adam, as head man, led off, holding a potato of formidable size in both hands over his head and trotting round the hall to the music. He then threw the potato to a woman of his choice —on this occasion Annie Wilde—who threw it in her turn to another man, and so on. Each person in turn held high the potato and led a growing line of dancers as they capered around the hall and the music went faster and faster. Cyril received the potato from Ellen Goodall, who thoughtfully offered him an easy catch, and passed it on to Polly. When the chain was complete, with only a handful of the most aged uncles and aunts outside it, the potato was thrown high through the air for a final catch by Adam; everyone cheered, and Robert's coming-of-age party was at an end.

Robert was proud but not altogether happy. It was good to be acknowledged as an adult. In accordance with custom, every active man on the island had patted him on the back and welcomed him into comradeship. And yet he didn't quite feel he was a man—not while he was bound so closely to his mother. Taking Tilda to the Dell had given him an unsettled feeling. He shouldn't have wrestled with her, the way things were at present. It was all very difficult. Emotional matters were hard to cope with. Maybe tomorrow the wind would have dropped and he'd be out fishing with the men. That would be a relief.

Cyril, in the end, had quite enjoyed his second day on

Halcyon. He was a sociable being, and delivering the mail had introduced him to most of the inhabitants. He hadn't minded at all being asked to read people's letters for them. And though it had been a bit of a bore watching islanders galumphing around in their jigs and polkas and whatnot, he'd triumphed in the gramophone interlude. The island girls had been impressed by him, and they weren't bad-looking. Maybe he'd be able to have fun here after all.

Grandma Molly lay in bed in her cottage, drifting towards sleep and thinking back to her youth. She thought, as so often, of Otipo, with honey skin and high cheek-bones and wide-set brown eyes, who'd arrived on Halcyon when disaster struck his own island of Rikofia all those years ago. Once there'd been a dozen Rikofians; they were all dead now, and their descendants had blended into the population. Molly had married Dan Wilde, but she'd always loved Otipo. Dan had been a decent man, though dull, and their son George was like him; but Tilda was like Molly herself, a wild creature at heart. Molly loved Tilda as she loved no one else alive, and wished for Tilda's happiness, whatever way it might come.

Adam Goodall lay awake, with Ellen asleep beside him. Adam had a worry that no one else on Halcyon knew about. It was the official letter that had come in the mail, addressed to 'The Head Man, Halcyon Island, Southern Ocean,' and marked PRIVATE AND CONFIDENTIAL; IM-PERIAL ADMINISTRATION FOR THE COLONIES.

Adam had known even before opening it what it would contain. The Mother Country was taking an interest again. In his grandfather's fifty years as Reader, there had been two such letters. They had flung the island into panic and turmoil; and it had all been unnecessary. In the end, nothing had come of them. Maybe nothing would come of this one, either. Should he shatter the islanders' peace by telling them, or should he await developments? The latter, he thought, since there was nothing any of them could do. But he wished he knew what was going on in the world outside.

Chapter 4

CYRIL's third day on Halcyon began with the winds as high as ever. No boat could go out. The men stayed in their houses, smoked their pipes, did domestic jobs or sat silently by the fire, whittling wood or carving scenes on bits of whalebone. Time dragged, and meals were dreary. There'd been no fresh fish for a week, and after the brief plenty of yesterday's party most islanders had little to eat today but potatoes and thin stew.

Grandma Molly wasn't daunted by wind or flying spray. She roused Cyril early, gave him porridge in a cracked bowl and goat's milk in a cracked cup, and took him on a second visit to the goat, which he tried again to milk, with little success.

'You'll learn,' said Molly. 'I hope. Now we'll go over to the vegetable patches.'

'We'll get blown off our feet,' Cyril objected.

'It's a bit more sheltered over there. And there's digging and clearing to be done. Maybe you're better at digging than you are at milking goats.'

'Maybe,' said Cyril without enthusiasm. He and Molly battled their way along the track that led across the grassland and past the Lookout and a scatter of boulders to the vegetable plots, a couple of miles from the village.

The wind was a little less fierce, but not much. Several women and girls, as tough as Molly, were working on their plots already. Cyril was chagrined to find that Molly, for all her age, could work faster and more steadily than he could. They stopped for a snack of cold potatoes, then worked on. By early afternoon, he was weary and had blistered hands.

'We done enough for today,' said Molly eventually, to Cyril's relief, and they set off back toward the cottage.

'It's clearing now,' said Molly; and it was. Suddenly and swiftly, the clouds were swept away and the sky was blue; the ferocious wind declined to a fresh breeze. The sea was a vivid blue-green, flecked with white horses; the black edge of the mountainside, plunging to the water, was outlined dramatically by sunlight. Far out on the horizon, a violet-grey hump emerged: the uninhabited companion island, named Kingfisher.

As Molly and Cyril arrived in the village, Adam met them.

'I've been thinking about what Cyril can best do on Halcyon,' he said. 'I don't think fishing's quite in his line, somehow.'

'Nor is digging,' said Molly. 'Nor milking a goat.'

Cyril reddened.

'But I've got just the job for you, Cyril,' Adam went on. 'What about teaching people to read?'

Cyril was startled.

'Me a teacher?' he said.

'He needn't think he's starting on *me*!' said Molly, alarmed. 'Not at my time of life!'

'Nobody'd be *forced*,' said Adam. 'But it's an opportunity for us, isn't it?'

Cyril said thoughtfully, 'I never taught anyone anything. Wasn't much good at school, neither. I wouldn't know how to start. What we got in the way of books?'

'We've got old Charlie Herrick's library,' Adam said. 'He was a ship's mate, wrecked on Kingfisher half a century ago. We brought his books over here when he died. There's some very good ones, I'm told.'

'You've read them?' Cyril asked.

'Well . . . not exactly. I've looked at them, but I've always been too busy. Tell you the truth, Cyril'—Adam was embarrassed—'I'm not much of a reader myself. I can read a letter, mind you . . . ' His expression was suddenly thoughtful.

Cyril grinned.

'I'll have a go at anything,' he said. 'Even teaching. But now can I set my wireless up?'

'What does that involve?'

'Mostly it's a matter of putting up an aerial. That's a high wire. The higher the better. I've got a coil of wire, and a fixture that goes on the end of it. I need something to attach it to. Then when we've got the set working you can hear music and stuff from the mainland.'

Molly sniffed. She wasn't sure she wanted stuff from the mainland. But Adam was interested. 'Do you get *news*?' he asked.

'Oh, yes, lots of it. Doesn't interest *me* much. Dance music, that's what I like. Crooners. Saxophones.'

Neither Molly nor Adam knew what a crooner or a saxophone was, but they didn't like to ask.

Cyril added, 'Robert said he'd help me.'

'No reason why he shouldn't. The boats won't go out today; it's cleared up too late.'

Adam and Cyril went down the hill to Adam's house, picking up Robert as they went. The wireless set sat in its packing-case, wedged in with screwed-up newspaper. Cyril extracted it and gazed at it fondly. It was a plywood box, with a circular grid in one face of it.

'Want to see inside?' he asked. He lifted off the top, back and sides in one piece, revealing a baseboard and a mysterious assembly of components, intricately wired together.

Adam and Robert inspected it with interest.

'How's it work?' asked Robert.

'Well . . . '

Cyril wondered how to explain radio theory to somebody who only knew about sheep, fish and potatoes. He wasn't really too sure of it himself.

'It's waves,' he said. 'There's a transmitter, that turns sounds into radio waves and sends them out, and we pick 'em up with the aerial and turn them back into sound.' He added proudly, 'This is a short-wave set.'

'What's short waves?'

'Well . . . Short waves are indirect waves. They don't come straight from the transmitter, they sort of bounce back off the Heaviside layer . . . '

39

'The *what*?'

'The Heaviside layer. It's . . . it's up in the sky somewhere. About sixty miles up.' Cyril foresaw a request to explain the Heaviside layer, and went on hastily, 'What it boils down to is, you need a short-wave set to receive over long distances, like we have to do here.'

Robert could see the point of that. He knew it was fifteen hundred miles to the Mainland Colony.

'What's those?' he asked, pointing into the set.

'Those are the valves. And those are condensers, and those are resistances.'

'What do *they* do?'

Cyril was defeated. He said, 'I've got a book about it. I'll lend you it.'

Robert's face fell. Cyril realized too late that Robert couldn't read. He went on with the guided tour of the set.

'This is what you tune it with,' he said, 'so as to get different transmissions. Here's where you join up the batteries. Here's terminals for putting in headphones, if you want to listen by yourself and save current. And here's where the aerial comes in and the earth wire goes out.'

Robert was frowning. It was too much to take in. Adam said, 'Well, now, what do you need to put your aerial up?'

'A high place,' Cyril said. 'Higher the better.'

'There's Jonathan Wilde's house, just round the headland,' Adam said. 'It's empty. And it's the highest house on the island. It'd be looking straight across at the mainland, if we could see that far.'

Robert pulled a face.

'That house is unlucky,' he said.

'I don't believe in ill-luck,' said Adam. He explained to Cyril, 'Jonathan Wilde was a mutineer on the *Susannah*, way back. He'd be Tilda Wilde's great-great-grandfather, or maybe great-great-uncle. He built his house on the mountainside, and was killed in it soon afterwards. Murdered by the other mutineers. No one's lived there since. As Robert says, it's supposed to be unlucky. Some say it's haunted, but nobody's ever seen a ghost there.'

'Nobody's *seen* one,' said Robert, 'but there's plenty who've *felt* it.'

'It does have a bad atmosphere,' Adam admitted. 'But it's a good house. Stone-built, and a flagged roof. It'll stand for ever.'

'Is there something we can use for a mast?' Cyril asked.

'We'll find something. But it's still windy. And we may need help. We'd better wait till Prayer Day.'

Next day was fine. The boats were out early and stayed out all day. They came back at dusk with excellent catches. There was plentiful fresh fish for island suppers that night.

The day after that was Prayer Day, when no work was done. Islanders put on their best clothes, and wore shoes if they had them. Adam conducted a simple morning service in the Meeting-House, and the rest of the day was free.

'I had an idea about your aerial,' Adam told Cyril. 'Down on Small Beach there's a spar from an old sailing ship. It's been there for years. I wouldn't let it be chopped up for firewood; always thought it'd come in useful some time.'

Old as it was, the spar was iron-hard. A party of islanders manoeuvred it from the beach and up a perilous, winding track to the house in which, long ago, Jonathan Wilde had been murdered. It was a mile and a half from the village; its front looked out to sea and the mountain loomed up behind it. It had a dark, vaguely sinister look, and Cyril—having by now heard gruesome details of the murder—shuddered and found himself reluctant to go into it. But it faced in the right direction; it was sound and fairly dry.

Putting up the aerial was a struggle. Robert and two or three others scrambled sure-footedly over the roof; Cyril gave advice from the ground, and by mid-afternoon the spar was bracketed firmly to the chimney and the aerial wire had been run up to the top of it. Everyone gathered round as Cyril connected and tuned the set.

At first there was nothing to be heard but hissing and an occasional crackle. Cyril fiddled with the tuner. Then, through the hiss, came faint, tinny sounds of speech, though it wasn't possible to tell what was being said. Cyril fiddled again. There was equally faint and tinny music from another source, then from a third source more speech, still undistinguishable. Cyril, who had hoped for better results, was disappointed. But the islanders were impressed. To them, it all seemed uncanny, like some mysterious communication from outer space.

'That was folk talking on the mainland?' asked Robert.

'Yes.'

'I can almost tell what they're saying!'

'Come back tonight,' said Cyril. 'It'll work better then. Short waves come across stronger after dark.'

News that the wireless set was working spread rapidly through the village. A sizeable party dared to brave the potential ghosts and straggled along the path round the mountainside to the cottage. Cyril tuned his set. And from the first station he located, voices now came over clearly.

'They're quarrelling!' said Tilda, shocked.

'It's a play,' Cyril explained.

'Doesn't sound like playing. It sounds as if they didn't like each other.'

'They're only pretending.'

'Why should people pretend to quarrel?'

Cyril tried to explain. But drama was a difficult concept for his hearers to grasp. He tuned out the play and found a news bulletin. This was just as baffling, and even more disturbing, since it was full of ominous warnings about trouble between nations. Adam listened with close and worried attention. World affairs had never impinged on the islanders, however, and most of them took little interest. A programme of dance music appealed to them for a while. But it was the mystery of wireless itself, and the capacity to change from one station to another, that most impressed them. Several asked for permission to turn the tuning knob themselves, and were delighted with the sounds they brought in.

At one point there was a burst of bleeping, much louder than the speech or music. Everyone looked to Cyril for the explanation.

'That's Morse code,' he said; and, as mouths opened to put the inevitable question, 'What's Morse code?' he added, 'That's another way of communicating by wireless.'

'Can you understand it?' Adam asked.

'Yes, I can read Morse. It's a ship. Reporting its position. It's quite close to here. That's why the signal's coming through so strongly.'

'It isn't coming to Halcyon, is it?'

'No. On its way from the Mainland Colony to Santa Cruz, the other side of the ocean.'

There was another burst of Morse; then music re-emerged from the background.

Cyril's prestige was rising sharply. By the time the islanders, who were early risers, drifted away to bed, he was being treated with considerable respect. Several people thanked him for giving them the new experience of wireless. Old Noah Attwood made a little speech to mark the occasion.

Adam was the last to leave. As Cyril put the cover on the set, he said, 'Come to my house, Cyril. There's something I want to consult you about.'

'What about the set?' Cyril asked. 'Will it be safe here?'

'Why shouldn't it be?'

'Well, it's valuable. I mean, at home I wouldn't leave something like this around. Somebody might tamper with it.'

'But they know it's yours,' Adam said.

'You mean, nobody ever touches anything that isn't theirs? Does nothing ever get stolen?'

'Stolen? People taking things that belong to other people?' Adam was startled. 'That doesn't happen here. How would we manage if it did?'

'You *are* out of the world!' said Cyril.

'That's what I want to talk to you about.'

They arrived at Adam's house. Adam produced the long

envelope he'd received in the mail and drew out the paper it contained.

'Tell me,' he said, 'does this say what I think it says?'

Cyril unfolded the letter.

'Dear Sir,' it began,

'I am directed by the Chief Minister for the Colonies to inform you that, in view of the uncertain international situation, it has been provisionally decided to establish a formal administration on Halcyon Island, and to set up a radio communication station there.

'Accordingly, a Commissioner for the island has been nominated. He is Brigadier H. J. W. Culpepper (retired), and if present plans are proceeded with he will be taking up office in a few weeks' time. He will be transported to the island on the cruiser *Indomitable* and will bring with him a small staff of aides and technicians. There will also be, initially, a platoon of engineers, whose task will be to erect the necessary buildings and later a small harbour on the island. They will be withdrawn when their assignment is completed.

'On his arrival, the Commissioner will take over the management of the island. You are required to assist him in any way he may specify, and in particular to supply him with any labour he may need.

'I have the honour to be, Sir,
    Your obedient Servant.'

The letter was signed with an indecipherable squiggle.

'Well!' said Cyril. 'Looks like Halcyon's going to come into the world!'

'Or the world come to Halcyon,' said Adam.

'It says at the top "Imperial Administration." Is Halcyon really part of the Empire, same as the Mainland Colony?'

'Well, yes. We run the Mother Country flag up the flagpole every year, on the King's birthday. But the Mother Country doesn't bother with us. Why should it? Just a few unimportant folk, scratching a living here in the back of beyond.'

'It's going to bother with you now.'

'Well, maybe,' Adam said. 'Something like this happened twice in my grandfather's time. When it looks as if there might be a war, they think they'd better occupy Halcyon before someone else does. But when the war doesn't happen, they drop the idea. Maybe they'll do so again. And, Cyril, everyone on the island will be scared stiff if I tell them about this letter. They don't think they can cope with the outside world: all those clever people doing clever things. Our folk are very humble. So I don't think I'll say anything about it yet, in case it blows over again. It's not as if we could *do* anything.'

'Maybe this time it won't blow over.'

'That's what I'm afraid of, especially since hearing what the wireless says. And that's why I'm talking to you now. What I'd like you to do, Cyril, is keep listening out with that set of yours, and tell me if a war starts or if you pick up anything that might affect us. And in the meantime, keep quiet about it. Nobody on the island knows but you and me and Ellen.'

'You can trust me,' said Cyril.

Inwardly, he glowed. His self-esteem, already boosted by the respect the wireless set had brought him, was raised still further by this sign of confidence. After four days on the island, he was beginning to think he might like it here. And he was beginning to feel, as the islanders did, that the outside world wasn't altogether real. He didn't quite believe in the imminence of war or of Brigadier H. J. W. Culpepper (retired). But it might be fun to teach islanders to read, especially the girls. And he would learn to milk that goat.

Chapter 5

SPRING came to Halcyon. Days lengthened and grew warmer, winds slackened, skies cleared. Good days for fishing came one after another instead of now and then. Children clambered perilously on the cliffs to plunder eggs from the thousands of indignant sea birds; and when the eggs they hadn't stolen hatched out, the nests were raided again and the young birds caught and eaten. A few stunted fruit trees struggled into flower in the Dell and other sheltered places. Long hours were worked in the vegetable plots. Sheep were sheared and spinning-wheels appeared in cottage doorways. Outer layers of clothing were discarded, though bodies remained well covered. Islanders ate well and, like their livestock, put on weight that they would lose again in winter. Jamie Campbell finished building his house and moved into it.

Nothing was heard of colonization or of Brigadier H. J. W. Culpepper (retired).

Amanda returned, and lay at anchor in the bay for the whole of a long, fine day. Islanders traded busily with her, and in the days that followed men had tobacco for their pipes and women tea for the pot. Bread and cake and biscuits appeared for a while on island tables; cans of fruit were secreted in cupboards but were too great a treat for every day. Captain Fisher brought replacement batteries for Cyril's wireless and asked if he was sure he didn't want a passage to the mainland. Cyril said he'd think about it next time.

Halcyon had accepted Cyril Jonas, as it always accepted incomers. Grandma Molly grew fond of him, and he knew it, though she never ceased to speak tartly to him, and to make it clear that she was in charge. He turned out to be an

able teacher, and before long was running three classes—
one for the children, one for the younger and brighter
islanders, and one for the slow and elderly. He made
friends with the goat, and before long could milk it almost
as well as its owner.

But the island girls were a problem. Cyril liked girls; and
whereas in the dance-halls of the Mainland Colony he'd
made headway easily enough, it was much harder on
Halcyon. Most of the girls were intended for young island
men, to whom they were doggedly faithful, being well
aware that plans for their future were a family matter
involving intricate negotiation in matters of sheep, vegetable plots, and building materials. They all admired Cyril,
and some might confess to their closest friends that they
fancied him, but they blushed and looked down when he
spoke to them. Any suggestion from Cyril of a walk in the
Dell caused instant alarm and flight.

The boys were impressed by what they saw as Cyril's
extreme cleverness, but mildly despised him all the same.
In their view, teaching and ballroom dancing were not
proper masculine occupations. He would never take his oar
in a longboat and become a real man. As for the wireless
set, it was all very well, but it didn't help you to catch fish
or grow potatoes.

Robert didn't share this attitude to the wireless set. He
spent a good deal of time with Cyril at Jonathan Wilde's
house fiddling with it, and asking questions about wireless
that Cyril couldn't answer. Cyril had books on the subject,
and Robert enrolled for a reading class in the hope of
learning from them. It soon became clear that this was an
extremely long-term aim, but Robert was not deterred and
applied himself industriously to the ABC.

Tilda was puzzled by Robert. On Prayer Day afternoons
he still took her to the Dell, but he didn't wrestle with her.
Tilda couldn't forget the warm glow she'd felt in her body
when their wrestling turned to kissing. Although at the
time she'd been shocked by her own responses, she had a
recurrent urge to wrestle and kiss again. But Robert

seemed to have drawn away from her. He had never been a great conversationalist, and on some Prayer Days they would just walk back and forth, side by side, not even holding hands, until it was time to go back to Tilda's house for tea. Occasionally, though, he would grow suddenly fierce, clutching her and pressing her close to him almost bruisingly, before abruptly releasing her and resuming the silent walk.

Tilda didn't know what to make of this. Grandma Molly could have told her. But she was too embarrassed to ask Grandma Molly; and Robert could neither understand nor discuss his own feelings. Both of them were frustrated. Tilda's parents however were satisfied that all was well. George Wilde, himself a silent man, would sit by the fireside on Prayer Day evenings, puffing at his pipe and looking with approval from one of them to the other. Several times he and Annie would remark to Tilda, when Robert had left for home, that Robert was a good, reliable boy. Tilda found this irritating. She didn't know quite what she wanted from Robert, but it was something more than goodness and reliability.

Lifting Day came. In accordance with tradition, Adam led a procession of the whole village to the vegetable patches for the ceremonial lifting of the first early potatoes. On the following Prayer Day Robert didn't come to Tilda's house. Tilda waited indoors for half the afternoon, while her mother sat at the spinning-wheel and her father just sat. Eventually her mother said, 'Maybe Robert's poorly.'

'He looked all right at Meeting this morning.'

'Why don't you go along and see?'

Tilda never liked going to Robert's house. She could always feel a chill in the way May Attwood greeted her. But she didn't want to sit at home all afternoon. She put a coat and shawl on and headed into the village.

On the wall in front of the Meeting-House were Sophy

Kane and her cousin Colin, for whom she was intended. They were sitting side by side, watching the world go by. For courting couples this was a recognized alternative to walking in the Dell.

'You looking for Robert?' Sophy asked.

Tilda nodded.

'He went towards Jonathan Wilde's house with Cyril. I expect they'll be playing with that wireless.'

Tilda said nothing, but her expression spoke for her. She didn't like being neglected in favour of the wireless.

'You know what lads are,' said Sophy. 'Some of them would rather fool around with other lads than walk out with their intendeds. Not all of them, of course.'

Colin smirked. Sophy snuggled closer to him. Tilda resisted a strong temptation to push the pair of them backwards off the wall, and stalked away.

'Hullo, Tilda,' said Robert when she arrived at Jonathan Wilde's house. 'I been here longer than I meant. I been helping Cyril get the reception better.'

'Pretty good now, isn't it?' Cyril said.

The cover was off the wireless set, and the two boys had in front of them a complex printed diagram, all lines and arrows and circles, intricately linked.

'Robert's better at understanding this than I am,' Cyril said. 'I reckon he has a natural gift for it.'

He twiddled the tuner. There were rising and falling squeals, snatches of music, a babel of chatter in different tongues, and, as always, a good deal of hiss and crackle. And then, unexpectedly, a silent background, and speech in their own language, as clear as if the speaker was in the room with them. Tilda listened, awed. Here at last was the voice of the outside world. It sounded portentous but puzzling.

'What's it all about?' she asked after a minute.

'It's a news bulletin,' Cyril said. 'From the Mainland Colony.'

'Sounds as if folks was having trouble somewhere.'

'Yes. There's a lot of talk about war. They say it might involve the Mother Country.'

'You mean the King and Queen?'

Tilda had seen old newspaper pictures of the King and Queen, pasted on cottage walls by loyal islanders. She'd seen pictures of the parliament buildings in the capital city, too. But apart from these few glimpses, she had little idea of the Mother Country.

'I suppose so,' Cyril said. 'But the King and Queen are kind of figureheads these days. If there's a war, it's generals and soldiers and things.'

'It won't have anything to do with *us*,' said Robert.

Momentarily the thought of Brigadier Culpepper crossed Cyril's mind. But he had kept his promise to Adam, and hadn't mentioned the letter from the Colonial Administration to anybody.

'Boring stuff,' Cyril said. 'Let's try and find some music.'

He twiddled again with the tuner. There were more squeals, some music that sounded serious and made Cyril pull a face, and finally—difficult to tune, and surrounded by squeals—came dance music. Cyril's foot tapped. So did Tilda's.

Cyril said, 'It's a slow foxtrot. Let's dance.'

'I can't do a slow foxtrot.'

'I'll show you.'

But the music faded, and a squeal began, on a rising and painful note. Cyril adjusted the knob. He stretched his hands towards Tilda, and the squeal began again.

Cyril pulled a face. Then he said, 'Tell you what. Let's ask Adam if we can get out the gramophone in the Meeting-House. We can dance to that.'

'*I* can't dance,' Robert said.

'You can learn. I'll teach you. I'm pretty good at teaching.'

'I'm not dancing with a *lad*!'

'You don't have to. I'll show you the steps. Then you can practise with Tilda.'

'I don't want to practise at all.'

'Then why don't me and Tilda go down to the Meeting-House?' said Cyril. 'Would you like that, Tilda?'

Tilda knew she'd like it. Her feet longed to learn the slow foxtrot. But this was unorthodox, when she was intended for Robert. At the very least, his permission was required. She looked at Robert questioningly.

'Adam won't let you,' said Robert. 'The gramophone's for dances and so on. He doesn't let anybody play with it.'

'I think he'll let *me*,' said Cyril confidently. 'Adam owes me a favour.'

He didn't want to say why, and added, 'If you don't want to come, Robert, you can stay here with the wireless.'

Robert's face lit up.

'You mean . . . ?'

'I trust you, Robert. I know you won't wreck it.'

'Th-thank you, Cyril. I'll stay.'

Robert didn't ask Tilda if she minded.

'And I don't,' she said to herself. Actually she did mind, a little. But the thought of dancing to the gramophone outweighed any resentment.

'C'mon, then,' Cyril said. 'Let's go.'

Robert was bending over the wireless set already. Cyril and Tilda walked down to Adam's cottage. Adam greeted Cyril warmly and asked him, 'Any news?'

'More talk about war. Trouble between the Mother Country and some place in South America.'

'But not the . . . other matter?'

'Nothing that I've heard.'

Adam made no objection to the use of the gramophone. He helped Cyril and Tilda carry it across to the Meeting-House, put a new needle into the pick-up, and wound the machine vigorously. Cyril chose a foxtrot from the pile of heavy records, and blew off the dust. Music ground out hoarsely from the great horn. Cyril took Tilda's right hand with his left; his other hand found the small of her back, and for the three minutes the record lasted he initiated her into the mysteries of the slow foxtrot.

'If you do it properly, you cover lots of ground,' he explained; and as they finished he told her, 'That was pretty good for a start.'

Adam, interested, stood by to change the records and put in fresh needles. Ellen came to join them. Cyril and Tilda waltzed, foxtrotted and quickstepped, Tilda gaining confidence as she went on. Other islanders heard the music and dropped in, one by one, until there was an audience of about twenty, including Sophy and Colin Kane, Nancy Oakes and Tom Reeves; but no other couple ventured to dance. A kind of wildness came over Tilda; she span at the end of Cyril's arm, leaned over at perilous angles, and improvised a few steps of her own. She was aware of little but the hall whirling around her and a sense of absolute confidence that nothing could go wrong. In the end it was Cyril who was exhausted.

As the last record ground to a halt, he relinquished her hand. 'Great!' he said. 'One of these days I'll teach you the tango.' On impulse, he leaned towards her and kissed her lightly on the cheek.

Tilda came suddenly to earth. The Meeting-House stopped swirling and settled into place. Cyril was moving away, thinking nothing of his gesture. But the islanders who were watching looked shocked and astonished. It was bad enough that Tilda had been dancing with Cyril—and in an abandoned manner—but to have allowed him to kiss her, without resisting, was hardly to be believed. And among those who had seen it happen were gossipy Marge Kane and censorious Alice Jonas. The news would be all round the village.

Tilda didn't think what to do now; she just did it. She said goodbye to Adam and Cyril, squared her shoulders, swept past the bystanders, and walked swiftly home.

Cyril was unaware of having caused a sensation. He'd enjoyed the interlude. He was mildly sorry that it was Tilda who danced with him, rather than Sophy, whom he thought more attractive. He didn't specially fancy Tilda, though he quite liked her and she was a pretty good dancer, considering how little practice she'd had. Just now, he was thinking more about his wireless set. He wasn't entirely happy at having left somebody else in charge. He set off on the path round the mountainside to Jonathan Wilde's cottage, and, arriving there, was relieved to find that Robert had done his set no harm.

'Marge Kane should mind her own business,' Tilda said next day. 'What happened last night didn't mean nothing. Robert didn't mind me dancing with Cyril. He was glad to see us go. He wanted to fiddle with that wireless thing.'

'Robert should have known better,' said her father. 'He's old enough to understand what's right.'

'I can't see that there was anything *wrong*,' said Tilda.

'Maybe *you* can't, but everyone else will,' her mother said. 'It was bad enough dancing on Prayer Day, but to dance with another lad when you're intended for Robert. And to let him *kiss* you . . . '

'I spent a lot of trouble fixing up you and Robert,' said George. 'I don't want to start it all again. I don't even know that there's another lad available. If Robert turned against you, we mightn't get anyone else.'

'Robert won't turn against me. I told you, he didn't mind.'

'But did he know this lad was going to . . . ?' George couldn't bring himself to use the word.

'To kiss me? 'Course he didn't. He knows by now, I dare say. If he doesn't, he soon will. But it was only on my cheek, not my mouth.'

'I should think not, indeed!' said Annie grimly. 'But from what I was told, you didn't try to stop it. In fact, Marge said it looked as if you *liked* it. I know that ain't true, but it shows how tongues will wag.'

Tilda burst out, furiously, 'If you want to know, I *did* like it!'

She was surprised to hear herself say that. She wasn't

even sure it was true. Though perhaps it was. She could still feel the ghost of the kiss on her cheek.

There was a horrified silence. Then, 'I never thought I'd be so ashamed of my own daughter!' said Annie.

Grandma Molly, visiting George and Annie, had sat silent in the chimney corner. Now she said, 'If you ask me, it's a lot of fuss about nothing.'

'We didn't ask you, Mother,' said George.

'So don't egg her on!' added Annie.

'Kissing's natural,' said Molly. 'Why shouldn't young folk do it if they like each other?'

'But kissing somebody you're not even *intended* for, never mind married to? *That's* not natural. I'm getting worried about Cyril. He's a nice enough lad, but he comes here bringing these mainland customs. He could do us a lot of harm.'

'He could do us a lot of good, too,' said Molly.

'I been hearing things about you,' said Robert, when Cyril joined him at the wireless receiver. 'About you and Tilda, when you was dancing in the Meeting-House last night. Everyone's talking about it.'

'Yes, well, we were pretty good,' said Cyril complacently. 'You should have seen us.'

Robert frowned.

'From what I heard,' he said, 'dancing wasn't all that happened.'

Cyril looked puzzled.

'They say you kissed her,' Robert went on.

'Oh, that? So I did. I'd forgotten. It was nothing, Robert. Just a sort of thank you. We do it all the time on the Mainland.'

'Here on Halcyon,' said Robert, 'you don't kiss somebody else's girl. Specially not mine. Understand?'

Cyril nodded. He didn't really know why Robert was fussing, but if that was how he felt . . .

Robert put out a hand and shook Cyril's.

'That's that, then,' he said, and switched on the set.

A couple of hours later, Cyril yawned and said, 'I'm tired. Must be with teaching all day.'

'*I'm* not tired,' said Robert.

'You will be tomorrow. It's still fine. You'll be out fishing as soon's it's light.'

'Let's go on just a bit longer. Reception's the best tonight we've ever had.'

'You can if you like. I'm off to bed.'

Robert's fingers were on the tuning knob. Suddenly Morse code burst from the set, so loudly he had to reduce the volume. It went on for about a minute, was answered by a much weaker signal, then started again.

Robert asked, 'What's wrong, Cyril?'

Cyril hushed him. He was listening intently. The dialogue in Morse continued through two or three exchanges before coming to a stop. Cyril dashed for the doorway.

Robert said, 'Hey, where you going?'

Cyril was yards along the track already. He yelled over his shoulder, 'Close down when you've finished, Robert. I'll see you tomorrow!' And he raced away into the darkness.

A few minutes later, Adam, roused by hammering on his door, struggled into consciousness.

'What's the trouble?' he enquired sleepily. Then, 'Cyril! It isn't . . . ?'

'It is!' said Cyril. 'I just picked up a signal from *Indomitable* to the Mainland Colony. She's heading for Halcyon! Estimated time of arrival, ten o'clock tomorrow morning!'

Second Wave

Chapter 6

---

*T*HE Calling Bell rang before dawn. Men, already dressing to go down to the boats, went to the Meeting-House instead. Women joined them. There was a clamour of speculation. Last time the bell had been rung at this hour, three years ago, the longboat *Kittiwake* had been on the rocks after night fishing. A rescue party had gone out and four men had been saved, though two were drowned and the boat wrecked. But today everyone was safe at home.

Adam faced the gathering.

'There are folk coming from the Mother Country,' he said. 'Today.'

The news caused a sensation.

'Who are they?' demanded Jamie Campbell, shouting over the buzz of other voices.

'A party led by Brigadier Culpepper.'

'Who's he? What's a brigadier?'

'An important kind of soldier, I think. But he's retired. I suppose that means he's not a soldier now.'

'What are they coming for?'

'They're coming to set up a kind of outpost for the Mother Country.'

As Adam had expected, there were sounds of dismay from all over the hall. Islanders were loyal to the Mother Country, but all the same the Mother Country was part of the outside world, and they were fearful of the outside world. The outside world was large, formidable, unpredictable. They would rather be left alone.

'Why do they want to do that?' asked Jamie.

'There's talk of war. I expect they wouldn't want another country to take us over.'

That didn't make it any better.

'How did you know about this, Adam?' Johnny Oakes asked.

'Young Cyril picked it up last night. On his wireless set.'

'And that was the first you'd heard of it?'

'No. I had a letter in the mail, the day Cyril arrived here. But it didn't seem certain. I thought it might not happen.'

'And you didn't tell anyone?'

'I told Cyril.'

Jamie said, 'You told Cyril, but you didn't tell any of us?'

'There'd been alarms like that before,' said Adam. 'Twice while my grandfather was Reader.'

Old Noah Attwood chipped in.

'That's true,' he said. 'It gave us the fright of our lives. We was on tenterhooks for months, both times. And nothing ever happened.'

'I reckon you should have told us, all the same,' said Johnny.

'I'll go further than that,' said Jamie Campbell. 'I think it's disgraceful. You call yourself Reader, and you leave us in the dark, all but a laddie who only arrived the other day.'

Grandma Molly leaped to Adam's defence.

'What would you have done about it, Jamie, if you'd known? Put up a barbed wire fence?'

'We could have been prepared,' said Jamie. 'We could have worked out a policy.'

'Jamie's right,' Adam admitted. He asked the meeting, 'Do you want me to stand down so you can choose Jamie or somebody else as Reader?'

There were a few mutterings in support of Jamie. But Adam was liked and respected, and still shared in the esteem that his grandfather had earned. Voices were raised all over the hall telling him to carry on.

Jamie could see how matters stood.

'No need for that,' he said. 'Most folk are backing you, Adam. I'll back you myself—for the time being.'

Grandma Molly said, 'The real question is how we're going to deal with these folk.'

'That,' said Adam, 'depends on how they deal with *us*. But it seems to me that, seeing we've always thought of ourselves as belonging to the Mother Country, we should start by welcoming them and trying to help. They're due to arrive this morning, and I think we should go out to meet them. And before that, we'll raise the flag, to show them we're loyal . . . '

But as he spoke, Colin Kane rushed in, shouting, 'There's a ship in the bay! You can see it through the mist. A great big ship! Looks like a warship!'

'That'll be it!' said Adam.

The warship was indeed the *Indomitable*, ahead of its schedule. Adam went out to it in *Shearwater*, with Jamie and Robert among the crew. They returned half an hour later, guiding a naval motor-boat ashore between the reefs and rocks. The petty-officer in charge of the motor-boat was impressed by the islanders' seamanship.

'I wouldn't like to do that without an engine,' he said.

'It's calm today,' said Adam.

'Doesn't seem all that calm to me.'

'A bit of swell, that's all.'

'I wouldn't like to see it when it's rough, then,' said the petty-officer.

'When will we see the important folk?' Jamie asked.

'The bigwigs'll be at breakfast now. I don't know when they'll come ashore. We're going to be here three or four days. We've a big job on hand. There's a supply ship as well, and a hell of a lot of stuff to be landed.'

And for most of the day there was nothing for the

islanders to do but stand and watch in amazement as a motor-boat and two flat landing-craft brought load after load of supplies ashore. Mostly these took the form of huge crates, whose contents could only be guessed at. A squad of soldiers, directed by a young officer, a sergeant and a corporal, stacked them up. Besides the crates, there were a great many sections of wooden buildings and other construction materials; there were innumerable barrels, which might have been of fuel or tar; there was a squat motorized vehicle of rugged appearance, with a trailer; there were twenty or thirty wheelbarrows and as many baggage-trolleys. The flat vessel, riding perilously low in the water, delivered five loads of gravel, which made a small mountain on the shore above the high water mark. There were scores of tea-chests, scores more of wooden cases of bottles, enormous quantities of everything. The day was warm, and the soldiers worked hard. Islanders who approached the motor vehicle—most of them had never seen one before—were told by a tall sergeant with a moustache to keep their distance.

Island reactions were divided. A few were full of wonder, excitement and curiosity. But most were apprehensive. There wasn't any room for self-deception. Whoever had set this operation in motion meant business. It wasn't a visit, it was an invasion.

In mid-afternoon, a fourth boat came ashore from the ship: a spruce, freshly-painted boat with a flag flying at its stern. Soldiers, themselves splashed with seawater and wet sand, dragged its bows to the beach, and the sailor who'd helmed the boat put out a gangplank. Down the plank came, with some care, an elderly gentleman in a tweed jacket and deerstalker hat, a grey-haired lady in a trouser suit, an extremely pretty blonde girl wearing a blue beret, a sweater and a short skirt, and a tall, thin middle-aged man in a suit, carrying a sheaf of papers.

The officer directing the working squad called his men to attention, marched up to the elderly gentleman, stood at a respectful distance, and uttered the one word, 'Sir!'

'All right, stand easy,' said the gentleman; and the tall man added, 'Tell your squad to carry on working.'

The gentleman looked around him, taking his time. At length he said, wearily, 'I thought as much. It's the end of the world.' And, to the lady, 'Well, Daphne my dear, this will be your abode, if you can bear it. And here, I suppose, are some of the inhabitants.'

The group of islanders had waited patiently, a few paces away. Now Adam approached and said respectfully, 'Welcome to Halcyon, sir!'

The grey-haired lady looked round the circle of villagers, then turned to the gentleman.

'My God, Henry!' she said, in a voice which was meant to be low but was clear and carrying. 'They're a bunch of half-castes!'

Most of the islanders didn't know what she meant. Their skin colours ranged through every shade of fawn and brown, and they never noticed any difference.

Jamie, who did understand, was furious. That he happened to have the whitest skin on Halcyon didn't make him less so.

'We're as good as any folk alive!' he declared.

'Careful, my dear,' said the gentleman to his wife. 'I expect they have their feelings. And they can't help their descent.' He said to Adam, in a slow, clear voice, 'Are—you—the—head—man?'

'Yes, sir,' said Adam. He added, with dignity, 'I speak your language.'

'And we're not halfwits!' Jamie chipped in angrily.

The gentleman ignored Jamie.

'You look very young,' he said to Adam.

The thin upright man referred to his sheaf of papers and enquired sharply, 'What's your name?'

'Adam Goodall.'

'That's odd. It's the right name. But according to my brief, Adam Goodall has been head man for more than fifty years. He should be elderly.'

'He was my grandfather, sir. He died last year, and I succeeded him.'

'Who appointed you?'

'Nobody appointed me, exactly. People just kind of thought I should take over.'

'Extraordinary!' observed the thin man.

'Well, it's one way of doing things,' said the elderly gentleman. He extended a hand. 'Glad to meet you, Goodall.'

The thin man said, 'This is Brigadier Culpepper, Goodall. He is the Commissioner. From now on, you take orders from him, you understand. They will normally come through me. I am Philip Saunders, and I am the Civil Administrator, appointed to assist him in non-military matters. I was appointed, Goodall, not because people "kind of thought I should take over", but by the official action of the Imperial Government. Is that clear to you?'

'Yes.'

'You may continue as head man for the present. I shall review the matter later. In the meantime, orders to your people will be issued through you.'

'Isn't that coming over a little heavy, Philip?' said the Brigadier.

'You will allow me to use my judgement, sir,' said Mr Saunders stiffly. 'In my view, these people must be told firmly from the beginning where they stand. It is in their own interest.'

'Of course, of course. I'm sure young Goodall will co-operate. And, Goodall, my wife and daughter wish to see something of your village. So, indeed, do I. We must find a site for a house. Lieutenant Willett will come with us.'

He motioned to the young officer directing the working party. 'Leave your sergeant in charge, Peter,' he said, 'and come with us. This will concern you.'

The little group of people moved off the beach. The Brigadier looked around him with interest as they went. His wife also looked around her, but with apparent disapproval of what she saw. The girl hardly looked around at all. Her expression was resentful.

A handful of villagers trailed behind at a distance. They were deeply interested in the incomers, and both shocked and fascinated by the girl's bare legs. Halcyon women didn't show their legs.

Philip Saunders waved the spectators away with a gesture. On the way up the dirt track from beach to settlement, Saunders said to the lieutenant, 'As soon as everything's ashore, we must start improving this surface.'

'See to it, Peter, will you?' said the Brigadier to Lieutenant Willett.

They arrived in the village. It was at its best, for the day was fine and the wind light. The Brigadier was still showing interest and the girl beginning to do so, but Mrs Culpepper was clearly unimpressed, and Saunders looked around him with equal distaste.

'It's nothing but a scatter of hovels,' he said.

'Would you like to see inside one?' Adam asked.

'I think I'd better.'

'This is my house we're just coming to. This is my wife, Ellen.'

Ellen curtsied to the visitors. Philip Saunders poked into each corner of the cottage, examined the inside walls and remarked 'Damp.' He prodded a bed, enquired 'What's in the mattress? Potatoes?', and ran a finger along a shelf, without picking up any dust.

'Where's your water tap?' he asked.

'We get our water from the stream.'

'There are animals wandering around. Where do *they* drink?'

'From the stream.'

Philip Saunders frowned.

'What kind of sanitation do you have?' he asked finally.

'We have an earth closet, sir. Out at the back.'

'Oh, my God!' said the Brigadier's wife. 'I do believe I can smell it!'

'No, ma'am, it doesn't smell at all,' Ellen said. 'Maybe in

hot weather some of them do, just a bit, but not ours. Would you like to go into it?'

'Heaven forbid!' said Daphne Culpepper. She turned to her husband. 'Henry, it's impossible! We've had some grim postings in our time, but this . . . '

Philip Saunders said, 'The village is hopeless. No point in requisitioning hovels like these. Our men will have to sleep in tents on the beach until we've run up some accommodation. But don't worry, Mrs Culpepper, we'll work on your house first. We'll choose a site away from the village and we'll lay on water and drainage. Willett here's a trained civil engineer, remember. That's how he got the posting. It'll all be in the day's work for you, eh, Willett?'

'It's not as simple as that,' said Lieutenant Willett. 'Depends on finding a site. And there's the wireless transmitter as well. The radio officer will be involved in siting that.'

Saunders frowned.

'He should have come ashore by now. Had a heavy night on board last night, I understand. Frankly, I'm not too happy about that fellow Rawson. Drinks too much.'

'One way and another,' said Willett, 'with the roads and the construction, there's a lot of work. More than my chaps can do on their own.'

'That's understood,' Saunders said impatiently. 'I've told you, you'll get help with the labouring jobs. We need to get a move on if life's to be tolerable here.'

Leaving Adam's cottage, the little party came to the Meeting-House. Adam pointed out with some pride that the flag of the Mother Country was flying from the mast.

'Yes,' said the Brigadier. 'Flying upside-down.'

He was amused. Mr Saunders wasn't.

'Get it replaced with one in decent condition and the right way up, will you?' he said to Lieutenant Willett. 'A torn and faded thing like that is a disgrace.'

Adam was chagrined. Mr Saunders walked round the outside of the Meeting-House.

'This is better built than most,' he observed. 'Let's have a look inside.'

He spent a little time inspecting the building. Then he said to the Brigadier, 'We can use this, sir, I think. Will it do as temporary quarters for you and your family, until your house is built?'

'Totally unacceptable,' said Mrs Culpepper.

'It isn't luxury, my dear,' said the Brigadier, 'but we can survive it for a week or two. It's a good deal better than the trenches, I can tell you.'

'The Great War has been over for years, Henry,' said Mrs Culpepper, 'and your experiences in the trenches are beside the point. To begin with, there is no privacy here.'

'Willett's men can put in a few partitions. And that little room to the left of the entrance can be my office for the time being.'

'But, sir,' protested Adam, 'this is our Meeting-House. We need it. We use it on Prayer Day, and for everything that happens in the village.'

'You can have it back later,' said the Civil Administrator. 'Unless of course we decide to use it for something else.'

They returned to the beach. The Brigadier and his wife and daughter were ferried back to the cruiser, where they would be sleeping so long as it was anchored off Halcyon. The Civil Administrator stayed behind a while for a discussion with Lieutenant Willett. Adam asked if he could help, and was told that he couldn't. His request for further information about the intentions of the new regime was dismissed by Mr Saunders with a terse 'Not now, I'm busy.'

Retreating disconsolate to a waiting group of islanders, Adam told them the little he knew of what was going to happen. There was instant outrage.

'They can't take our Meeting-House from us!' declared Jamie Campbell.

'How are we to stop them?'

'We . . . well, there's more of us than there are them.'

'Have a bit of sense, Jamie,' said Adam. 'We can't fight them. What do you think *that* stands for?' He indicated the cruiser, lying out in the bay. 'It's the power of the Mother Country. But we won't let the Meeting-House go without a protest.'

There hadn't been any fishing that day, so most of the island men were within call. Adam assembled them. Led by him and Jamie, a group of some ten or twelve approached Mr Saunders, who was still in conversation with Lieutenant Willett. The Administrator turned towards them.

'Well, what is it?' he enquired.

'We want to talk to you, sir. About the Meeting-House.'

'I've told you, I'm busy just now. Come and see me there tomorrow at noon.'

Johnny Oakes said, 'Most of us'll be out in the boats. We can't lose another day's fishing. We have to eat.'

'That's *your* problem,' said the Civil Administrator. 'If you really want to see me, you'll manage it.'

Adam said to the islanders, 'The boats had better come in early tomorrow.'

There was reluctant assent. The weather looked set fair, and no one wanted to give up half a good fishing day. The men stumped away, grim-faced. The Civil Administrator didn't watch them go; he was already continuing his discussion with the lieutenant.

The spick-and-span boat returned and took the Administrator back to the cruiser. Lieutenant Willett and his working party remained on shore. They went on working until dusk, when the remaining boats also went back to the ship. A cluster of bell-tents was erected on the level ground close to the beach; a rudimentary field kitchen was set up and the soldiers, sitting around in little groups, ate out of mess-tins. Islanders came down from the village from time to time to peer at the men from a safe distance, and to make guesses about what was in the crates and what the soldiers were eating. But most of the time was spent by people in their own homes, where the invasion was discussed all evening. Most islanders were deeply worried, though some had vague hopes of benefiting from the supposed wealth of the Outside World and some younger folk were excited by the very fact that things were happening.

Cyril and Robert came down after dark from Jonathan Wilde's house, where they had spent the evening with the wireless set. Cyril was feeling frustrated. He'd hoped to overhear an exchange of messages between the *Indomitable* and its base, and to be able to tear down the hillside with news for Adam. But all he picked up that had any bearing on events in Halcyon was a brief report from the cruiser to its base in the Mainland Colony that unloading was going according to plan and was expected to continue for another two days.

By the time he and Robert were back in the village, the soldiers were all in their tents. Lamps could be seen glowing dimly through the canvas of two or three of them, but most were in darkness and there was no sign of activity.

'They'll be worn out after a day like they've had,' Cyril speculated. 'Gone to sleep early, I dare say.'

A little way from the beach, the motor-vehicle was outlined by moonlight. Robert was entranced by the sight. 'Look at that!' he said; and then, 'I never seen a motor car before.'

Cyril said, 'I've seen lots, and driven them, too. It's not a thrill to me. That one's nothing special, except it's had some kind of adaptation for rough ground. They'll certainly find it rough enough here.'

Robert said, 'I'm going to take a closer look at it.'

He walked openly up to the motor car. Nobody stopped him. Cyril, a little worried, followed. Robert studied the car with interest. It was obvious what the steering-wheel was for. He opened the door and sat behind the wheel, gripping it instinctively with both hands. He looked around him, trying to imagine what it would be like to drive it. Then he got out and walked round the outside of the vehicle. He didn't know what made a car go, but whatever it was, it must be hidden under that lid at the front. He yearned to examine it.

'Come away, Robert!' Cyril urged him. 'Someone'll see you in a minute!'

Robert felt around the bonnet, hoping to find a catch that would release it, but he didn't find one. Then a flashlight shone upon him and somebody grabbed him from behind.

'What d'you think *you're* doing?' a voice demanded. The tall sergeant with the moustache spun Robert round and stared fiercely into his face.

Robert didn't say anything. He was bewildered. Islanders were sometimes rough in the way they treated animals, but they never laid hands on each other in anger. And he couldn't see what he was doing wrong.

'Cat got your tongue?' the man enquired.

Cyril appeared out of the darkness and rallied round Robert.

'He only wanted to look at the motor car,' he explained. 'He's never seen one before.'

'He can tell my officer about that.'

The man gripped Robert's arm and marched him to one of the tents. Cyril went along with them.

Lieutenant Willett was sitting on a camp bed in a tent which he obviously occupied alone. He was studying some papers by the light of an oil lamp.

'What's all this about, sergeant?' he enquired.

'This young feller was trying to break into the motor,' the sergeant said. 'And the other one was with him. I don't know what *he* was up to. Lurking around.'

'Well?' said Peter Willett. 'What *were* you up to?'

Robert was still tongue-tied. Cyril said, 'We weren't up to anything. Robert here was interested in the motor car, that's all. Cars are new to him.'

'Is that right, Robert?'

Robert nodded.

Peter Willett said, 'Well, you can't have been planning to steal it, that's for sure. Even if you could start it, there's nowhere to drive it to. Did you mean to damage it?'

'No, sir,' said Robert, shocked at the idea.

'I believe you. You were just inquisitive. Well, if you want to see something, why not ask?'

Cyril said, 'The sergeant told us earlier on to keep away.'

The sergeant said, 'That's correct, sir. Administrator's orders.'

'H'm. Actually, sergeant, the Administrator has no right to give you orders. He isn't in the Army. I am. However, these lads were told to keep away and didn't. I'll have to deal with them.' He put on a fierce expression.

'You know what I'm going to do?' he said to Cyril and Robert.

They shook their heads.

'I'm going to turn my back on you while I have a word with Sergeant Young. And when I look round again, it would be a good idea if you weren't here.'

He said to the sergeant, 'I think we'll forget that little episode.'

The sergeant said, 'Right you are, sir. But lads wants watching, you know. Lads is always getting up to something.'

'Didn't *you* ever get up to anything when you were a lad, sergeant?'

The sergeant grinned.

'We got up to worse things than looking at motor cars,' he said.

'I thought so. So did I . . . Shall I turn round now, sergeant?'

'I think you might, sir,' said the sergeant. 'They've gone.'

Chapter 7

THE island boats set out before dawn next morning, hoisted sails, and made for the fishing ground just short of Kingfisher. Adam was at the helm of *Shearwater*, while Johnny Oakes helmed *Petrel* and Dick Kane *Seamew*. The names were traditional; there was always a *Shearwater*, always a *Petrel*, always a *Seamew*, unless one of them had recently been wrecked. They came in, shortly before midday, with a good catch. Women and girls were left to sort and distribute the fish; the men ate a hasty meal and gathered in front of the Meeting-House.

There was a shock for them. The Civil Administrator had acted already. A big notice on the Meeting-House door said NO ADMITTANCE, and a soldier stood in front of it.

The islanders could hardly believe it. The Meeting-House had always been open at all hours. They all looked towards Adam.

Adam said to the soldier, 'We've come to see the Civil Administrator.'

The soldier said, 'He can't see you yet. He's talking to the Brig.'

They waited outside. Time passed. Men fidgeted. Adam looked glum. It was a long while before the Brigadier emerged. The soldier sprang to attention and saluted. The Brigadier looked around him with mild surprise.

'Quite a gathering,' he observed.

'We're supposed to be seeing Mr Saunders,' said Adam. 'You remember?'

'Oh, yes, of course. You're Goodall, aren't you? Let me see, what was it about?'

'About our Meeting-House being taken over.'

'Yes. Well, I'm sure Mr Saunders will put you in the picture.'

'Sir, could we talk to *you* about it?'

'Not a lot of point, really. He's in charge of this kind of thing. I wouldn't like to shove my oar in.' And the Brigadier walked away in the direction of the beach.

Adam asked the soldier, 'Can we go in now?'

'I'll find out.' And a moment later, 'He'll see you when he's ready. Not more than five of you, he says.'

Adam pulled a face. 'He didn't tell me he'd only see five,' he protested.

'Sorry, chum. Nothing to do with me. He gives the orders, I take 'em.'

There was another long wait. Eventually five islanders, headed by Adam and Jamie, filed into the Meeting-House. The Administrator had installed himself in the little room which had been the missionary's office when first the Meeting-House was built. He was sitting at a trestle table with papers in front of him, and looked up irritably.

'This is a waste of time, Goodall,' he said. 'I told you yesterday all you need to know, which is that I am requisitioning this building. However, for your informa-tion, the room we are in now will be my headquarters for the time being. The main hall will be partitioned to make temporary accommodation for the Brigadier and his family. When the building work is done, there will be a house for the Brigadier, and you may get your building back. I can't decide at this stage.'

Adam said quietly, 'Islanders built the Meeting-House with their own hands. It's a hundred years old. This is where we come for every Prayer Day service, every meeting we have, all our socials and dances, everything. The whole community revolves around it.'

'Then it will have to stop revolving for the time being.'

Jamie burst out, 'There's no fairness in that. The Meeting-House is *ours!*'

Philip Saunders said, 'I don't *have* to explain matters to you, but I will. Listen carefully. My Government is not taking this island into administration out of some whim or other. Halcyon is totally valueless. There would be no reason to go to trouble and expense over it, if it were not for the world situation. There may be a war at any time. We are a far-flung empire, and may be threatened from any quarter. At this moment the potential enemy is a powerful and unpleasant dictatorship, the Republic of Santa Cruz. I suppose you know where that is?'

'It's to the west of us,' said Adam.

'That's correct. I'm glad to find you're not totally ignorant. Santa Cruz is to the west and our own Mainland Colony is to the east, both of them fifteen hundred miles away. Halcyon is in the middle. If Santa Cruz were to seize it and then there were a war, it could cause mayhem to shipping. That's why we're here, Goodall—a vital national interest. In comparison, the socials and dances in your Meeting-House don't matter a damn.'

Jamie asked, 'How many men have you here?'

'That's not a secret. About thirty.'

'And you reckon they could defend Halcyon against an invasion?'

'Of course not. What we're doing at the moment is asserting ownership. Once we're here, Santa Cruz can't invade without making it an act of war. And also we're setting up a wireless listening post. It will help us keep in touch with what's going on.'

'Might the Mother Country send a *big* force before long?' asked Adam thoughtfully.

'I don't know, and if I did know I wouldn't tell you. But now you're here I've something else to say to you. I'm going to need your labour. We've to make roads and put buildings up, quickly. That will take more men than we've brought with us.'

The islanders looked at one another in dismay. Philip Saunders went on, 'You'll be paid, of course.'

Adam said, 'Money's no use to us here. We just live from hand to mouth. We'd rather be left to get on with our lives.'

'I'm afraid that option isn't open to you. The work must be done. As for payment, there'll be no need of actual money. It's all been thought of in advance. We shall give you tokens, according to the amount of time you put in, and when everything has been landed we shall open a store here and you can spend what you earn. There will be ample supplies of canned, dried and packeted foods.'

Jamie Campbell said fiercely, 'We're free men. We don't want your roads and we don't want your tokens and we don't want your cans and packets! I've seen the Outside World myself, and I know what it's like. I don't want anything more to do with it.'

'I've told you, you have no choice. The island is a colony of the Mother Country. Brigadier Culpepper has been appointed Commissioner. He has the powers of a Governor. In words of one syllable, you have to do as he tells you. He is also Justice of the Peace. That means he can send you to jail if you don't. Do you have a lock-up here?'

Adam said, 'We've never had to lock anybody up.'

'There'll be a lock-up now,' Saunders said. 'I dare say the soldiery will keep it busy if you don't. Anyway, hold yourselves prepared to be called on for work.'

There was an angry murmur from the group. Adam said, 'It's all we can do to keep alive. We haven't time for making roads.'

'I'm afraid you'll have to find it. You'll have to adjust yourselves, that's all. If you do as you're told you won't come to any harm. Before long you'll be grateful to us. And I'll tell you one thing. You can thank your lucky stars it's the Mother Country and not the Santa Cruzians. They're nasty.'

'Oh? And what are *you*?' demanded Jamie truculently.

Saunders had spoken all through the interview in a cold, detached voice. Now he flushed and looked momentarily angry.

'What's *your* name?' he asked.

'James Campbell.'

'Watch your step, Campbell. I shall keep an eye on you.

You have the look to me of a trouble-maker. And now, I have other things to do. You've had more of my time than I intended. I wish you all good day.'

Sonia Culpepper stood beside her father on the deck of the cruiser. It was the second day after *Indomitable*'s arrival at Halcyon: another fine day and the sea still calm.

Sonia said, 'Daddy, you are *stupid*. You tell me all that rubbish about the joys of island life, and then the island turns out to be *this*.'

'At least, my dear, it's a change from boarding school. You complained enough about school.'

'It was dreadful. *Everything* in my life is dreadful. I wish I'd been born in a slum and sent to work at fourteen in a cotton mill.'

'I think you'd have found that even more dreadful.'

'It would be more like *living* than anything in my life so far. Nothing has ever happened to me. Nothing at all. Nothing.'

'Travelling five thousand miles to a distant colony isn't exactly nothing. And you have to do something between now and going to that place in Switzerland next autumn. The alternative was staying with Aunt Bertha. Would you rather have stayed with Aunt Bertha?'

'Aunt Bertha is *dreadful*.'

'What would you *really* like to do, Sonia?'

'Play tennis and swim and go to parties and dances, that's what I'd like to do. And what I *could* do, if you'd only stay at home in Surrey like anybody else's father. Instead of which, here we are, about to be put ashore in a godforsaken place with nothing but a few soldiers and peasants. No company, no young people, nothing to do but listen to that pompous ass Saunders . . . It's *dreadful*.'

'Saunders may be a pompous ass, but Peter Willett isn't. And I think he's rather taken with you.'

'I know he is. He makes eyes at me all the time. But I'm not taken with Peter Willett. I know he's every mother's dream. "The Willetts are such a good family." Oh, yes, Mummy approves of him. So reliable. Won't lead me into temptation. I wonder what she'd think if I took up with one of the soldiers. I rather like Sergeant Young's moustache. Or maybe a husky island fisherman. Some of them look quite sexy.'

'You described them as peasants a minute ago.'

'Yes, well. What if I became a peasant's woman? How would you like that?'

'I don't think you'll have the chance. I'm told the island men are all married, and very faithful to their wives.'

'As dull as anybody else, in fact? Oh, Daddy, why *did* you bring me to this place?'

'Actually, I like your company. I'm rather fond of you, my dear.'

'I don't know why. I'm not fond of myself these days. You're a silly old duffer. I suppose you're rather nice, really. But that's no excuse. I'm not going to forgive you.'

'Never mind forgiving me,' said the Brigadier. 'I'm about to go ashore. Are you coming with me?'

'Oh, I suppose so. After all, what else is there to do?'

The Brigadier and Sonia went ashore with Philip Saunders in the spick-and-span launch. Saunders bore the Brigadier away to the Meeting-House, where work on partitioning the interior had begun. Sonia told them she would take a walk into the village, declining an offer by Peter Willett to go with her. Saunders said, 'Quite right too, Miss Culpepper. Lieutenant Willett has duties to perform.' Willett bit his lip and said nothing.

Sonia set off on her own. Her spirits were cheered as she walked uphill through the village, glimpsing between cottages the cliffs and sea and mountainside. Boats were still plying between cruiser and shore; the unloading was due to be completed today. Far beyond the grey shape of the cruiser could be seen the pale, mirage-like outline of the companion island, Kingfisher. Stretching her legs, glad to be striding out in the open after so much confinement on board ship, she was unexpectedly conscious of her health and energy. She was almost enjoying herself. Yet there was something missing.

Sonia knew what it was. She needed a friend. Not, at the moment, a boy-friend. Somebody to chat and laugh and share confidences with: a girl-friend. She would be the only girl in the colonial community. It was a bit hard, she reflected, that there would be nobody of her own sex to talk to on the whole island except her mother . . .

With this thought in her mind, Sonia crossed the stream, close by the washpool, where Lizzie Oakes and Marge Kane were scrubbing clothes and spreading them on the grass to dry. She smiled at them but didn't speak; she wouldn't have known what to say. Lizzie Oakes stood up and curtsied but likewise didn't speak; she didn't know what to say any more than Sonia.

Sonia was some distance along the track when the dog appeared. It was a large mongrel, wild or semi-wild; and it took an instant dislike to Sonia's bare legs. It made a little rush at her. She shouted, loudly, 'Get away!' It retreated snarling, half-circled her and moved in again. Sonia, frightened, drew back. The dog, scenting fear, leaped in, and she felt its teeth in her calf.

Then a rescuer came: a hefty, handsome girl with a stick. Tilda. She thwacked the dog on back and side, hard. The dog turned from Sonia towards her, and Tilda hit it on the snout. The dog howled and made off. Tilda pursued it for a few yards, but the dog ran faster. Tilda returned to Sonia and asked, 'Did he bite you, miss?'

Sonia, shaken, showed her the tooth-marks. Tilda said, 'You better come into our cottage.' She took Sonia's arm, half-supporting her, and walked her to the Wilde cottage. George was out fishing, Annie at the spinning-wheel. Annie took one look at the bite and told Tilda, 'Go for your grandma. She knows what to do.' In very little time, Sonia was sitting in one of the cottage's two battered armchairs and Grandma Molly was applying a mysterious and rather sinister-looking salve which she assured Sonia would prevent any harm coming from the bite.

Annie Wilde made a cup of tea for Sonia, but none for anyone else because she only had two or three spoonfuls of tea in the bottom of her caddy. The large spoonful of sugar she put in the tea was the last of the sugar, too. Sonia sat sipping the hot sweet liquid and still trembling.

Tilda said, 'I'm sorry about that, miss. Those dogs can be nasty, specially if they think you're scared of them. We don't stand no nonsense ourselves. Even the children just send them packing.'

'I must be a fearful coward,' Sonia said.

'Oh, I wouldn't say that, miss. It's frightening if you're not used to it. And the dog knows you're not one of us. I'd carry a stick another time, if I were you. That'll show 'em you're not going to stand no nonsense.'

'Probably they'd still know I was frightened,' Sonia said.

Grandma Molly said, 'I been having frights all my life, and I'm still here. It's natural to be frit. But I reckon if you face up to whatever it is, even if you're scared, things turn out all right, and then you're not frit any more. I'd like to see the dog that could scare *me*!'

'Don't boast, Gran,' said Tilda.

There was a silence. Sonia was gradually recovering. Tilda said, 'I been admiring that jumper of yours.'

'Yes. It *is* rather nice, isn't it?'

'Did you make it? Or maybe somebody made it for you?'

'I'm afraid not. I bought it in a shop.'

'Oh, a shop.'

Tilda couldn't quite envisage a shop. She had never seen one.

'Are you intended?' she enquired.

'Am I what?'

'Intended.'

Sonia looked blank.

'I mean, are you going to marry somebody?'

'I expect so, some day. I'm not really thinking about it yet.'

76

'You look old enough.'

'I'm seventeen.'

'And there's nothing arranged for you?'

'Arranged? Oh, goodness, you mean an arranged marriage? No. We don't have arranged marriages in the Mother Country. I shall marry who I like, when I like, if I like.'

Tilda was round-eyed. Sonia went on, 'I expect I'll live on my own, or with a girl-friend or a group of young people, before I marry. I'd like to have a job and earn my living.'

Her hearers were astonished. Tilda said, 'So you don't stay in your mum and dad's house till the day you get wed?'

'I expect they'd like me to. But I shan't.'

'Well! Maybe there's things about the Outside World that I'd like,' said Tilda.

Annie Wilde was frowning.

'Tilda's always been a rebel,' she said. 'Like her grandma.'

'That's right,' said Grandma Molly smugly.

'So you're a rebel, Tilda!' said Sonia. 'Shake hands. Rebels of the world, unite. I mean to be a rebel myself, if I have the nerve.'

She put down her teacup.

'But I'd better go,' she said. 'They'll be wondering what's become of me.'

'Does your bite still hurt?' asked Annie.

' 'Course it don't,' said Molly, 'after what I put on it.'

'Well, actually,' Sonia admitted, 'I was forgetting about it. No, it doesn't hurt much.'

'I'll give you a stick,' said Tilda, 'in case you meet any more dogs. Just show it to 'em. That'll do the trick.'

'I'll be seeing you again, I hope,' said Sonia. 'It's good to have someone to talk to.'

Chapter 8

Sonia's dog-bite made news. She was ferried straight back to the ship and taken to the sick bay, where the bite was dressed again and she was given an injection.

Philip Saunders sent for Adam.

'I'm not having this,' he said. 'Doesn't anyone own these dogs?'

'Some are owned,' said Adam. 'Some have gone wild, or are born wild. They live on the mountain and come to the village scavenging.'

'They must be got rid of at once. No telling what diseases they might carry. Tell your people to put a collar on any dog they want to stay alive. I'll give them twenty-four hours.'

'We don't have dog collars,' Adam said.

'You'll have to improvise them, then. Even if it's only with a bit of rope. When the twenty-fours hours are up, I shall have a squad sent out, and any dog without a collar will be shot. And after *that*, any dog that bites a person—I mean bites one of our people, naturally—will be shot and its owner punished. By the way, Goodall, I thought I felt an earth tremor the other day. Could that be so?'

'Yes, sir, we get them sometimes; we always have done. The Peak's an old volcano.'

'But not a dead one?'

'Well, a geologist came here once, in my grandfather's time. He said it might erupt some day, but maybe not for centuries. We don't worry about it.'

'I hope you're right. Anyway, we have more immediate problems. There's another thing I meant to ask you about. Whose is the empty house a mile away, round the mountain?'

'That's Jonathan Wilde's house.'

'And who's he?'

'He's dead, sir. Died two hundred years ago. He was one of the mutineers on the *Susannah*.'

'Oh, the *Susannah* mutineers. A famous story. That mob who put the captain overboard and then all murdered each other. Not very edifying . . . But whose house is it now?'

'It hasn't been lived in ever since.'

'Then we shan't be upsetting anyone by requisitioning it. Lieutenant Rawson says it's in the best situation for our radio transmitter and I've told him to go ahead. We shall be setting that up as quickly as we can.'

Adam looked unhappy but said nothing. Saunders went on, 'I gather they found a wireless set and aerial there. If it's nobody's house, how does that come about?'

'Oh, that's Cyril's. A boy who came from the mainland a few months ago.'

'Well, we're impounding it. I'm told it's quite powerful. We can't have somebody in a position to eavesdrop on our messages.'

'But that set *belongs* to Cyril. He's very proud of it.'

'Too bad.'

Adam said, doggedly, 'But do you have any right to confiscate somebody's property?'

Philip Saunders was angry. He said, in a cold, controlled voice, 'Obviously I haven't yet made you understand, Goodall. Any day now, we may find ourselves at war. Under threat of war, the defence of the Mother Country's interests takes precedence over everything else. Brigadier Culpepper is empowered to take any measures he thinks necessary. And he will do so. It's a security matter, and I'm not going to argue with you about it . . . Well, Goodall, what are you hanging about for?'

Adam said, 'I think you ought to know, sir, that the weather looks like changing.'

'It still looks fine to me.'

'You haven't been here long, sir. We get to know the signs. It'll be stormy by morning. And there's a lot of stuff on the beach. You should lash down anything that could be blown away. The winds are strong here.'

'Thank you for the warning, Goodall,' said Saunders. 'I shall bear it in mind. And remember, I mean what I say about those dogs. Act on my words, please, and jump to it.'

In Grandma Molly's cottage, Cyril dismissed Polly Attwood and two other children whom he was teaching to read. The children dashed out at once to the open air. Cyril mopped his forehead.

'That's hard work,' he told Grandma Molly. 'Ever tried explaining why CAT is spelled with a C and KITTEN with a K?'

But Grandma Molly had never spelled either word.

'It's above my head, that stuff,' she said. 'My brother Thomas was clever. *He* learned to read. Taught himself. And what came of it was, he left Halcyon and he's hardly been back since. But I never had time, somehow. There was always so much else to do.'

'I'll teach you, Gran,' Cyril offered.

Molly ruffled his immaculate hair. 'It's too late,' she said. 'I'll not learn now.'

Cyril would have been furious with anyone else who touched his hair. He still spent time every day getting it just right. But Molly was privileged. Though no word of affection had ever passed between them, they'd become fond of each other. He grinned.

'All right,' he said. 'If you're not interested in my amazing offer, I'll be going over to Jonathan's.'

Molly decided that the story of Sonia and the dog-bite would keep until supper.

'Off you go, then,' she told him.

Robert was out fishing, and Cyril was looking forward to having the wireless set to himself for once. He walked smartly through the village and round the headland to Jonathan Wilde's cottage. And he was astonished to find people there before him. They were a loose-limbed lieutenant, a few years older than Lieutenant Willett, and two young soldiers.

'W-what are you doing?' he asked.

'Taking over, I should think,' said the lieutenant casually. 'My name's Rawson, by the way, Andrew Rawson. We have to set up a transmitter. This is just the right place, as somebody knew already. We were told before we came there was no radio on the island. So whose is the receiver?'

'Mine.'

'Not a bad set at all. Whoever built that knew what he was doing.'

'That's right,' said Cyril, pleased. 'It was a mate of mine who built it. Well, a fellow I used to know, anyway. I got a little bit of money from my dad's estate to remember him by, and that's what I spent it on.'

'I dare say it pulls the stations in, eh? Even here?'

'Yeh, it does. Night time, I hear all kinds of languages, jabbering away. And the Mainland Colony, of course. And the Mother Country sometimes. It's great.'

'Good for you.' Lieutenant Rawson yawned and said, 'Sorry, I'm not quite at my best today. Had a heavy night on the ship.' Then, 'Pity you won't be able to go on using it.'

'*What*?'

Rawson seemed mildly amused by Cyril's consternation. 'I said, Pity you won't be able to go on using your set.'

'Why not?'

'Orders from the Brig. Well, orders from the Saunders, anyway. I suppose the Brig must know. Saunders tells him some things, sometimes.'

'But *what* orders?'

'No private wireless sets allowed. Security risk.'

'B-but . . .'

Cyril spluttered with indignation. 'What security risk is that? It's only a receiver, it won't transmit.'

'Question is, *what* will it receive? There'll be plain language signals passing between us and ships, us and the Mainland Colony, us and the Mother Country . . .

Saunders doesn't want the whole island knowing every move in the game.'

'If it's in plain language it can't be all that secret,' said Cyril.

Rawson yawned again.

'You have a point there. Anything really secret would be in code. And I have the code book. Sleep with it under my pillow. So there isn't really any risk. But what is it Mr Saunders says, chaps?'

The two men had been silent during this conversation. Now they said in unison, 'Walls have ears!' and grinned.

'That's the Saunders theory. Walls have ears. Or maybe, "Never tell anybody anything if you can help it." Sorry about that, laddie, but don't blame me. We're just a service department here. We carry out orders.'

'So do I have to take my set away?' Cyril asked.

'No such luck. We have to impound it.'

'But you can't. It's mine. I bought it and paid for it.'

'Too bad. I told you, I'm sorry, lad . . . What's your name, by the way?'

'Cyril Jonas.'

'Well, Cyril, you'll get your set back as soon as I'm told I can release it. But it won't be while we're in a state of alert, which we are now, in case you didn't know. If Santa Cruz backs off, it'll be another matter.'

'What are you going to do with it?'

'Keep it here. One of my chaps will sleep in here tonight. Tomorrow there'll be glass in the windows and a lock on the door. And I'll give you a bit of advice, Cyril. Don't try to break in. You can't get away with it.'

Cyril said, 'I'm not standing for this.'

'If you're not satisfied, laddie, you can go and argue with Philip Saunders. But in my opinion, you might as well save your breath.'

Cyril stormed into the Meeting-House, brushing aside the soldier on guard. His face was white with fury.

'You can't take my set away!' he shouted. 'It's theft!'

Philip Saunders said, 'Shut up.'

'I won't shut up!'

'Yes, you will. And you'll stop your bloody impudence. Who the hell are you, anyway?'

'Cyril Jonas.'

'You don't sound like an islander.'

'I'm not an islander.'

'Then you should know better how to behave. If you're not an islander, what are you doing here?'

'Just at present,' said Cyril, 'I'm teaching them to read.'

'You're a teacher? You?'

'Not a real teacher. I do my best. They hadn't any teacher at all until I came.'

'I presume—' with a hint of sarcasm '—that you're literate.'

'I can read and write, sure, and do sums.'

'And you can operate a wireless set. You can't be totally stupid . . . ' Philip Saunders was moderating his tone. 'I think I can use you, Jonas. I have a job for you.'

'I didn't come to ask for a job.'

'You may get one all the same. We need a civilian clerk, and it's hard to find one in a place where everyone's illiterate.'

Cyril was taken aback. He said, still furious, 'I don't *want* a job as a clerk. And what about the people I'm teaching? Ten children and sixteen grown-ups.'

'If they managed without a teacher before, they can manage without one again.'

'But . . . I won't do it!'

Philip Saunders enquired, evenly, 'Would you rather work on making roads? That's the alternative, Jonas. Think about it, will you? I have a feeling that when you've done so you'll realize that you're in luck.'

Cyril marched out, still furious. Outside, he was hailed by a soldier.

'Hi there, Cyril.'

Cyril recognized one of the two men who'd been with Lieutenant Rawson in Jonathan's house.

'Hullo,' he said cautiously.

'I'm Gerry Baines. Wireless mechanic. Just going off duty. I wanted to say I'm sorry about losing your set.'

'Thanks,' said Cyril, not feeling much cheered.

'I've built a few sets in my time, Cyril. I guess that's why I became a wireless mech. Where do you live?'

'At Grandma Molly's. Last house in the village.'

'I'd like to come and see you.' Gerry Baines dropped his voice. 'Fact is,' he said, 'if there's somewhere to keep it, I'd like to build a set with you on the quiet. I've got a few components in my kit, and I can borrow some from the Army when all our gear's been unloaded. Rawson won't notice. More often than not, he gets drunk at night and has a thick head next day. And even when he's sober he's not really interested. We might steal a few bits of your set back if we need 'em. How about that?'

Cyril's face brightened.

'Sounds terrific,' he said.

'We'll beat the bastards, eh?' said Gerry Baines.

'You bet we will,' said Cyril. 'Shake, pal.'

Later, Philip Saunders remarked to the Brigadier, 'The head man gave me a storm warning this afternoon. Whether it amounts to anything I don't know. He's only a peasant like the rest.'

The Brigadier said, 'Peasant or not, I expect he knows more about the weather here than we do.'

'Maybe, maybe not. It still looks set fair.'

Both men's minds were on the following morning, when the *Indomitable* was due to sail for the Mainland Colony. Its last action before leaving would be the final delivery to Halcyon of the Brigadier, his family, the radio officer and Philip Saunders. Tonight would be their last night on board.

Neither of them remembered to pass the warning on to Lieutenant Willett, who was staying on shore with his men.

Chapter 9

*T*HE sun had shone all day, and went on shining, but towards dark a heavy haze began to build up on the western horizon. The breeze dropped to nothing; the air became sultry. There was an ominous sense of falling pressure. Sergeant Young said to Lieutenant Willett, 'Feels as if there's going to be a storm, sir.'

Willett concurred. 'I've been thinking that myself,' he said. 'Have all the tent-pegs and guy-ropes checked, will you? And get any loose stuff on the beach fastened down tight.'

'Yes, sir. We better get moving.'

The men were tired. In a long, strenuous day they'd just managed to finish unloading. Now, wearily, they tightened the tarpaulins that covered the more vulnerable stores. A motor launch had been left for the use of the Halcyon detachment; they drew it up well above the high-water mark, fastened a canvas cover over it and roped it to a huge boulder. They ate supper out of their mess-tins; it was stew for the third time in their three days on Halcyon. A strong gust of wind sprang from the sea and was followed by the same expectant calm as before. The men retreated to their tents, drew the flaps tight, and settled to playing cards or draughts, reading books or comics, or grousing idly together. A few, utterly weary, went to sleep almost at once.

The wind rose, becoming steadier and stronger. First drops of rain pattered on the tent-canvas.

In the village, the islanders began to be alarmed. Storms were a regular occurrence on Halcyon, but everyone could tell from long experience that this would be a bad one. The houses wouldn't come to any harm; they were built of stone and had been tested many times. The sheep were hardy and the lambs well grown; they would survive. The few stunted fruit trees were in the relative shelter of the Dell; they would probably lose the unformed fruit, but that was not a fatal loss. The real worry was the potato crop. This was the time when it was most vulnerable. There were fifty acres of flourishing plants; if the gale lasted long it would wither the lot and the main crop would fail.

Many islanders worried about the soldiers. There was a long tradition of looking after anyone in danger. Rough seas and vile weather were old enemies of human life on Halcyon, and it was basic morality that no one should be abandoned to them. Against such enemies all were on the same side.

Adam consulted Jamie. Jamie said, 'We've worries enough of our own. We don't owe that lot anything. They think they're so clever. Let them look out for themselves.'

Adam was shocked.

'They can't know what they're in for,' he said. 'How we feel about having them here isn't the point. We still have to help them.'

'After the way they've treated you, Adam, you must be crazy to think like that.'

'It's our tradition,' said Adam unhappily. 'I ask myself what my grandfather would have said, and I know the answer. He'd have said they're human beings, same as us, and we got to do what we can for them.'

'You can count me out,' said Jamie.

But he didn't mean it. In the middle of the night, as the gale howled round the houses and the sea pounded the rocks below, Jamie was one of a phalanx of islanders in oilskins, heads bent low, arms linked together to form one body and prevent them from being blown away, who forced their way through walls of rain and spray down the track to the landing-place.

An Army tent, flying through the air like a monstrous bird, with force enough to kill, just missed them; a dozen of the soldiers' tents had gone already, and the last of all, bellied out by the gale, strained hard at its moorings, urgent to take off and fly after the rest. Men, battered to the ground, soaked almost to drowning, some of them hurt by flying planks and building sections, lay flat on their faces, unable to stand upright against the storm.

Peter Willett crawled from one to another, trying to assemble them. Adam yelled into his ear, 'We'll get them to the houses!' One by one they were half-dragged, half-carried by stumbling, bent-double groups of islanders to the nearest cottages, and each was thrust in through a briefly-opened door, along with enough of the gale to shake every moveable thing in the house and wet the inside walls.

Only the big, powerful Sergeant Young, sodden uniform plastered to his body, had strength enough to be rescuer rather than rescued; and when all were saved he bawled at Adam, barely audible against the storm though at six inches' range, 'What about the boat?'

The sea, driven above high water mark and pressing on with the gale behind it, had shifted the colonists' motor boat already and was about to hurl it on the rocks. A boat could no more be abandoned than a man; Adam and Robert and Johnny Oakes, with Peter Willett and Young himself, grabbed at its gunwales and urged it along, bucking and kicking, to a point beyond the reach of any tide. They didn't feel the bruises and sores that would give them agonies later.

Nearly every cottage in the settlement ended the night with a soldier as guest. Peat fires had been banked up; men were stripped to the skin and a few had the luxury of stepping into a tin bath with an inch or so of hot water. Women modestly withdrew to the sleeping-places until the men were dressed in whatever oddments of dry clothing could be found for them. Most were offered stew from the pot and cups of tea; a few islanders who had no tea could only give their guests hot water to drink.

But as the howl of the wind rose to repeated crescendos and the rain crashed against the windows and the sea pounded with a menacing boom against the rocks below, there was no one on the island who wasn't thankful to be warm and dry and sheltered from the storm.

Lieutenant Willett would have liked to check that his men were all safe, but it was impossible in the conditions. Not until the gale slackened was it found that there was a man missing.

During the next day the storm grew slowly less ferocious, though winds were still violent and no island boat could go out. Nor could any boat come ashore from the *Indomitable*. As the Brigadier and his party had still to be landed, the cruiser lay at anchor in the bay all day. Islanders, tough as they were, were confined to their homes. Usually when this happened the men did any odd jobs they could find, then sat around the house, bored, puffing their pipes if they had any tobacco, and grousing about the weather; the women still had plenty to do.

This time there was no boredom. Every house, except those of the very elderly and of one or two unsociable people like Ben and Alice Jonas, had its guest from the Outside World. The islanders, who had been awed by such august figures as the Brigadier and the Civil Administrator, identified themselves readily with the rank-and-file soldiers, whom they perceived as being plain ordinary people like themselves. An initial tendency to address even privates as 'sir' was soon dropped, and first-name terms were established all round.

The soldiers for their part were happier in people's homes, with fires to sit round as the storm raged outside, than under canvas. And it soon became clear that their hosts would hang upon every word they said. Such marvels as aircraft, underground railways, double-decker buses, cinemas and football stadiums were described to round-eyed listeners. Some men yielded to temptation and told tall stories— readily believed—of their own amazing experiences. Within a day, a score of friendships were flourishing.

Cyril was lucky. The man who arrived, drenched but cheerful, to be taken in by Grandma Molly was Gerry Baines, the wireless mechanic, who had worked out which was her house and had managed to get there first. He and Cyril cemented their friendship rapidly.

But islanders were worried about the damage the gale might have done. By late afternoon, the winds had dropped sufficiently for Adam and Jamie to lead a party over to the vegetable patches. What they found could have been worse, but was bad enough. The potato plants had all suffered in the gale; the earlies were safe, but the main crop would be poor. Potatoes were the staple of island diet. If other food sources failed—and all were precarious—next winter could be a hungry one.

Adam returned to the village and joined Peter Willett and Sergeant Young in checking round the houses. None of the soldiers was seriously hurt. But Private William Boothroyd, aged twenty, from the northern part of the Mother Country, could not be found. They called at every house and peered into every outhouse, every corner where a man might have taken refuge from the storm, without result. Now alarmed, they went down to the beach, where Willett and Young pulled faces to see that the stores that had been landed were scattered over the sands. Some of the building sections were damaged; there was oil and tar where barrels had broken against rocks; the gravel mountain was partly demolished. There was no sign anywhere of Private Boothroyd.

Next morning's tide brought in his mangled body. It was clear from his injuries how he had died: by falling from a height to the rocks below. He must have struggled up the cliff face alone and either had lost his footing or had reached the top and been instantly blown away by the wind. Such deaths had happened on Halcyon before, and would happen again.

Indomitable, already a day behind schedule, stayed at

anchor off Halcyon for a few more hours. The weather had changed beyond recognition, as if to deny its recent villainy. The sea was calm and deeply blue; the sky smiled innocently; the only cloud was the soft white halo that ringed the Peak. The cruiser's chaplain came ashore in the launch to conduct a hasty funeral service for Private Boothroyd. The body was buried in an open windy spot, not far from the Lookout, where generations of islanders and thirty or forty sailors from wrecked ships had found their last rest. Everyone on Halcyon who was able-bodied enough to get there was at the funeral as an act of natural piety, though another morning's fishing was lost. Death from the elements was a sombre and familiar hazard, to be treated with respect.

The chaplain returned to *Indomitable* in the spick-and-span launch. The cruiser's siren sounded; the grey shape slid slowly out of sight. The supply ship had gone already. Brigadier Culpepper, with Philip Saunders and the Army detachment, was left to govern Halcyon in the name of imperial power.

The Brigadier was distressed by Boothroyd's death.

'I feel responsible for it,' he said to Saunders. 'You told me of young Goodall's warning, and I forgot.'

Saunders had also forgotten Adam's warning, but was not the man to feel guilty.

'We didn't realize it would be a storm like *that*,' he said.

'We could have authorized Willett to put the men in the Meeting-House,' the Brigadier went on. 'Or we could have had them billeted in the village before the storm really blew up. I must confess, I half-thought we should have billeted them in the village anyway, until the building work's done.'

'With hindsight, perhaps so,' said Saunders. 'But I'm not sure about it, even now. It isn't a good thing to have our men too friendly with the natives. It's best we should keep our distance. And now, sir, there's something more important than the death of one private soldier. Did you hear the news on the ship's radio today?'

'No.'

'The Santa Cruzians are making threatening noises. They claim that our colonies in the Southern Ocean really belong to them. That includes Halcyon. We must get out, they say, before we're thrown out.'

'That isn't new,' said the Brigadier.

'No, but they're turning up the sound. We must get our building work done and the transmitter operating, pretty damn quick.'

With Lieutenants Willett and Rawson, they inspected the damage to the landed stores.

'Looks worse than it is,' said Peter Willett. 'The food and drink seem to be all right, thank God, and the tools and timber. Some of the building sections have been knocked about, but we can probably repair them. The main problem is to get everything together from where the storm's left it. And half the gravel's in the sea. We'll have to shovel it out before we lose it. It's all going to keep our chaps busy for the next day or two.'

'We have to get *on!*' said Saunders testily. 'Most of this is pick-and-shovel work. We can't put skilled men on it!'

Further along the beach, the island men were carrying their longboats down to the water. *Shearwater*, *Petrel* and *Seamew* had been safe from the storm, tucked tightly away in a cave. Saunders shouted, 'Put those boats down! Come over here!'

The men, bewildered, came slowly across. The Brigadier said, 'I'd like to thank you chaps for the help you gave our men last night. I shall come into the village later and thank all your wives.'

Some of the islanders couldn't understand his accent, but all of them got the sense of what was being said. Two or three grinned, others made gestures approximating to salutes, and Adam, as spokesman, said 'We were glad to do it, sir.'

Saunders took over.

'However,' he said, 'that's not all we need from you. You can see the situation we're in. We shall have to have a working squad to help clear this mess and start on the road.'

They stared at him.

'You mean *us*?' said Adam.

'Indeed I do.'

'But . . . we've only had half a day's fishing in five days. People are getting hungry.'

The Brigadier said, frowning, 'They've got to eat, Philip. We can't interfere with that.'

'With respect, sir,' Saunders said, 'we haven't time to waste. We can make an issue of food from the stores. In the circumstances, a free issue.'

The Brigadier's face cleared.

'Well, there you are,' he said. 'It seems a fair offer.'

Jamie said, 'We're not used to working under orders. We do things our own way. And we want to live our own lives.' He faced Adam. 'I say we should have nothing to do with this. We go fishing!'

Philip Saunders was white with fury. He said, 'I will not —the Brigadier will not—have this kind of insurbordination. You will do as you're told!'

The Brigadier said, peaceably, 'Let's put it like this. You tell me you're loyal subjects of the Mother Country. The Mother Country is under threat. What's more, this island is under threat. I hope that by being here we shall deter any invasion. Now you can see by looking around you that we have a great deal to do. You've helped us once; I appeal to you to help us again.'

The islanders looked from Jamie to Adam. Adam told them, 'We don't only live by fishing. Or by the vegetable plots or the sheep. You know what my grandfather used to say: we live by working together and helping each other. I think we should help the Brigadier.'

'You mean we should be pushed around!' snorted Jamie. 'Your grandpa had more spirit than that. He'd have stood up for our rights!' He added, 'We don't want their canned muck anyway. We want real food!'

This last declaration was a tactical error. To island

families, canned food was a scarce luxury, obtainable only by bargaining with Captain Fisher of the *Amanda*; and Captain Fisher drove a hard bargain. Fish, on the other hand, was ordinary, a staple diet. Not that it could be taken for granted; on Halcyon no food could be taken for granted; but it couldn't compete with the glamour of food that came in a tin. There was a murmur among the men which Adam correctly interpreted as indicating that they were willing to work in return for a distribution of food.

He didn't feel too easy about it himself. His instincts were on Jamie's side: better to live in your own independent way than to sell your labour for a handout from someone else's stores. But the island tradition of giving help where needed was strong, and the loyalty the Brigadier had mentioned was powerful, too.

'When do we start?' he asked.

The Brigadier beamed.

'That's the spirit,' he said. 'I'm glad to see it.' He walked round the group, shaking each man's hand in turn. Adam recalled a newspaper picture on the wall of May Attwood's house, showing Royalty similarly shaking hands all round. Brigadier Culpepper was the nearest Halcyon would ever get to Royalty. But when the Brigadier came to Jamie, Jamie put his hand firmly behind his back and stared challengingly into the Brigadier's eyes.

Culpepper said, 'I'm sorry you feel like that.'

Philip Saunders said, 'That man's trying to make trouble. We shouldn't give him any work.'

'He doesn't seem to want any,' said the Brigadier. Jamie, his face thunderous, was stalking away on his own. 'I don't think we'll pursue him, Philip, do you?'

They watched Jamie go before sending the remaining islanders round to Sergeant Young to be issued with wheelbarrows and shovels.

Chapter 10

LIEUTENANT Peter Willett and his men worked hard. The track that led from the beach was widened, the turf cut to a spade's depth, and gravel brought up on wheelbarrows spread to make a rough-and-ready road. With a hundred yards of road laid, the motor-vehicle was started, and from then on the gravel was brought up on the trailer. Ignoring the village, the new road went straight to the site Willett had chosen for the soldiers' quarters; and then the building work began.

The sections were designed to go up quickly, and they did. For the Brigadier's house—a bungalow—Willett had found a clifftop site with splendid views. It was habitable, though not comfortable, in just over a week, and a one-storey barrack block was ready for occupation by the end of a second week. A conduit tapped the stream above the washpool and brought water; a huge earthenware pipe going straight to the sea produced a primitive sewage system. A second one-storey block provided kitchen, cookhouse, washplace and social institute for the men, and a third was laid out as the officers' mess and common room, with quarters for Philip Saunders, the two lieutenants, and any visitors of like status who might arrive. A petrol generator supplied electric light. The settlement was the wonder of the islanders' world.

The soldiers were moved from their billets in the village to the new barrack-block. Most of them had mixed feelings about it. They now had better amenities, including the institute, in which they could smoke, play cards and drink a few beers, but they often preferred to spend evenings in the homes of their former island hosts.

The Brigadier moved out of the Meeting-House, but the

islanders didn't get it back. Mr Saunders installed Cyril, who'd reluctantly accepted the job of civilian clerk and was trying to keep his classes going as well, in the little room he himself had first occupied. Meanwhile Saunders expanded his own domain into the main part of the Meeting-House. He also requisitioned a nearby cottage, the home of Old Isaac Reeves who had played the fiddle at village dances. A sign over the cottage door now said ISLAND STORE. Beady-eyed, dough-faced Corporal Reg Wainwright took charge of the store, while Old Isaac, a solitary widower, moved into another tiny cottage in which his son Jack, Jack's wife and younger brother, and five children were already living.

Philip Saunders found plenty of assorted tasks for Cyril. One of them was working out the number of tokens to be paid each week to island workers, and the prices in tokens of the food, drinks and tobacco that they could buy in the newly-opened store. Cyril devised a scheme whereby an average worker's earnings would be enough to support an average-sized family. Saunders scaled it down, pointing out that most islanders had a few sheep and hens and a vegetable plot, and wouldn't be totally dependent on the tokens.

'But, sir,' objected Cyril, 'if they do a full day's work, shouldn't they get a full day's pay?'

'I am not here,' said Saunders, 'to scatter my Government's resources around. Halcyon is costing the Mother Country a lot of money.'

'There's another thing,' Cyril said. 'When the men go fishing, they give the old people a share of the catch. But there's hardly any fishing now. And we don't have old age pensions. Shouldn't we issue some tokens to old people?'

'That's not our responsibility. The islanders can look after their own. No doubt they will manage somehow.'

'I think that's a bit mean, sir,' said Cyril, greatly daring.

'When I want your views on the matter, Jonas, I shall ask you for them. In the meantime, you can get on with your work.'

Cyril got on with his work. In spite of its defects, the

token system was popular with many island wives. Dry goods, packets and above all canned foods expanded their menus. For every islander who didn't think this was real food there was another who delighted in the gastronomic joys of cornflakes, baked beans, pressed beef and canned tomato soup.

It was also Cyril's job to issue the tokens and to cancel them when they came back, used, from the store. And before long he came to the conclusion that no one except himself was checking on the numbers of tokens issued. He began to slip a few extra tokens into the hands of those islanders he knew to have elderly relatives or more than average-sized families.

It seemed a satisfying piece of social justice until the day when the storekeeper, Reg Wainwright, came into Cyril's tiny office and observed, 'I know what you're up to.'

'What do you mean?'

'Come off it, lad. You know what I mean. There's tokens around that ought not to be. I'm not blaming you. We all have to look after Number One. I've been wondering what you're getting out of it, that's all.'

'I'm not getting anything out of it. It's to help the old people, mainly.'

'Oh.' Reg was thoughtful. 'Well, you *could* benefit yourself, you know. I've been thinking on these lines myself. Next time the supply ship comes, we'll have toiletries in the store. Nothing fancy, mind you—just a few things like scented soap and cold cream and face powder—but for a woman on this island they're things she's never had in her life before. Now if you was to slip a few tokens to a young lady you fancied, she might be willing to do you a favour, eh?' He winked.

'Don't be daft,' Cyril said. 'This is Halcyon. They don't behave like that.'

'Oh, no? Let me tell you, money talks, the world over, and on this island tokens is money. You got a girl friend, Cyril?'

'As a matter of fact, no. But that's not how I'd get one.'

'I hear gossip, you know, being in the store. I hear that you're something of a dancer and you was dancing with that girl, Tilda, like nobody's business. So much so that the old biddies was all shocked. I bet you wouldn't mind getting a bit further with *her*.'

Cyril found himself feeling indignant on Tilda's behalf.

'She's not the sort of girl you could buy with a bottle of scent,' he said.

'She's a fine lass,' said Reg, unperturbed. 'Moves well. Lots of vitality. I could fancy her myself.'

'If I was you, I'd keep my hands off her,' said Cyril.

'All right, lad, all right. I was just pointing out that where stores is concerned there's always possibilities. And two can play at keeping secrets. If you don't get as many tokens back from me as there's goods gone out of the shop, you'll keep quiet about it, eh, Cyril, same as I keep quiet about you handing out too many tokens?'

Reg walked out without waiting for an answer. Cyril agonized for days, but couldn't bring himself to stop giving out the extra tokens. Philip Saunders took no interest, having weightier matters on his mind. But the satisfaction Cyril had felt with his activities evaporated. It all seemed rather sleazy now. In spite of good intentions, he wished he hadn't started.

Bella Reeves, with five children to keep, got a job cleaning the Brigadier's bungalow and earned a few extra tokens each week. But Daphne Culpepper felt that Bella didn't amount to an adequate household staff. Her status as wife of the Commissioner and therefore First Lady of Halcyon required her at the very least to have a maid.

'It really will not do,' she said to Sonia, 'for you and me, and sometimes even your father himself, to have to answer the door. We need someone from the village. Not a slow-witted middle-aged woman. A *girl*, with something about her, capable of being trained. Does such a person exist?'

'There's Tilda Wilde,' Sonia said, 'the girl who beat off that dog. *She* has her wits about her.'

'Speak to her, Sonia, will you? Tell her to come and see me.'

Sonia went into the village to look for Tilda. But Tilda was away, working on the family vegetable plot, and Sonia decided to try again later. Her way home took her past the cottage which Jamie Campbell had just finished building for himself.

Alone of the able-bodied men, Jamie never reported for work. Nobody compelled him; he earned no tokens and could buy no food or tobacco. He couldn't go sea-fishing; a longboat and crew were needed for that. But he had his vegetable plot and a few sheep and chickens, and he collected shellfish on the shore. He could live. Today was fine, warm and almost windless, and he was whitewashing the outside of the cottage.

Jamie knew very well who Sonia was. His first impulse was to scowl and turn away. But she was a very pretty girl, and Jamie was no natural bachelor. He had dallied, and more than dallied, with girls on the Mainland. When deciding to return to Halcyon, he had been well aware of strict island morals, but the island had called to him, and he considered he could abide by the code, provided he found himself a wife. It had, however, been harder than he thought. Only Lucy Reeves was currently available. Lucy was shy and homely and only sixteen, and although Jamie had begun discussions with her father, Jack Reeves, Jack was in no hurry, and not much progress had been made. Sonia was an appealing sight; and Sonia was smiling at him.

Sonia was quite aware of Jamie. She had heard Philip Saunders complaining about him at the dinner-table. But this didn't set her against him; if anything it made him more interesting. And Sonia found Jamie attractive. His thick, wavy red hair and pale skin went intriguingly with a muscular seaman's body.

'You're Jamie,' she said.

'Aye,' said Jamie cautiously. 'And you're Miss Culpepper.'

'Sonia. I've heard about you, Jamie.'

'I don't suppose it was anything good.'

'It wasn't *meant* to be good. But that doesn't worry me
. . . Is this your cottage, Jamie?'

'Aye. I built it myself.'

'Are you married?'

Sonia knew he wasn't.

'No.'

'Or—what do they say?—intended?'

'No.'

'I expect you'll get married some time, won't you? This
house is too nice to be wasted on a single man. I love the
white walls of the cottages. They make the village look so
attractive. At least, in the sunshine.'

'We don't get too much of *that*.'

'I know.' Sonia shuddered at the recollection of Halcyon
rain. 'But I bet they're nice and cosy when the weather's
bad.'

Jamie sensed that an invitation to come inside would be
accepted, and asked, 'Would you like to have a look in
mine?'

'I'd love to.'

'It's a bit primitive, you know,' Jamie said, guiding her
inside. 'Not like the Mainland. No running water. But I'm
doing my best with it.'

There were two tiny rooms with low ceilings and little
square windows. Sonia couldn't imagine it as a place to live
in permanently. But it appealed to her instantly as the kind
of place where, a few years ago, as a child, she would have
loved to play a game of house.

A game of house . . .

'And you've a kettle boiling on the fire,' she said.

'Aye. Would you like a cup of tea, Miss Culpepper?'

'I told you, my name's Sonia. I'd love a cup of tea.'

Jamie scraped the last of the tea out of his caddy. They
sat side by side on a broken-down sofa, obtained by barter
from Captain Fisher in exchange for two sacks of potatoes.
Jamie said, over tea, '*What* was it you heard about me?'

'Well, perhaps I shouldn't tell you, but I will. Mr

Saunders says all the island men are shiftless, but you're the worst of all, because you're a disruptive influence. He says he wishes you could be deported.'

'The bastard! . . . I'm sorry, that was a slip of the tongue.'

'Don't apologize. I've heard ruder words than that. But actually I don't think he's *that* bad. He's just stiff and starchy and bossy and walks all over people and doesn't care about anybody's feelings.'

'That's right. He's a bastard.'

Sonia giggled. 'He's a pompous ass, anyway. Do you still go out fishing, Jamie? I haven't seen any of the boats out lately.'

'The other men are all on building work. Except on Prayer Day, and we've had some wet Prayer Days lately. If I can get a crew together I mean to go out in spite of Mr Saunders. Next time I've fresh fish I'll bring you some. Or' —Jamie hesitated, then plunged—'I could give you it for supper here. Fresh from the sea. Would your dad let you come?'

'I'd like to see him stop me,' said Sonia.

When she left the cottage a few minutes later, Jamie put an arm lightly across her shoulders in showing her out, and Sonia didn't remove it. They thought about each other for the rest of the day.

On the following day, Sonia remembered her mission and went again to look for Tilda. This time Tilda was at home. Sonia outlined her mother's proposal and explained the duties of a housemaid.

Tilda's response was unhesitating.

'I'm sorry, miss,' she said, 'but I don't want to be a maid. It ain't the way we live on Halcyon, being at somebody's beck and call. And I'm used to working in the open air. I'd feel all shut in.'

'Will you think it over, Tilda?' Sonia asked. It was in her mind that it would be useful to have a reason for going into the village again.

'There's no point in thinking it over,' Tilda said. 'I *know*.'

'I could come back in a day or two, in case you change your mind.'

'I shan't change my mind.'

Tilda spoke with dignity. Belatedly, Sonia wondered how she could ever have made the suggestion. She abandoned her quest; but she didn't go straight home. When, three hours later, she got back to the bungalow, Mrs Culpepper complained that the errand had taken her a long time.

'I tried to persuade Tilda,' Sonia told her mother, omitting to say where she'd been in the meantime, 'but there's nothing doing. We'll have to look for someone else. Tilda's too independent. She hasn't the *soul* of a servant.' She added, suddenly inspired, and with feeling, 'Actually, I'd rather have her as a friend.'

'A *friend*!' said Mrs Culpepper faintly. 'Whatever next?'

Chapter 11

*J*AMIE had gone round the village several times in the evenings, trying to persuade the other men to join him in rebellion and take a boat out in defiance of orders. He had not had any success. Most of the men were married, had wives and children to support, and didn't want to invite trouble. Jamie believed that Robert was in sympathy with him; but so far Robert had been restrained by his own responsibilities.

Prayer Days were now the only time for fishing. Women and children looked after the sheep and worked on the vegetable patches, but were not thought able to manage the longboats. That was hard work even for the strongest muscles; and there were the endless Halcyon wind and swell, the frequently rough seas, the rapid vicious currents, the rocks and reefs, the sharks that over the years had taken off many a man's limb. Deliberately, island men never learned to swim; and they went out fishing with their pockets full of stones, so that if they drowned they would drown quickly. Yet they were always glad to get out to sea; it was in their blood, and if prevented for long they were deeply unhappy.

On several successive Prayer Days after construction work began, the weather was poor and fishing impossible. And by now another sea-going expedition was due: the yearly visit to Kingfisher to gather guano. Guano was the word for sea bird droppings. With the breeding season over and the birds gone, the stacked cliffs of the companion island would be rich in this smelly but valuable material, used by islanders to fertilize the vegetable plots. It was vital to collect it before the rain had had time to wash most of it away. In the week in which Jamie and Sonia met, the weather looked set fair at last, and Adam applied to Peter Willett for the necessary two days off for the island men.

Willett referred the application to the Civil Administrator. Saunders refused it. There was too much still to do, he said.

'You're not taking that from him, are you?' Jamie demanded angrily of Adam.

Adam had sounded out the men already, and had found no backing for an act of defiance. Islanders were awed by Authority, and Mr Saunders was Authority.

'I've no choice,' he said. 'They won't stay away from work.'

'You've no backbone!' Jamie declared. 'But maybe there are some who have.'

Jamie came to the Wildes' cottage at dawn. There was a golden haze on the horizon and a sky of slightly-misted silky blue that promised a fine day when the early chill wore off. George and Annie Wilde were up already, Tilda still in her sleeping-place.

'You been outside this morning, George?' Jamie asked.

'Yes. Why?'

'How's the weather look to you?'

'Fine for a couple of days.'

'That's how it looks to me, too,' said Jamie. 'So I'm thinking of taking *Petrel* over for the guano.'

George stared.

'You can't do that,' he said. 'The trip's off until further notice. Saunders's orders.'

'I'm thinking I'll go anyway. Saunders didn't give any orders to *me*.'

'You're daft, Jamie Campbell. You're asking for trouble. Anyway, you can't take a boat out all by yourself.'

'That's why I've come, George. I'm making up a crew. I want you to be in it.'

George said, 'I'm not getting on the wrong side of Saunders. It's all very well for you, Jamie, you ain't got nobody depending on you. I'm a family man.'

Tilda was awake now, and struggling to pull on her bulky clothes in the little cell, not much bigger than herself, which was where she slept. Now she came out, angry and defiant.

'Go back to bed, girl,' said George. 'This ain't nothing to do with you.'

'It *is* to do with me! I heard what you were saying. Seems to me Jamie's right. It's time we stopped being pushed around.'

'Be quiet, Tilda!' said Annie. 'Don't you dare talk like that to your father!'

'I'll say what I have to say. I reckon you should go with Jamie, Dad. They can't shoot you for it.'

'They could make things very hard for us,' George said.

'If you won't go,' said Tilda, 'I will.'

''Course you won't. Women don't go in the boats.'

'Why not? I can row and sail. You know I can. I was best of all the kids, boys *and* girls.'

'You sound like your grandma talking. Well, I can't control your grandma, but I can control you.'

'Can you?'

Father and daughter glared at each other. It wasn't their first confrontation. Tilda had been a spirited child, and hadn't got less so as she grew up. But this was more serious than any previous clash, and both of them knew it.

Tradition was on George's side. It had always been understood on Halcyon that while a girl was under her father's roof she obeyed her father. But the incomers, whether they knew it or not, were changing the established order. In the strange new world the islanders now inhabited, anything might happen. Suddenly Tilda and her father knew that the old rules didn't apply any more. It was a battle of wills. And George knew whose will was stronger. He wasn't prepared to impose his authority by force; it was doubtful whether he even could. Tilda would go whether he permitted her or not.

He backed away.

'Well,' he said, 'it don't look dangerous today. Let's

hope it's still fine tomorrow. Go if you must, girl, and on your own head be it. And the sooner you get married and it's Robert's job to keep you in order, the better I'll be pleased.'

Jamie said, 'You haven't asked me what *I* think.'

'I think you'll have trouble getting a crew,' said Tilda. 'They'll all be like my dad.'

'You could be right. Ah well, you're a good strong lass, Tilda. I'll take you.'

Jamie was indeed finding it hard to get a crew together. Most of the men thought like George. They grumbled at Philip Saunders and would have liked to defy him, but they didn't dare. Only Tom Reeves, who was a younger brother and an adventurous spirit, agreed to go.

A boat crew was normally six. In light seas, four could handle a boat, but with fewer than four it was impossible.

Jamie said, 'If we could get one more, we'd be all right. In fact four's better than six on this trip; there's room for more guano. But who . . . ?'

He and Tilda looked at each other. There was one able-bodied oarsman who hadn't been asked. Both were reluctant to suggest him, but Tom Reeves wasn't.

'Robert!' he said. 'He's as able as any man on Halcyon!'

'His mother won't let him,' said Jamie.

'His mother, his mother! Time he let go of his mum's apron-strings!'

'He feels responsible,' said Tilda, defending Robert. 'She keeps telling him, he's the man of the family now.'

Jamie and Tom brushed objections aside.

'He's not like the others,' said Jamie. 'He's only a lad. They won't blame *him*, they'll blame Tom and me for leading him astray. And *I* don't mind being blamed, do you, Tom?'

'No, I don't mind,' said Tom cheerfully. 'I'll soon be in trouble with this lot, one way or another. Once they've built a lock-up, I'll be in it!'

'Unless I'm in it first!' said Jamie.

'Then we'll be in it together!'

Stimulated by rebellion, the two were egging each other on.

'Come on, then!' said Tom. 'We'll go and persuade young Robert!'

Tilda waited outside May Attwood's cottage when the other two went in. She wasn't sure how she felt about Robert these days. She hadn't even spoken to him lately. But when he emerged from the cottage with Tom and Jamie, the emotional fog that had surrounded her feelings suddenly lifted. She was glad that he was coming. Her body remembered afresh that embrace in the Dell. Her spirits soared; her face shone.

'He's come away without telling his mum,' said Jamie.

'She's asleep,' Robert said. 'Polly'll tell her when she wakes up.'

'I never thought you'd do such a thing!' said Tilda, astonished.

'They persuaded me, Tilda,' said Robert.

'I reckon it was knowing *you* were coming that persuaded him,' said Jamie; and Robert blushed. He suffered a few minutes of reaction, in which he could hardly believe he'd been so daring, but then took his tone from the cheerful defiance of the two men and the obvious elation of Tilda. He too seemed buoyed up by the excitement of action.

Petrel was in the cave by the beach where the longboats and two or three dinghies always lay. There were also, among much other gear, huge canvas sacks for the guano. Sergeant Young approached as they dragged the boat out.

'Going somewhere?' he enquired.

'Yes.'

'Where?'

'To sea.'

'Care to tell me anything more?'

'No,' said Jamie. 'You going to stop us?'

'Can't see that I have any right,' said the sergeant. 'It's your boat, not ours. But when Saunders gets to know about this, there'll be trouble. He won't have anyone stepping out of line.'

'I don't give a fig for Saunders!' said Jamie.

For a moment there was a grin on Sergeant Young's face, but it was instantly suppressed.

'Don't say I haven't warned you,' he told them, and turned away.

'We'll hitch a dinghy behind,' Jamie said. 'May as well bring back all the guano we can.'

And with the dinghy to get afloat, it was hard work launching the longboat, and hard work again pulling out against the tide until they were beyond the reef. Before they reached that point, there were figures to be seen waving from the cliff top. Jamie took a hand off his oar long enough to wave back.

Then they were out at sea. Jamie raised the sail and took the helm. The breeze was fresh now; it was a perfect sailing day and they were reaching southward past Halcyon's series of ragged headlands, backed by the cloud-haloed Peak. Past the southernmost point of the island, there were fierce currents, pushing *Petrel* to leeward and perilously close to a jagged fringe of rocks; but Jamie steered expertly clear of them and took the boat safely round through the wind to head directly for Kingfisher, still no more than a small grey blob on the horizon.

Jamie relaxed.

'Plain sailing now,' he said to Tilda. 'Want to have a go?' and they changed places.

Holding to helm and sheet, feeling the boat heel beneath her, sensing the power of wind and wave under her hands and watching the wake cream away behind, Tilda felt a wild delight; she was like a bird on the wing; she could hardly bear the intensity of her joy. This was what life was for. Tom, who had a fine baritone voice, began to sing— sea shanties and old folk songs, some in uncomprehended languages, that had got into Halcyon's repertoire from heaven knew where. The others joined in; sang at the tops of their voices against the breeze.

When the sun had moved some way across the sky, Kingfisher began to take shape: forbiddingly high and volcanic like Halcyon, but with a row of lesser summits in place of the single Peak, and one end much higher than the other. Facing them as they approached was a sheer, immensely high cliff face; before it a beach and a patch of flatland.

Tilda gave up the helm and Tom took it; he and Jamie had been to Kingfisher several times and knew the hazards.

'Tons of guano there,' said Jamie, 'but the cliff's no good. There's not a man alive on Halcyon can climb it. Grandma Molly says she climbed it as a young lass, but it's hard to believe. We go the other side.'

They rounded the cliff and the headland it fronted, and were at the far side of Kingfisher, away from Halcyon. The steep, stacked cliffs at this side didn't look much less sheer than the one they'd seen first, but Tom and Jamie asserted that they could be climbed, with care. There were hundreds of ledges, which in the breeding season would be alive with untold numbers of sea birds; but the breeding season was past and there were only stragglers now. There was an inlet with a little beach of black volcanic sand, protected by a thick belt of kelp; Tom lowered the sail and they paddled over the tangled mass of weed into safe water.

A tiny stream, consisting largely of waterfalls, came leaping down from the heights above. Close to the inlet, in a sheltered space, was a decrepit wooden structure which seemed to have been built from ships' timbers, and beside it a little patch of land that might once have been cultivated.

'Charlie's House,' said Tom. 'And Charlie's Garden.'

'Who was Charlie?' Tilda asked.

They couldn't tell her. They thought he was a ship-wrecked sailor who'd once lived here alone. He had some connection with the history of Halcyon, but they didn't know what. Old Noah Attwood would probably remember.

Jamie had brought cold potatoes from his plot and hard-boiled eggs from his hens; Tom, who'd been working on the road, had two cans of corned beef and a packet of biscuits. They ate. The water from the stream was fresh and sparkling.

Then the work began. The day was now well on, and it was hard, nasty, dangerous work. Carrying shovels stored in the hut and the sacks they'd brought with them, they clambered over the cliff from ledge to ledge, scooping up the slimy, smelly droppings. To slip or put a foot wrong would have been fatal. But islanders were sure-footed, used both to hard work and to danger, and the guano represented food for the hungry months ahead. They worked steadily while daylight lasted.

Tilda worked higher and higher up the cliff. She was still happy; it gave her pleasure to see the men around her, treading with practised confidence from ledge to ledge, and it didn't worry her to look far out over the sea or far down to the tiny black beach and toy-sized boats. She climbed up and down a dozen times with sack loaded or empty, knowing that she wouldn't—almost that she couldn't—fall.

Towards dusk, Jamie suggested that she and Robert should go and collect driftwood for a fire. He and Tom didn't stop work until dark, when the dinghy was nearly full of guano. Then they all sat around the fire and ate their remaining food. The night was clear and starlit, but cold. The men tipped the longboat on its side and turned it two-thirds over, resting it on stones so that it formed a kind of cave with its opening towards the fire. Jamie and Tom lit their pipes and sat, sometimes silent, sometimes reminiscing about past visits to Kingfisher. Robert and Tilda walked along the beach, collecting more driftwood, then sat with the other two. From time to time, Robert fed the fire; he seemed thoughtful now, and Tilda wondered whether he was worrying over his rashness in joining the expedition. She herself wasn't worried at all; she was immeasurably contented, full of a kind of inner glory.

The men knocked out their pipes and lay down at one end of the boat, drawing sheepskins over themselves. After a long day in the open air they were weary and soon asleep.

Tom snored; Jamie occasionally muttered; but the sound of the sea nearby was louder than either.

Robert fed the fire again and sat with hands clasped round knees, looking into it. Tilda sat beside him. They were silent for a long time. There was no need to say anything. Then they drew the remaining sheepskins together and fell asleep, fully dressed, in each other's arms. From time to time, one of them half woke, shifted a little, sighed contentedly and went back to sleep. They stank of seagull muck and were blissfully happy.

By dawn the fire had gone out and it was bitterly cold. All four were awake and up early. Nothing was left of the food but a bit of cold potato. They ate that and drank from the stream. The longboat was turned right way up, moved to the water's edge and tethered to a boulder; the tide was coming in. The hard, filthy, dangerous work began again. It went on until nearly midday, and Tilda's muscles were aching from unaccustomed uses when Jamie called a halt.

Petrel was now afloat, and the launch of longboat and dinghy was not too difficult. But both boats sat low in the water, and a passage through the belt of kelp had to be forced by strenuous work with all four oars. Tom Reeves told a story of a return trip from Kingfisher in which sack after sack of guano, the product of just such labours as their own, had had to be jettisoned to save the boat from foundering in a heavy swell. But today, when they were out beyond the kelp, they found the sea still peaceable. Before long, the sail could be raised. Robert took a turn at the helm; the outline of Kingfisher receded behind them. It was Halcyon now that was barely perceptible on the horizon, and as before it seemed a long time before it grew any bigger.

Petrel in fact was making less and less way. The wind had dropped; for these seas it was exceptionally light. Eventually the sail began to sag and flap, and there was hardly any wake.

'It's not another storm coming, is it?' Tilda asked.

Jamie and Tom agreed that it wasn't; there were none of the signs.

'Just a calm day,' said Jamie. 'And a damn nuisance. We may as well drop the sail and get rowing.'

Rowing the heavily-laden boat, with the equally laden dinghy behind it, was back-breaking. And slow. They laboured for hour after hour, making little headway. Halcyon remained tiny; all that could be seen over the curvature of the earth was the upper part of the Peak. When darkness came, they were still miles out. Tilda wondered if they were really moving forward at all.

The sky was still clear, and Halcyon men could navigate by the stars. That wasn't a problem, but exhaustion was. They had to take spells of sleeping at the oars, and in those spells the boat drifted. And when they were rowing they were increasingly weary. They were hungry and thirsty, too.

Dawn showed still only the Peak on the horizon. They rowed doggedly on. Jamie and Tom were philosophical. Such things had happened before. On more than one occasion, a second boat had gone out from Halcyon to help the first one ashore.

'But there won't be that today,' Robert said. 'Saunders would stop it.'

Jamie pulled a face. Then he said, 'I think there's a wind.'

Tilda could hardly feel it. But Jamie was right. Gently, almost caressingly, the wind came up to them: a fair wind. Before long, the sail could be raised. Jamie took the helm. At first the boat barely ghosted along; then it gathered speed, a line of wake appeared, and they were running before a moderate breeze. And now at last Halcyon started growing, and grew gradually bigger until its familiar outline filled most of the sky and they were heading for the landing-place.

'They'll have seen us,' Jamie said. 'They'll be there.'

It was still early. Work on the roads and site hadn't started yet. As *Petrel* came in through the surf, every able-bodied islander seemed to be on the beach. Men waded into the water, as expected, to haul in the boat and dinghy. But nobody cheered as the four filthy, crumpled people staggered wearily ashore, their stinking cargo landed at last.

Adam stood in front of Jamie, looking him in the eye.

Jamie looked back at him, challengingly.

'Well, we made it,' he said. 'Somebody has to show a little spirit, even if the Reader doesn't.'

Adam said, 'Yes, Jamie, you showed spirit. And it's a disaster.'

'How so? What did our friend Mr Saunders say?'

'He's sacked Tom and Robert for missing work. They won't be employed again. And neither will you, in any circumstances.'

Jamie grinned broadly.

'That's fine,' he said. 'Why should Tom or Robert work for him? They can work with me instead. And Tilda's as good as any man. I have a crew, Adam! He can put that in his pipe and smoke it. We shall go out fishing every day that's fit. Saunders can keep his tomato soup; there'll be fish on the tables!'

'Not so fast, Jamie!' said Adam grimly. 'Why do you think they're not all cheering you?'

'Wishing they'd had enough guts to do it themselves, maybe.'

'No. Not that at all. Saunders has condemned the boats as unseaworthy. Brigadier's orders, he says. Seems the Brigadier's been worried about our boats ever since he first saw them. He heard about your trip, and when you weren't back yesterday it decided him. He's signed an order saying they're not to go out any more. You've done for us, Jamie! We're at Philip Saunders's mercy!'

Chapter 12

MAY Attwood ran to Robert and flung both arms round him.

'Thanks be that you're safe home!' she cried. 'When you weren't back last night I was scared. Oh, Robert, I was scared!'

'You needn't have been. It was calm as calm. You must have known.'

'There's boats been lost in all weathers, you well know. And your Great-uncle Ted was saying yesterday, when he was a young man, a boat loaded with guano went down. Sprung a leak and foundered in no time, and four good men drownded . . . Oh, Robert, how *could* you worry your poor mum like that?'

May's relief was turning rapidly to reproach and indignation.

'And you know what's the result of what you done! No work for you, no food for us!'

'We still got the goat and the hens,' Robert said. 'And the plot. And I can find shellfish like anyone else. We won't go short. Adam says he'll see you get your share of the store food, just as if I was working. Anyway, I got a job for days, carting the guano over to the patches.'

'That's all very well. But the disgrace! There's some that don't see why we should get a share, after the trouble you caused. Alice Jonas for one. She says them that step out of line should pay the price . . . And you was with Tilda, too! How did you sleep on Kingfisher?'

'I slept all right.'

'Don't be stupid. You know what I mean.'

'We all four slept under the boat. With our clothes on. And listen, Mum. Tilda and me's intended. I got a right to be with her.'

'From what I hear, Tilda doesn't take being intended seriously. Dancing and carrying on with that Cyril! I'm disappointed in her. Well, I suppose it was your turn last night, kissing and cuddling and so on. And *I* know what such behaviour leads to. If Tilda was to get . . . ' May reddened but went on. ' . . . You know!'

She had gone too far. Robert was furious now.

'Don't you talk like that!' he said. 'There ain't been nothing wrong between us. And there won't be. Not unless you drive us to it.'

Polly had been sitting quietly in the corner, listening. Now she flew at her mother.

'You're not fair to Robert!' she protested. '*Nobody's* fair to Robert. It wasn't wrong, going for guano. He shouldn't be punished. And now you're being horrid to him!' She took Robert's hand. '*I'm* on your side, Robbie!'

'Robert and the others was punished for disobedience,' said May, 'not for getting guano.'

'Disobeying who?'

'Disobeying *them*. Mr Saunders is the boss, and we got to do what he says.'

Polly said, 'You should be sticking up for Robert. Why don't you go and *see* Mr Saunders?'

'That wouldn't do no good. Everybody says, Saunders don't change his mind.'

'Then go and see the other man. The Brigadoon or whatever he is.'

'Brigadier. He's the head of them all. I wouldn't dare.'

'Well, *I* would!' said Polly.

'Don't be so silly, child!' said May. 'Stop being tiresome. And you'll have to get out of here. I'm heating water for Robert, so he can clean himself up a bit. Coming back all smelly like that!'

'Daphne, my dear,' said Brigadier Culpepper, 'I don't like the noises coming out of Santa Cruz one bit. I think you and Sonia should leave when the supply ship next comes.'

'I thought the Mother Country's occupation was meant to frighten the Santa Cruzians off. A tinpot dictatorship wouldn't risk tangling with a Great Power, wasn't that the theory?'

'It was. But Marshal Gomez—he's the dictator—wants a bit of glory. There are half a dozen other generals waiting to boot him out if they get an opportunity. He'd treble his chances of staying in power if he could tweak the Mother Country's tail and get away with it. And the latest thinking back home is that he'll probably try. The fact is that our being here is a bluff, and Gomez may call it.'

'Henry, dear,' said Daphne Culpepper, 'you are a tiresome man, and you have taken me to some dreadful places, of which this is not the least dreadful. But if you think I am going to leave you in what seems to be becoming a hot spot while I leg it for home, you have another think coming. Absurd it may be, but I happen to believe that my place is with you.'

The Brigadier put a hand on hers.

'I knew that was what you'd say,' he said. 'It won't be any good arguing with you. But Sonia? Shouldn't we try packing her off to Aunt Bertha after all?'

'We could try. I'm not too happy about her anyway. I think she's hobnobbing with the natives. The girl she was suggesting as a maid has refused—says she prefers to be out of doors—and now Sonia wants to bring her here as a *friend*.'

'The girl who drove off the dog? Good idea. Why not?'

'Really, Henry! One should *never* get involved with the natives . . . What's that?'

'Someone at the door.'

'As we're still without a maid, I'd better answer it.'

But as Daphne Culpepper got up there was the sound of footsteps from an adjoining room and then of voices in the doorway. Sonia Culpepper appeared.

'Somebody wants to see you, Daddy,' she said.

The child who came through the door was barefoot and skinny, and wore a faded, ragged frock two or three sizes too small. Her face was round and nut-brown, her nose small and tip-tilted, her hair dark and curly.

Brigadier Culpepper looked at the child's face and was charmed. His wife looked at the child's clothes and was appalled.

'You can't come in here!' she said. 'This is a private house!' And, in a whisper that wasn't very soft, 'She probably has fleas. Most of them have fleas.'

'Just a minute, Daphne!' said the Brigadier. 'Let me find out what this is about.'

He bent towards Polly. 'Well, my dear,' he said, 'what can I do for you?'

'Are you the head man?' Polly enquired.

'Well, yes, I suppose you could call me that.'

'It's about Robert. It's not fair, what Mr Saunders done to him.'

'And who is Robert, and what has Mr Saunders done to him?' The Brigadier's tone was kindly.

'Robert's my brother. He went to Kingfisher for the guano.'

'Oh, yes, I heard about that expedition.'

'And Mr Saunders is punishing him. He says he isn't to work on the roads any more. And Jamie and Tom the same. And it's not fair, because we need the guano for the vegetable patches, and if they hadn't gone we'd never have got any because the men haven't been able to go fishing except on Prayer Day. And Robert works ever so hard for my mum and me, because my dad's dead. And now Mr Saunders says they can't go fishing at all.'

'Hold on a minute, not so fast!' said the Brigadier. 'How old is Robert?'

'He's nearly seventeen.'

'H'm. A family to support at sixteen . . . I dare say I could have a word with Mr Saunders. But I'm not promising anything, Polly. Mr Saunders is the Civil Administrator. Do you know what that means?'

'No.'

'It means that really it's up to him to decide. And as for the fishing, I'm afraid those boats aren't safe. You wouldn't want your brother and all the men to go out to sea in unsafe boats, would you?'

'They been going out in them for years and years,' said Polly.

'And quite a lot of men have been drowned. Isn't that right?'

'Yes, sir,' Polly admitted.

'You see, Mr Saunders and I have been made responsible for this island, and we don't feel we can allow unsafe boats to be used. If there were another tragedy, we should be to blame.'

'Really, Henry!' said Daphne Culpepper. 'You can't discuss such matters with a child!' She turned to Polly and said, coldly, 'The Brigadier has listened to you very carefully and told you what he'll do. Run along now, and don't come bothering him any more.'

The Brigadier said, mildly, 'She isn't bothering me at all. I like to talk to young people. Do you like sweets, Polly?'

'Sweets?'

'Don't you know what sweets are?'

'I don't think they have them here,' said Sonia.

'Have *you* any, Sonia?'

'I think I have, in my room.' Sonia fetched a tube of fruit gums and put them in Polly's hand. Polly looked at the tube in some bafflement, and Sonia showed her how to open it. Polly smiled radiantly at her and at the Brigadier. Daphne Culpepper steered her from the room.

Sonia said, 'I think those four showed courage, defying old Saunders.'

'Perhaps so,' said the Brigadier, 'but I have to uphold his authority.'

'My view of the matter is, Good old Jamie!' said Sonia.

The Brigadier studied his daughter thoughtfully.

'You know the fellow?' he enquired.

'Slightly.'

'Don't get to know him too well, will you?'

Philip Saunders was not pleased by the suggestion that he should cancel his dismissal of Robert. 'But of course, if you insist, sir . . . ' he said coldly.

'I'm not insisting. I'm not even telling you, I'm asking you. The lad has a mother and sister to support.'

'He should have thought of that before he let himself get involved,' said Saunders. 'However, perhaps in the circumstances . . . In fairness I shall have to reinstate Reeves as well. But nothing would persuade me to employ that man Campbell.'

'Fortunately,' said the Brigadier, 'the question seems unlikely to arise. I understand that Campbell has no intention of accepting employment.'

'I told you, miss,' said Tilda, 'I shan't change my mind. It isn't my kind of work.'

'Don't call me miss. My name's Sonia. And I didn't come to ask you the same question again. As a matter of fact, I came to apologize for having asked you in the first place. I realize it might seem a kind of insult. If you ask a person to be your maid—or even your mother's maid— you're not treating them as an equal. What I really wanted was to have you as a friend.'

Tilda looked startled.

'Don't you like the idea?' Sonia asked.

'I never thought of it. I mean, I'm our sort of people and you're your sort of people. Different.'

'Is it a difference that matters?'

'I don't know. We don't have no polite ways, the way you have. We just say what we think.'

'And *we* don't? Go on, Tilda, show me how it's done. Say what you think.'

For a moment Tilda looked blank. Then a grin spread across her face.

118

'All right,' she said. 'Just this minute, what I'm thinking is, I like your trousers.'

Sonia was wearing slacks.

'They *are* rather comfortable,' she said. 'And useful in Halcyon weather, with all the wind. I can understand why you island women are so covered up. Though you do all look a bit old-fashioned.'

'I reckon we look awful,' said Tilda with feeling. 'Every time I see you I wish I could wear clothes like yours.'

'Well, why don't you?'

'Because I ain't got any. And if I had, my mum would have a fit if I tried to wear them. All the other women would say it was disgusting.'

'They think *I'm* disgusting, do they?'

'No, not exactly. They think it's different for you, being from the Outside World.'

'Tilda, I have lots of clothes. Come home with me. Try some on.'

'I couldn't wear them trousers, that's for sure. I'm broader in the hips than what you are.'

'I've other things you could wear. Come on. Meet my mother.'

Tilda looked dubious.

'Do I have to tell her why I don't want to work for her?'

'Not unless she asks. And she won't.'

'I never talked to a person like that before.'

'She's only human, Tilda. You're not scared of her, are you?'

Tilda was in fact somewhat apprehensive. But, as she often did when in doubt, she asked herself what Grandma Molly would have said. And the answer was clear.

''Course I'm not scared,' she said. 'I'll meet her any time.'

'Make it now,' said Sonia.

'You mean you're not on your way to see Jamie?'

This time Sonia was startled.

'What makes you ask that?'

'Well, you've been to his house before, haven't you?

Three times, they say in the village, and stayed there quite a while. They say you're sweet on him.'

To her surprise, Sonia found herself blushing. But she didn't deny it.

'They seem to know a lot in the village,' she said ruefully. 'And I'm not looking for Jamie this morning. He's working on his plot. My goodness, if my mother got to know about Jamie . . . '

'It ain't up to me to tell her,' said Tilda.

'I've been at Sonia's house,' Tilda told her mother later.

'You mean Miss Culpepper? You call her Sonia?' Annie said.

'She told me to. We're pals. Leastways, she says we are. I met her mum, too.'

'They say her mum's all stuck-up.'

'She wasn't with me. She was nice. She gave me a cup of tea. And Sonia took me to her bedroom.'

'Was it very posh?'

'Not like what they're used to in the Mother Country, Sonia says. But it looked posh to me. Curtains and a bedspread and things, all looking new. And a dressing-table. And you know what she's got? She's got cosmetics.'

'Cosmetics?'

'Things you put on your face. Like powder and rouge and eye-shadow and lipstick . . . '

'*Lipstick!*' Annie had heard of lipstick. The tattered magazines that arrived on Halcyon by way of the *Amanda* and were passed from cottage to cottage until they fell to bits had sometimes had coloured pictures of film stars with scarlet lips and thin, pencilled eyebrows. Such creatures, Annie was sure, led scandalous, sinful lives.

'I ain't seen Miss Culpepper wearing lipstick,' she said.

'She doesn't when she's walking round Halcyon. But when they have the officers to dinner she does. She's going to give me a lipstick, she says, that's right for my colouring . . . '

'And when would *you* wear lipstick, my girl?'

'Sonia's dad's talking about giving a dance in the Army institute. If he does, I could wear it then. And Sonia's giving me a skirt, a new one that's too big for her but fits me just right.'

'Not a *short* skirt?'

'Yes. It only comes down to here.' Tilda indicated a point on her thigh.

'Your dad won't have that, I can tell you.'

'What happened last time he tried to stop me doing something?'

Annie remembered, and changed tack.

'And what's Robert going to say?'

'Robert can say what he likes. He'll have to put up with me the way I am. Times are changing.'

'Times are changing on Halcyon all right.' Annie sighed. 'But are they changing for the better?'

'Some ways yes and some ways no, I reckon,' said Tilda. 'We can't be like we used to be, whether we want to or not.'

Philip Saunders and Peter Willett dined with the Culpeppers that night.

'The girl came to see me,' said Daphne Culpepper. 'Tilda. I rather took to her. A nice straightforward girl, and surprisingly intelligent.'

'Why surprisingly?' asked the Brigadier.

'Well, one doesn't expect too much from these people. But Tilda is quite bright. She'd make a tennis player, I dare say. Well made, strong limbs, well co-ordinated. And pleasant. Uneducated, of course, but she can't help that. I believe if one had time one could turn her into a lady.'

'Do you think she'd want to be a lady?'

'No.'

'I worry a little over what we're doing to these people,' the Brigadier said. 'Here they were, perfectly contented with their own way of life, and we've come in and started turning their world upside down.'

'They needed shaking up,' said Saunders.

'Why? They're strong and healthy, they don't know what crime means, they live to a ripe old age . . . '

'If they survive accident,' said Willett. 'There are a lot of deaths from drowning or cliff falls.'

'I must admit, both the boats and the cliffs give me the horrors,' said the Brigadier. 'We can't do anything about the cliffs, but those boats of theirs won't do at all. Totally unfit to go to sea. Made of driftwood, leaky, with ancient patched canvas. I've issued orders that they're not to go out. I'm in charge now, for better or worse, and I don't want the responsibility of tolerating unsafe boats.'

'I gather the island men are indignant,' said Peter Willett. 'They say it's not the boats that are dangerous, it's the seas.'

'That's a fine distinction,' said the Brigadier.

'But the boats are their livelihood,' said Sonia.

'Just at the moment, *we're* their livelihood,' said Saunders, 'and likely to be so for quite a while, if Santa Cruz will let us alone. There's a lot of development work needed. Including a proper, organized fishing industry instead of the crazy set-up we found here.'

'For myself,' said the Brigadier, 'I'd rather give the men good seaworthy boats free of charge and let them get on with it in their own way. In fact I've asked the powers-that-be to finance them. The trouble is that Halcyon isn't of any use to the Mother Country except as a strategic outpost, and even that's marginal. It has nothing to give us: no oil, no minerals, poor soil, wretched climate. All it can do is cost money. No wonder it's been left to itself for all these years. Strategic interest apart, why should the taxpayer in the Mother Country fork out for Halcyon?'

'Common humanity, maybe,' suggested Willett.

'That doesn't seem to be a powerful argument, I'm afraid, especially when times are hard.'

'The fact is,' said Sonia, 'that we're piling problems on these people. You're not going to solve them with sweets and cigarettes, or even with cans of fruit salad.'

Brigadier Culpepper sighed.

'You are absolutely right, my dear,' he said. 'We are invaders. We don't know what harm we may be doing. But there are others who would be worse.'

Peter Willett was responsible for all construction on Halcyon. He worked hard and seldom took a day off. But he was a keen walker, and anxious to explore the island on foot. In fact there was no other way, for there was still little more than a mile of road that the motor vehicle could use. Willett also yearned for more of Sonia's company than he ever got, and when eventually he gave himself a free day she took pity and agreed to go walking with him. They needed a guide.

'Let's ask Tilda,' Sonia suggested. 'She knows all the paths, and how to get to the viewpoints.'

Tilda did know the paths, which were not much more than sheep-tracks. She also knew a good deal about the island's plants and animals; but she insisted that Robert knew more than she did, and she was aware that he needed any extra tokens he could earn. The party became a foursome.

Peter and Sonia wished to see the south coast, and Robert and Tilda took them by a route that led uphill from the village past a subsidiary crater of the Peak. The ground here was slightly warm, though not enough to cause discomfort.

'It's always like that,' Robert said, in reply to a comment from Sonia.

A little further on there was a long, ragged crack in the volcanic soil, and from it rose wisps of pungent smoke.

'Is *that* always the same?' Peter asked.

'Not always. Sometimes. There's other cracks, too. When they're like this we say they've got the smokes.'

'Got the *smokes*? Is nobody worried?'

'No. It's always been the same. All my Great-uncle Noah's lifetime there's been the smokes, and he says all his grandfather's lifetime before him. It don't mean anything. It's same as the rumbling.'

'What rumbling?' asked Sonia.

'There's rumbles from time to time,' said Tilda. 'Sometimes more than others. There haven't been any lately, but they come and go. And sometimes there's tremors.'

'But we don't worry about them,' Robert said.

'Sounds a bit worrying to *me*,' said Peter.

Later, Willett mentioned the cracks to the Brigadier.

'I know about the cracks,' the Brigadier said. 'I haven't seen them, but they're mentioned in our briefing. Seems the volcano hasn't erupted for three hundred years, and the geologist who looked at it forty years ago said it could go another three hundred.'

'Forty years is a long time,' Peter said. 'Don't you think it should be looked at again?'

'Perhaps so. Glad you raised the matter, Peter. I'll send a signal to the authorities, asking them to send somebody. They may oblige, they may not. It's not the kind of thing they're worrying about at the moment.'

Chapter 13

MIDSUMMER came and went. The threat from Santa Cruz hung fire. Warlike noises were still being emitted in a routine way, but nothing actually happened. Life on Halcyon settled down, with varying degrees of satisfaction for different people. The supply ship came twice more. The administrators and the soldiers were made more comfortable as more equipment arrived. A cold store made it possible to bring in fresh food. The Brigadier's house and the officers' mess were carpeted. A cine projector, adapted by Gerry Baines to run from the generators, was installed in the men's institute, and the soldiers had old crackly films, often shown three or four times over, to alleviate their boredom. A superior gramophone also arrived.

At the village store, there was now a wider choice of foods, and islanders could buy bottled beer, ice cream and sweets with their tokens. The longboats, still under prohibition, remained in their cave; but fish was imported and could be bought in the store, if you had the tokens.

There was no sign that the demand for the islanders' labour would end. A road, poor but passable, now reached in one direction to the vegetable patches and in the other to the radio post at Jonathan Wilde's house. A motor car had arrived for the Brigadier, in which he could drive the whole two and a half miles of it. Peter Willett drew up plans for a harbour; there was talk of blasting and excavation work, to begin next spring. Philip Saunders applied for authority and materials to instal water and sewage systems in the village. The Mother Country government picked up the bills without much complaint. But it didn't send anyone to look at the cracks beside the old craters.

Daphne Culpepper hired Bella Reeves's daughter Lucy as

maid. Lucy was young, timid and not very bright; and Daphne, without actually meaning to bully her, gave her a hard time. But Lucy had four smaller brothers and sisters, and the extra tokens were needed. Daphne also had a patch of ground adjoining the house fenced off as a garden, for which she had grand but improbable plans. Next to it, a slightly bumpy tennis court was laid out, and was used frequently by Sonia, the two lieutenants and Philip Saunders. Occasionally the Brigadier played; he was getting slow on his legs and a little stiff, but with superior skill in placing the ball he could still beat his juniors. Two or three times, Sergeant Young was invited to play, and trounced the lot of them.

Sonia was often seen by her mother in Peter Willett's company and never in Jamie Campbell's; but she frequently went into the village and, contrary to Daphne Culpepper's impression, more often to visit Jamie than Tilda. Tilda knew what was going on, and although she had promised not to give Sonia away, she shared Halcyon morality to the extent of feeling uneasy about it.

Cyril was suffering even greater pangs of conscience. He was still distributing tokens to those in need, and there was no sign that he would be found out; but he disliked Corporal Wainwright more and more, and when the corporal winked or made conspiratorial remarks he felt sickened.

The day came when Grandma Molly remarked thoughtfully, 'You look worried, lad. Been looking worried for quite a while, haven't you?'

Under pledge of secrecy, Cyril told her of his misdeeds.

'I want to get out of it,' he said. 'But there's folk that'll go hungry if I do.'

'You'll be found out, Cyril. That fellow Saunders will get curious sooner or later, and you'll be in real trouble. You'll have to own up. Sooner the better.'

'And Wainwright?'

'I can't see that you need to bring him into it. What he does is up to himself.'

'All right, Gran,' said Cyril after some thought. 'I'll do what you say.'

Molly spoke to Tilda, Tilda spoke to Sonia, Sonia spoke to her father, and Cyril found himself in the Brigadier's office confessing his crimes.

'How many tokens do the men get for a day's work?' the Brigadier asked.

Cyril told him.

'And what can they buy with that number of tokens?'

Cyril gave him two or three possible shopping-lists.

Brigadier Culpepper exploded.

'It's villainy!' he said. 'Sheer exploitation on our part! We can't employ men on those terms. I suppose it was Saunders who fixed them? Well, he'd better re-fix them at once. Sounds to me as if the proper rate would be about double. As for you, young Jonas . . . I suppose you think you're a kind of Robin Hood. Well, maybe you are, but what you've been doing is theft of Government property, and I can't allow it.'

The Brigadier looked at Cyril severely.

'You ought to be sacked!' he said.

Cyril looked alarmed. The Brigadier's face relaxed.

'However,' he said, 'we haven't a replacement for you. And somehow I think that by the time I've talked to Mr Saunders he won't be thinking of sacking you anyway. Don't do it again, you understand?'

'Yessir.'

'If I have anything to do with it, you won't need to.'

The following day the issue of tokens for island labour was increased by eighty per cent.

Philip Saunders, smarting under a rebuke from his chief, instructed Sergeant Young to carry out an inquiry into the running of the entire stores section. A remarkable number of items were discovered to have found their way into the quarters of Corporal Wainwright or to have been sold to fellow-soldiers. The corporal was charged before his unit commander, lost his stripes and was transferred to work on the roads.

'That's your doing, you little bastard!' he said to Cyril.

Cyril protested, truthfully, that he hadn't mentioned Wainwright to anyone and it hadn't been his aim to get him into trouble. But Wainwright was not mollified.

'I'll get you for this!' he declared; and it sounded as if he meant it.

In Robert's home there was a transformation. Isaac Reeves, who'd been dislodged from his cottage and had moved in with his married son Jack, was keenly aware that he'd made Jack's cottage even more overcrowded. Isaac was a widower and May Attwood a widow. He walked over to her house and proposed marriage.

May saw the advantages at once. However hard she clung to Robert, the boy would leave her before long. Isaac was a healthy sixty and she'd known him all her life. She accepted him, on the understanding that he didn't play his fiddle more than once a week. Three weeks later Adam married them. Robert, though still the apple of his mother's eye, was no longer breadwinner for a family. Isaac had given him his freedom.

Cyril and Gerry, with help from Robert, finished building a new wireless set and devised a way of rigging a quickly-removable aerial from Grandma Molly's roof. For fear of its being seen, they could only use it after dark, but that was when reception was best. As summer drew to an end and the hours of darkness grew, they could listen more. And there was more to listen to, for the Santa Cruzian threat was being voiced again, more and more loudly, until the news bulletins from the Mainland Colony were full of it.

The messages received at the Halcyon radio post from the mainland or the Mother Country were increasingly in code. There were also signals from the Mother Country's southern ocean fleet.

'Rawson's fed up with it,' said Gerry. 'He has to decipher them. It's keeping him busy when he'd rather be drinking in the Mess.'

128

'Do you get to see them?' Cyril asked.

'No. They're all top secret. Rawson takes them straight to the Brig. The only thing he'll tell *us* is that the Brig is looking worried. And it takes a good deal to worry the Brig.'

The Brigadier had decided some time ago to give a dance for the islanders, in compensation for the loss of their Meeting-House. Now that the soldiers' institute was fully equipped, there was a place where it could be held. He himself was fully occupied with the international problem, and delegated the arrangements to Philip Saunders.

Saunders had not changed his opinion of the islanders or his methods of proceeding. He auditioned Isaac Reeves, decided, with some justice, that his fiddle-playing was appalling, and opted for the gramophone. This meant a programme of modern dances, since Isaac's hotchpotch of traditional tunes was not available on record. It didn't occur to Saunders that for many islanders a dance without the familiar jigs and reels was hardly a dance at all. It did occur to him that the presence of thirty-odd soldiers meant there were not enough women to go round. He solved this problem by inviting all the women on the island but ordaining that men could only come as partners.

The system worked fairly well. There were many friendships between islanders and soldiers, and island men were seldom jealous, having never questioned the faithfulness of their womenfolk. Many a husband who couldn't or wouldn't dance in modern ballroom style had no objection to his wife's being partnered by a soldier.

Tilda, being intended for Robert, should by rights have gone with him. She would have done so if Robert had been willing. But Robert wasn't a dancer of any kind. Having declined to be her partner, he knew Tilda well enough to accept the inevitable.

'I suppose you'll want to go with *him*,' he said.

'Cyril? Yes, I will. Do you mind?'

'I don't mind. Cyril knows where he stands. He's my pal but you're my girl, and everything's fine so long as he don't forget it.'

Robert didn't think Cyril would forget it. None the less, in the days that led up to the dance, he felt emotions that he failed to recognize as jealousy.

Cyril was delighted. He'd gone off Sophy Kane a bit. He'd grown fond of Tilda and thought her looks had improved; and in an odd way the suggestive remarks of Corporal Wainwright had made her seem more exciting.

Sonia also had a problem. Her parents expected her to go with Peter Willett. She would have preferred to go with Jamie, and seriously considered whether she should come out openly and say so. But it would have meant trouble that she couldn't face. She was spared embarrassment when Lucy Reeves, who'd been half-intended for Jamie, plucked up courage to invite him. Jamie was content to go with Lucy.

Tilda and Sonia dressed for the dance together in Sonia's room. Sonia lent Tilda an ankle-length dress of modern design which, since Tilda's proportions were more generous than Sonia's, looked slinky on her. Sonia also made up Tilda's face. Seeing herself in the glass, Tilda had a brief fit of nerves, wondering if she dared appear in public thus beautified. She referred the question, in her own mind, to Grandma Molly. Molly had certainly never worn make-up. But surely Molly would have been on the side of daring.

'Here we go!' said Tilda.

'Why, Tilda dear, you look lovely,' said Daphne Culpepper.

'Hmm. Fine gel!' said the Brigadier to his wife.

Brigadier and Mrs Culpepper opened the dance and accomplished a stately waltz and foxtrot; but the Brigadier had urgent signals from the Mother Country to deal with, and he and his wife soon left. After they'd gone, Sonia danced mainly with Jamie, causing some increase in the level of gossip. But Tilda was the sensation of the evening, and she and Cyril were the stars. Tilda felt she had grown into Cyril's style; she swayed and spun and floated and seemed to herself to have left the face of the earth. Towards the end of the evening, other couples stopped dancing to watch them. The older women were agreeably shocked by Tilda's appearance and her abandoned manner of dancing, and predicted that she would come to a bad end.

Afterwards, Cyril walked Tilda home. She was excited and needed to wind down; they went a long way round by the cliff edge and all was quiet when they reached her house. Cyril's first reaction to Tilda's changed appearance had been a swiftly-suppressed whistle. Now he wanted to kiss her, wondered whether he was prohibited by Robert's warning, considered how she would take it, and by hesitating allowed the moment to pass. All he said was, 'One day we'll do the tango.'

'You told me that before,' she said, and slipped indoors.

As Cyril turned away, a figure emerged from behind the outhouse. Reg Wainwright flung himself on Cyril from behind and brought him down with a thud. They tussled on the ground. Wainwright was heavier and had the advantage of surprise, but Cyril struggled free, only to get a vicious knee in the groin. He doubled up in agony. Wainwright was pummelling him about the head, had given him a burst nose, was going to knock him unconscious . . . Then someone else came running up at speed and entered the fight.

Cyril recovered enough to see Wainwright in his turn knocked down and lying on the ground, defeated, curled up and sheltering his head in his arms. The new arrival seemed for a moment poised to kick him in the ribs, then apparently changed his mind and stood clear. Wainwright crawled two or three feet, then stood up and ran for all he was worth.

Cyril turned to his rescuer.

Robert.

Cyril, shocked and breathless, his nose streaming blood,

could only gasp out, 'Thank you.' Then he sank to a sitting position, tipping his head back to stop the bleeding. No one in Tilda's house seemed to have heard the commotion, and there was no point in causing alarm. Robert sat beside him. They were silent for a while.

'Who was he?' Robert asked in a low voice.

'The storekeeper. Has a grudge against me.'

'Why?'

'It's a long story. I'll tell you another time . . . Robert, what were you doing? How did you come to be here just at that moment?'

'I . . . I was just passing.'

Robert's tone was embarrassed.

'Don't tell Tilda about this,' he said.

Cyril realized that Robert had followed to see him bid Tilda good-night. If he'd gone beyond what Robert thought proper, might it have been Robert who would have set upon him? He would never know.

'I won't tell her,' he promised. 'If she asks what's happened to my face, I'll tell her I walked into a door or something.'

Robert said thoughtfully, 'I never been in a fight before. I never even seen one. We used not to have fights on Halcyon.'

As the threat from outside grew, tension was also growing within the island community. The Halcyon men were dividing into two groups. Some of them, headed by Jamie Campbell, felt increasingly rebellious, declaring that they wanted nothing to do with the new way of life, and muttering about taking the boats out regardless of orders. Others had adapted to the regime and were building their lives round the concepts of going to work and acquiring tokens. Adam sympathized with the rebels, but as head man felt obliged to act as peacemaker. The result was that Adam and Jamie didn't trust each other.

Jamie and Tom Reeves were in fact planning another act

of defiance. They didn't say anything to Adam about it. Jamie didn't even tell Sonia, though there were few days now when he and Sonia didn't meet. On a fine morning at the end of summer, Sergeant Young, waking early and going outside to stretch his legs, saw all three of the island longboats heading out to sea in defiance of orders.

Young wasted no time. Within minutes the covers were off the motor boat. It was launched with himself at the wheel. The sergeant handled the motor boat as confidently as he handled a tennis racquet. Before the islanders had hoisted their sails he was racing round them like a sheepdog rounding up stray sheep. A crew member signalled with waving arms that the islanders were to turn back. *Petrel*, ignoring the instruction, had the starboard oars knocked from the rowlocks in a quick dash by the motor boat. The islanders then complied, and the three boats were herded back to the beach. But over-confidence brought Sergeant Young to grief. He ran his boat at high speed on to a rock; it split and filled with water. The crew escaped, but sea-water got into the engine. Until new parts could be obtained the boat was useless.

Jamie and the others were brought before Brigadier Culpepper, sitting as magistrate, and charged with a breach of regulations leading to damage to Government property. Jamie, in court, maintained with passion and eloquence that the boats belonged to the islanders and were essential to their way of life. The Brigadier said that he sympathized with this argument but it wouldn't wash. The island was unquestionably a colony of the Mother Country, and as Commissioner he had been given power to make any regulations he chose. He had made this regulation in the interest of safety; it had been broken and the men were guilty. He would release them all with a warning, but he wasn't going to risk having the same order defied again. The boats would be destroyed. They must be kept under guard tonight and broken up tomorrow morning.

'And that will be a relief,' he said to Saunders at dinner.

'You let Campbell off lightly,' Saunders said. 'That man will go on to make more trouble.'

'Maybe so,' said the Brigadier. 'Frankly, we have more important things to worry about just now than James Campbell.'

He and Saunders worked on into the night, poring over maps and charts, sending and responding to a succession of signals. Next morning, Saunders was roused at dawn by Lieutenant Willett with the news that the island boats had gone.

'Young left a man to guard them overnight,' Willett said, 'and he staggered back to the barracks an hour or two ago, having been hit over the head from behind and knocked unconscious. A dozen island men are missing, too.'

Saunders was dismayed. 'Send for Goodall,' he said. 'Perhaps *he* can tell us where they've gone.'

But Adam didn't know.

'They *could* be on the way to Kingfisher,' he said doubtfully. 'If so, we'll be able to spot them from the Lookout.'

But as far as the eye could see from the Lookout, the seas were empty.

'Then they haven't left the island,' Adam said. 'My guess is that they've been hiding the boats, somewhere on the west coast. There's hundreds of caves and little inlets. Finding something in one of them would be looking for a needle in a haystack. And you'd never get to them anyway. It's a rugged coast, all rocks and high sheer cliffs, and the sea pounding away all the time. It's suicide to try to put a boat in there unless you know it like the palm of your hand and have years of practice in these seas.'

'If the men have hidden the boats there, how will they get back?' demanded Saunders.

'Overland. There's ways up the cliff if you're a good climber. *We* can do it. I wouldn't advise it for *your* folk.'

'Then you'd better get a party together, Goodall. Go and find them, and bring them to me.'

But this was pushing Adam too far.

'No, sir,' he said firmly.

Saunders and Adam looked each other in the eye. Saunders dropped the idea. Together with Willett, they walked down to the village, where the women, denying knowledge of the men's intentions, were waiting anxiously for their return. Most of the morning passed. At last, to the general relief, a few figures were seen straggling round the side of the mountain. Everyone went to meet them.

They were wet and muddy, and tramping with heads down. And there were not twelve of them.

Jamie was in the lead. He spat at Saunders.

'You bastards!' he said. 'You drove us to it!'

'What happened, Jamie?' Adam asked quietly.

'Lost four men, all in *Seamew*. Misjudged the run-in, and the boat split like matchwood. None of us could do a thing.'

'They were all drowned?' Saunders asked.

''Course they were. Drowned and smashed. A nasty death, Mister Bloody Saunders. I wouldn't wish it even on you!'

Brigadier Culpepper, called from his desk, faced the assembled islanders. His face was haggard.

'I don't know what I can say to you,' he said, 'except that I'm profoundly sorry. I gave that order for the best. It was meant to save lives, not to *cost* them. The pity is that I didn't have it carried out at once. It seemed late in the day to start, that was all.'

There were jeers from the back of the crowd.

'It's no good being sorry!' Jamie snarled. 'We were happy here till you arrived. You come here, making yourselves comfortable but interfering with all our ways, and now this! And *you* represent the Mother Country! If this is what the Mother Country does to us, the Mother Country be damned!'

'Hold hard, Jamie!' said Adam. 'This was a disaster, but it wasn't intended. The Brigadier couldn't have known.'

There was a note of authority in Adam's voice which recalled his grandfather, revered on Halcyon for many years. Jamie said no more, though there were mutterings in the crowd that suggested most were on his side.

'Will the bodies be recovered?' the Brigadier asked.

'Not from that coast,' Adam said. 'With the currents round there, they'll be swept a long way south. No telling where they'll finish up. I think we'll have a service for them up at the burial ground tomorrow.'

'Shall I conduct it?' the Brigadier asked. 'Or read the lesson?'

'No, sir,' said Adam. 'I think you should keep away.'

No work was done on Halcyon that day. The next morning, in a fine drizzle, Adam conducted the service for the four drowned men. The private soldiers and non-commissioned officers, all of whom had friends in the village, were given leave by Lieutenant Willett and trudged up the hill to the burial ground to join the islanders. It was indicated gently to Peter Willett that he too would be welcome, and he stood with villagers and soldiers in the rain to hear the words so often heard, and to sing, as the islanders always did after a death at sea, the hymn 'Eternal Father, strong to save.'

No one approached the Culpeppers or Philip Saunders. They were left to endure the silence around them.

But for Saunders and the Brigadier, this uneasy peace didn't last long, for by midday the signals from the Mother Country, its Mainland Colony and its southern ocean fleet were arriving in nonstop flow. Cyril, returning from the service, was kept busy trekking back and forth between the administrative headquarters in the former Meeting-House and the radio post at Jonathan Wilde's.

Over at the radio post, in his little makeshift office, Lieutenant Rawson was at his wits' end. The signals were all in code. No one but himself was entitled to use the code book. He had no cipher machine, and manual coding and decoding was slow, laborious work.

Rawson missed lunch and dinner, and even so fell further and further behind. He kept a bottle of whisky in the room, and felt justified in resorting to it on this occasion. As time went by, he resorted to it more frequently and poured it more generously. He had been working hard for days, and became sleepy, but struggled to continue decoding, though he did so more and more slowly and inaccurately. In the end, he fell deeply asleep. Gerry Baines, coming in from the transmitting room in late evening with a signal just received that carried the top priority rating EMERGENCY, found Rawson sprawling face down over the code book, and could not stir him into activity.

Not being a commissioned officer, Baines was not supposed to use or even open the code book. He thought of going for the Brigadier or Lieutenant Willett, but it was over a mile to the village or the settlement, and they probably had even less idea of decoding than he had; besides, though he hadn't much respect for Rawson, he didn't want to get his officer into trouble. He extracted the code book and began, painfully, to decipher the signal himself.

When Cyril arrived from headquarters with a message to be sent out, he found Rawson still sprawling, head between arms, at his table, and Gerry completing a shaky decipher- ment, with several missing letters, of the emergency signal.

'What's up, Gerry?' demanded Cyril. 'You look like you'd seen a ghost.'

'It's worse than that,' Gerry said. 'Take a look at this. No, half a minute, you're not supposed to see it. Nor am I, for that matter. It's top secret. But if you look over my shoulder you might catch a glimpse. And I'm warning you, it'll shake you.'

Cyril peered at the message. Gerry pencilled in the missing letters; there wasn't any doubt what they were. Reconstructed, it read:

MOST SECRET: CULPEPPER FROM COMMANDER-IN-CHIEF SOUTHERN OCEAN. FOLLOWING ORDERS ORIGINATE FROM

IMPERIAL WAR MINISTRY. ALL REPEAT ALL MOTHER COUNTRY PERSONNEL CIVILIAN AND MILITARY TO BE EVACUATED INSTANTLY FROM HALCYON. ALL TO REPORT FOUR A.M. LOCAL TIME BRINGING ONLY KIT THEY CAN CARRY TO POTATO BEACH, WHERE UNLIT MOTOR VESSELS WILL AWAIT THEM. ACKNOWLEDGE THIS MESSAGE, THEN DESTROY SIGNAL STATION AND ALL SECRET DOCUMENTS.

Chapter 14

CYRIL arrived breathless at the former Meeting-House, now the administrative headquarters, to find that the Brigadier had gone home. At the Culpeppers' house, he was admitted by the Brigadier himself, and thrust the message, in an envelope, into his hands. The Brigadier tore the envelope open and stared for a moment at its contents. Then he rapped out, in the tones of the army officer on active service in World War I rather than those of the mellowed, retired gentleman, 'Get over to the officers' quarters. Root out Saunders and Willett. Tell them to come over at the double, pronto, no messing. And where's Rawson? This is urgent and top secret. Why hasn't he brought it himself?'

'I think Lieutenant Rawson's ill, sir.'

'Ill? Or drunk?'

'Dunno, sir.'

The Brigadier gave Cyril a hard look.

'Half a minute, lad. Have *you* seen this?'

Cyril hesitated, looked down, mumbled something.

'You have, haven't you?'

'Yes, sir.'

'Just as well. No harm done. Your people have to know. When you've done as I told you, go to young Goodall's cottage and send him over. And get the wireless op. to acknowledge the signal. He can send it plain-language, it won't matter. Just, "Message received. Orders will be carried out."'

The Brigadier hesitated for a moment. Then, 'No. Make it just "Message received".'

'You realize what this means?' the Brigadier said.

'It means we're pulling out,' Peter Willett said. 'Or rather, they're pulling us out.'

'Yes, yes, of course,' said Brigadier Culpepper testily. 'But beyond that, you realize what it means?'

'It means,' said Philip Saunders, 'that we have been made fools of. We have devoted all this time and effort, to say nothing of the Mother Country's money, to taking this place in hand and making it fit to be a colony, and just when we're getting somewhere it's all to be thrown away.'

'Seems to me,' said Peter Willett, 'it means that Santa Cruz has called our bluff. When it came to the point, the Mother Country never meant to defend Halcyon.'

'Correct,' said the Brigadier. 'In fact, inescapable. But that's still not the whole of it. What else does it mean?'

Saunders and Willett looked blank. The Brigadier answered his own question. 'It means we're supposed to bale out and leave the poor devils who live here to the tender mercies of Marshal Gomez. As nasty a dictator as ever strutted the face of the earth.'

'I wish the Santa Cruzians joy of the islanders,' said Saunders. 'Maybe Santa Cruzian methods will get better results than ours. I've never known such a hopeless workforce. No sense of time, no discipline, nothing. I'm sorry to abandon what we're doing, but I'll be glad to see the back of them.'

The Brigadier said, with unusual asperity, 'I rather think, Philip, that they'll be glad to see the back of *you*.'

Saunders bit his lip. The Brigadier went on, 'Anyway, I have to tell you I'm not leaving.'

'But, *sir*!' expostulated Saunders. 'You can't do that! It's orders!'

'I have His Majesty's commission to govern Halcyon. I haven't been dismissed from my post, and whatever the Commander-in-Chief of the Southern Ocean Fleet may think, I don't take my orders from him. *Or* from the Imperial War Ministry. It's my job to stay here and help the people of Halcyon. And that's what I propose to do.'

'You'll be taken prisoner,' said Saunders. 'Or shot.'

'That's a risk I'm prepared to run.'

'But,' said Peter Willett, 'what about Mrs Culpepper? And Sonia?'

'They'll have to go, of course. I can't expose *them* to the risks of staying. It will be grim for us to split up, but I'm afraid there's no alternative. And now, Peter, we can't stay here chewing it over. Get over to the barracks, alert Sergeant Young, organize the men to be at Potato Bay with their kit at four o'clock. That's in just five hours' time. And make sure the chaps at the wireless post are on board. Including Rawson, even if they have to bring him down in a wheelbarrow. Though I must say, the Santa Cruzians would be welcome to *him*.'

As Peter Willett left the Brigadier's house, Adam Goodall arrived. The Brigadier took a deep breath and prepared to break the news.

'It's no good trying to bully me, Henry,' said Daphne Culpepper severely. 'I have stayed with you through five successive postings, and I am staying with you now. You *need* me, Henry. Who would make sure you ate at regular hours and had a clean shirt to wear?'

'I shall be lucky if I get either regular meals or a clean shirt under the Santa Cruzians,' said the Brigadier. 'And, my dear, it is quite impossible for you to remain here. I cannot allow it. Speaking as Commissioner, I insist that you obey my instructions and embark with the troops. I don't know where you'll be taken to in the first place, but it will be a Mother Country warship and you will be safe and comfortable.'

'You can speak as Commissioner if you like,' said Daphne, 'but I shall only hear you as my husband, and I tell you I am not going. Sonia will go, of course. I'm afraid, Sonia, it means a stay with Aunt Bertha after all.'

'I'm not going either,' said Sonia.

'Oh yes you are!' said the Brigadier.

'Oh no I'm not!'

'Sonia!' said Daphne in a warning tone. 'That is no way to speak to your father.'

The Brigadier said, 'Sonia, have a bit of sense. You wouldn't be safe with the Santa Cruzian soldiery around. I hate to think what might happen to you. That applies to you too, Daphne. An attractive woman and a pretty girl . . . '

'Flattery won't help you, Henry,' said his wife. 'As for the Santa Cruzians, well, it may be an unpleasant regime, but Santa Cruzian officers are still gentlemen. I remember their military attaché in the Mother Country. A charming young man, with exquisite manners. I'm sure they would not allow the common soldiers to trouble us. And although the Santa Cruzians do tend to shoot and imprison people and all that kind of thing, they always treat ladies with respect.'

The Brigadier had lived with Mrs Culpepper for thirty years. During most of that time, when her wishes had conflicted with his, she had got her way. But in an emergency he could put his foot down. Moreover, he was firmly convinced that a man was the head of the family and gave the orders; and in the last resort, as a woman brought up in the conventions of her time, Daphne Culpepper accepted it too.

'Daphne,' he said, 'and Sonia, you are in my care and I am not standing any nonsense. You will embark at Potato Bay at four o'clock. I shall be there myself to see that you do . . . *What* did you say, Sonia?'

'Nothing.'

'It sounded to me like an expression that no young lady should use.'

'I'm not a young lady,' said Sonia. 'I'm a young woman.'

Over at the barracks, the petrol-electric generator ran all night and lights shone from all the windows as the soldiers got their kit together. Most of them were philosophical about the sudden move. They'd been posted at short notice before; it was the service way of life. They hadn't been told that a Santa Cruzian invasion was imminent, but they knew it was threatened and they weren't sorry to be getting out of the way. They hadn't enlisted as combat troops, and had no wish to take part in any heroic rear-guard action.

But they were sad at having to part from friends they'd made on the island. Most of them, when they'd stuffed their back-packs and kitbags with what they could carry, went across to the village to say their farewells. There was no need for Adam to trudge around giving the news; within an hour every soul on the island had heard it. Lamps in cottage windows matched the lights from the barracks. Midnight pots of tea were made and drunk; addresses in the Mother Country were written on scraps of paper and handed over to be carefully preserved, though both soldiers and islanders knew that whatever happened to Halcyon there was little chance that they would exchange letters, and none that they would ever meet again.

Gerry Baines sent off the Brigadier's signal. He and Cyril removed a few portable pieces of equipment that they thought might usefully be taken over to Grandma Molly's; then they found hammers and, feeling sick as they did so, smashed the transmitter to bits. The din woke Lieutenant Rawson, who on being told the news yawned, rubbed his eyes, said he wasn't surprised, and shambled down to the officers' quarters, leaving the code book behind him. Gerry rescued it.

Gradually, in the small hours of the night, the soldiers straggled back to barracks. The cook had prepared a lavish final breakfast, for which the men lined up at three o'clock; they also collected ration packs. At half past three, Sergeant Young formed them into a squad and marched them—with some difficulty, for the night was moonless—along the road they'd made, past the Lookout and the vegetable patches, and down to Potato Beach. Lieutenants Willett and Rawson walked behind. On the way they were overtaken by the Brigadier, driving his wife and daughter and Philip Saunders in the official motor car, which had now covered a total of some twenty miles from new.

Afloat just off the beach, a trio of motor launches waited, commanded by Marine NCOs. The Marines were worried and impatient. Their job was to get their passengers safely conveyed to a waiting destroyer. This was to be done before daylight, unseen from any of the three Santa Cruzian warships that lurked around. An attempt by Sergeant Young to call the roll was sharply discouraged. Everyone embarked higgledy-piggledy in the darkness, wading through water and impeded by kit or baggage. The Brigadier, Willett and Young kept such watch as they could on the operation, and when it seemed that no one was left ashore, the two lieutenants and the sergeant shook the Brigadier's hand, saluted, and, still hustled by the Marines, clambered into the now-crowded boats.

The Brigadier, having kissed his wife and daughter and seen that they were safe aboard, stood alone on the beach as the unlit launches slid gently, under low power, out into the bay. Then he turned, climbed into the motor car, and drove away beneath a sky that hadn't yet become light. He didn't know that one of the launches turned round and circled two or three times before finally heading for the waiting warship.

Gerry Baines emerged from behind a pile of brush and driftwood. In the darkness it had been surprisingly easy to slip away. But his heart was thumping. He'd acted on impulse. He had been offered safety; in fact he'd been ordered into safety; but he'd felt more attached to Cyril and Grandma Molly and the island than to the Army. Now he was a deserter. He must be crazy.

Gerry heard one of the launches circling, and wondered if it was coming back for him. If it had returned to the beach and he'd been hailed, he might have let himself be picked up. He could have spun some tale about what had happened. But it didn't, and as the darkness faded he could just distinguish its shape as it dwindled away towards the horizon.

He was leaving the beach when he heard a voice call 'Hey there!' He turned. Incredibly, in the pale dawn light a girl was walking towards him out of the sea. Sodden clothing clung to her limbs.

Gerry rubbed his eyes, then recognized her.

'Miss Culpepper!' he said.

'Yes, it's me. Sonia.' She smiled uncertainly at him.

'I'm crazy,' she said. 'I decided at the last minute I wasn't going.'

'That makes two of us. How did you do it?'

'Slid overboard. Somebody must have seen me, but it was quite a while before the launch turned. I don't suppose the man in charge wanted to lose time. Anyway, they didn't search for long. And here I am.'

'It's a miracle you weren't drowned.'

'It wasn't that difficult. I'm a strong swimmer.'

'You *must* be . . . What happens now?'

'I don't know. My father thinks he's sent me to safety. I don't know how I can face him. P'raps I won't.'

'What do you mean?'

'I . . . might go somewhere else.'

Gerry said, 'You're shivering. Listen, for a start I'm going to Grandma Molly's. First house in the village when you come to it from this end. She'll have a fire. You can get dry. And we'll both think what we're going to do. Molly might have ideas as well. She's good at knowing what to do.'

Molly said to Sonia, 'It's the kind of daft thing I'd have done when I was a girl. Sometimes I think folk get more sense as they get older. And then again, sometimes I think being sensible ain't everything. Maybe there's times for being daft. Here, love, let me kiss you.'

Molly embraced Sonia vigorously.

'You're soaking wet,' she said. 'Take your clothes off. I

got enough hot water for you to have an inch or two in the bathtub. Then I'll find something dry for you to wear and you can sit by the fire a while. No need to hurry. Your dad won't be worrying about you, 'cause he don't know you're missing. But as for your mum . . . '

'She'll be furious, but she won't worry. She knows I can swim that distance. And she knows I didn't want to leave Halcyon. She'll think I've gone back to Dad.'

'And *aren't* you going back to your dad?'

'No. I'd be in his way. I shall go to Jamie.'

Molly knew all about Jamie.

'I won't tell you what to do,' she said. 'You're old enough to know your own mind. Don't be in too much of a hurry, that's all . . . Now, get yourself stripped and bathed. I'll send Gerry into Cyril's room.'

Cyril, after his late and busy night, was still asleep. Gerry sat on the foot of the bed and waited for him to wake up. Gerry hadn't asked whether he could stay at Molly's; he knew he could.

Third Wave

Chapter 15

*I*SLANDERS woke to a pale, grey, comparatively wind-less day, and a Halcyon that was suddenly empty of its occupying force and silent after the sounds of construction that had echoed through the settlement. All around them were relics of the short-lived colonial regime: the barracks and officers' quarters—unbelievably luxurious by Halcyon standards—with their plumbing and their cooking equip-ment; the stores, with food and drink and cigarettes and all the small luxuries that had been imported to ease the life of the troops; the dozens of picks and spades and wheel-barrows; the petrol-electric generators. It added up, by Halcyon standards, to incredible wealth. There was no sign of the Santa Cruzians. But the calm felt ominous.

In Grandma Molly's cottage, Sonia Culpepper slept. Neither her father nor her lover knew she was on Halcyon. Molly hadn't said a word to anyone. It was up to Sonia to tell.

The Calling-Bell, silent during the occupation by the Mother Country, brought adults to the Meeting-House. It was still partitioned into offices, and Adam and the Brigadier had to address the islanders from outside. There were signs of hostility to the Brigadier. The loss of four good men was too recent to be overlooked, even in a crisis. When Adam explained that Brigadier Culpepper had felt it his duty as Commissioner to stay on and give the islanders what help he could in their dealings with the Santa Cruzians, there were a few who muttered that he needn't have bothered and might as well have left with the rest.

But the Brigadier won the islanders over. They had little idea of what the Santa Cruzians might be like, but a considerable dread of the unknown. They felt that the Brigadier's high rank and presumed knowledge of the Outside World gave him better qualifications than any of them could have for coping with the invaders. And after all, he spoke their language and represented the Mother Country. Though their loyalty had been tested in recent weeks, it was deeply ingrained.

'We could pick off a few of the bastards with our rifles,' suggested Tom Reeves.

'Don't do any such thing!' the Brigadier told him. Then, 'How many of you have guns?'

Most of the men had ancient rifles. They used them for slaughtering livestock, and occasionally for killing wild dogs or for shooting goats on expeditions to Kingfisher.

'Hide them in the roof,' the Brigadier advised. 'Only use them in absolute emergency. Don't try to resist the Santa Cruzians, don't provoke them, carry on your normal lives as best you can.'

'How can we carry on our normal lives,' Jamie Campbell demanded, 'when we haven't got the boats?'

The Brigadier said, 'I made a mistake. I've said I'm sorry. All I can suggest is that you bring the boats back from the other side, if you can safely do it.'

'Of course we can't *safely* do it!' Jamie growled. 'But we can do it, and we'd better!'

'Then there's the food,' the Brigadier said. 'We have big stocks of canned and dry goods. I don't see why we should leave them for the Santa Cruzians. I propose that we distribute them round the village and that everybody hides away as much as they can. Adam, will you supervise and see fair play? And take and stow away any equipment of any kind that the village can use?'

'I hope they leave us time,' Adam said.

'Don't count on it,' said the Brigadier. He added thoughtfully, 'What about the motor car? I don't see why we should leave a valuable motor car for the Santa Cruzian blighters. But there's no way we can use it. Maybe we should push it over a cliff.'

Robert had stood silent among the crowd. But the thought of destroying the motor car was too painful to bear.

'We could hide that, too,' he said.

'Where?'

'Right under the headland where your house is, there's a good dry cave that they'll never find. It's too steep to climb down. You have to go beyond the wireless post to Billygoat Gulch, then down to the beach and back along the sand. We can make it at low tide. There's plenty of room in there for a motor car.'

'Isn't it all rough track when you get past the wireless station?'

'Yes. But it's been dry for a good few days. I reckon the car could make it.'

'When will it be low tide?' the Brigadier asked.

Every man on Halcyon knew the state of the tide at any time of any day.

'Just about now,' Robert said.

'All right. We're on our way. Come with me, Robert, and navigate.'

Adam said, 'Why not take some of the food stocks? An emergency supply. If the Santa Cruzians are as bad as Mr Saunders told us, they might confiscate anything they found in the houses.'

'A good idea,' the Brigadier said. 'Will two or three people help me load?'

Several islanders were willing. Robert said anxiously, 'We'd better hurry. The tide won't wait.'

The motor car was loaded rapidly with cans and with sacks of dry goods. With the Brigadier at the wheel and Robert beside him, it chugged away up the road towards Jonathan Wilde's house. Jamie and half a dozen men set off grimly on foot across country to pick up the boats they had hidden, at such risk and with such loss, on the west coast. Remaining able-bodied islanders began the task of removing what was of use to them from the Army stores and barracks. Some pushed hand-carts, some led donkeys carrying panniers, some had wheelbarrows that had been used in the building work.

They were alarmed and bewildered, and at the same time excited. The wealth that had been brought by the incomers from the Mother Country was suddenly theirs, though they didn't know for how long. They fell upon it. Stacks of cans, packets, jars and barrels disappeared rapidly: first from the stores, then from the cookhouse, then from the officers' quarters. Adam hurried around, making sure that shares were laid aside for those who were too old and infirm to collect for themselves.

Soon after the work began, an unaccustomed noise had people gazing into the sky. An aeroplane appeared over the horizon and flew over the village.

Islanders were startled. They had seen pictures of aircraft, but had never before seen an actual machine.

'Don't worry,' Cyril told those around him. 'It's one of ours. That's the Mother Country markings on its side. It's a light reconnaissance plane. There must be an aircraft carrier around.' He added knowledgeably, 'The ones like that with two wings are called biplanes, but new ones built now are mostly monoplanes. That means they only have one wing.'

The aeroplane circled twice, low enough for the pilot's helmeted head to be seen, then flew away out to sea.

'Does Santa Cruz have aeroplanes, too?' someone asked uneasily.

'A few. But it hasn't any carriers, and land-based planes won't get this far. If there's a war it'll be a sea war. And the Mother Country rules the seas, or so they say.'

'It isn't ruling Halcyon just now,' said Adam ruefully.

The Brigadier and Robert drove past Jonathan Wilde's house, now deserted again, and were at the end of the road. Beyond it was only a rough track, along which the motor car jolted uncomfortably over bumpy ground and perilously close to the cliff top. Here and there, the path had crumbled away and they had to divert their course away from the edge. Then they were on volcanic slopes, driving with the car tilted at an angle; there were boulders scattered around and patches of scree that slid from under the wheels.

'Murder on tyres,' said the Brigadier. 'Heaven preserve us from a puncture.'

It seemed a long drive, with the car in constant danger of slithering out of control, and was made more difficult by folds in the mountainside. At one point an upward slope brought the car to a standstill. Robert got out and pushed from behind; the Brigadier put his foot hard down, and with engine roaring and loose grit escaping under the wheels the car made its way up the next rise.

Billygoat Gulch, reached at last, was a wide, almost-dry watercourse, and the car could be driven down it to the shore.

'Now we head back the way we've come,' Robert said. 'And we'll only just make it. Tide's on its way in.'

Again the Brigadier put his foot down, and the car sped across firm sand. Robert had a minute in which to feel the joy of swift movement; then the car was slowing, running through shallow water to round a point. Then they were on dry sand again, and racing the tide.

'See the cave entrance over there?' Robert said. 'That's where we're going.'

'Fingers crossed,' the Brigadier said; and though water reached the hub-caps the car got through.

There was an upward slope to the mouth of the cave, which was above the water-line and plenty wide enough for the car. Inside, its front compartment was lit by daylight through a broad, high gap in the rock-face.

'There's an old blow-hole in one of these caves,' said

Robert, 'where the sea used to shoot up at high tide, till it broke into the next cave, and that took the pressure off. But the one we're in now is always dry.'

The Brigadier drove as far in as he could get.

'We haven't much time,' Robert said. 'Let's not unload.'

Outside, the tide was encroaching rapidly and the cliff was steep.

'Can you climb?' Robert asked.

The Brigadier was a man in his sixties. He looked up ruefully at the sheer face above him.

'I can try,' he said. 'You lead.'

The cliff was no problem to Robert, who had been climbing since he was a child and had gone up much stiffer ones in his day. He had a strong head for heights and a finely tuned sense of balance. He adjusted instinctively to each change of handhold or foothold; knew without having to think about it whether or not there was sufficient purchase. Below him the Brigadier laboured. His face grew red and sweat stood on his forehead; he didn't dare to look anywhere except at the cliff-face immediately in front of him. Three or four times Robert gave him a hand; once he was stuck and couldn't move until Robert came alongside, shifted his holds and got him going again. They reached a ledge on which the Brigadier, exhausted and shaken, had to rest for several minutes before he could attempt the last few feet of the climb.

'It'd be a bad joke,' he said, 'if I killed myself before the Santa Cruzians arrive.'

When they reached the top, he saw that they were only a little way from his own bungalow.

'We certainly are back at our starting-point,' he said. 'And thank you, Robert. You saved my life three or four times during that climb, and you were risking your own.'

Robert was startled. He was unaware of having saved Brigadier Culpepper's life, and didn't think he'd taken any great risk. It had been an easy climb.

The two remaining longboats arrived at the main beach just before dusk. The villagers, who had been busy all day removing stores and equipment from the deserted Army buildings, turned out to welcome Jamie and his companions and draw the boats up to their usual resting-place. There was general relief that the operation had been carried out without any further casualty. Adam said, 'We don't know what tomorrow's going to bring us. Let's all have hearty suppers at the Mother Country's expense. Tomorrow, if nothing's happened, we can start fishing. It's high time we had fresh fish.'

'Do you really think nothing will have happened, Adam?' asked Ellen later.

'No,' said Adam.

In Jamie's cottage, Sonia said, 'I've come to you, Jamie. I love you. This is home.'

'Maybe it is for now,' said Jamie. 'It's not what you'll always want.'

'It is.'

'I don't think so. Halcyon's small. Your world's much bigger. I don't belong to it.'

'But I *love* you, Jamie. Don't you love me?'

'Yes. But what about your dad? He'll have to know. What's he going to say?'

'I shall tell him tomorrow, when I've spent a night with you. He'll know for sure then that we're lovers and it's too late to stop us. I think he'll accept it. He's mostly worried about the island and his responsibilities. He hasn't time to worry about me.'

'I think he *will* worry, Sonia.'

'Are you afraid he'll take a horsewhip to you?'

'I'm not afraid of any man. But . . .'

'Do you *really* love me, Jamie?'

'Of course I do.'

'Then stop talking and put your arms round me. Now.'

Gerry Baines was installed in Grandma Molly's cottage, where he shared Cyril's room. Molly gave him a set of shabby civilian clothes, once the property of her late husband, Dan. She had accepted his presence calmly.

'He may as well be here as anywhere,' she said. 'I know this lad. He wants to stay on Halcyon, and if I can help him I will.'

Gerry and Cyril sat with the rebuilt wireless set until late in the night. Gerry had worked hard and ingeniously on it, and considered it equal to its predecessor. He was anxious to pick up the source from which he'd received the instruction to Brigadier Culpepper to withdraw from the island.

'I'm hoping they don't know yet that the code book's adrift,' he said. 'As soon as they do, they'll change it.'

Long after midnight, with Cyril nodding but Gerry still alert, the Morse signal came in at full strength. Gerry jotted down letters on a notepad, and after the sign-off reached for the code book. He smiled with quiet satisfaction as the apparent mumbo-jumbo began to transform itself into sense. But the message itself was nothing to smile at.

He shook Cyril awake.

'Here it is,' he said, and pushed it across.

MOST IMMEDIATE MOST SECRET, it said. COMMANDER-IN-CHIEF TO ALL SHIPS SOUTHERN OCEAN FLEET. SANTA CRUZIAN WARSHIPS MOVING IN. LANDING ON HALCYON AT FIRST LIGHT CLEARLY IMMINENT. DO NOT ATTEMPT INTER-CEPTION. AWAIT FURTHER ORDERS.

'That's it,' said Gerry.

'It's enough, isn't it?' Butterflies fluttered in Cyril's stomach.

'Sure is. Look, I'd better stay on watch in case there's more. You run down and tell them. Good luck.'

Cyril pushed open the door, trod lightly through Molly's room, and ran out into the night with his news.

Chapter 16

*I*T was a dark night still, and starless, but a shade or two lighter to the east. A calm night, too, by Halcyon standards—well chosen for an invasion. Cyril dismissed from his mind any picture of an invasion fleet driven straight on to the rocks. They would get ashore all right.

For the moment he wasn't frightened but strangely exhilarated. Here he was at the very centre of things. With Gerry he was the first person to know what was happening. He ran downhill through the village to Adam's cottage, where Ellen opened the door. Her face was anxious.

'He's not here,' she said. 'He's at the Meeting-House.' And in the Meeting-House Cyril found Adam and the Brigadier conferring together. Both jumped up.

'Cyril! What's the news?' the Brigadier demanded.

'Arriving at first light,' Cyril said.

'I thought as much. It's what I was betting on.'

Cyril stared open-mouthed at the Brigadier, who was dressed as no one on Halcyon had ever seen him, in full dress uniform, with epaulettes and a chest resplendent with medals.

'I never thought I'd wear all this stuff,' he said. 'It's only for state occasions. But this may be a state occasion. Adam, will you go round the village and warn people? Tell them to make sure they have water, feed the animals if there's time, and be prepared to stay inside and bar the doors. And I think somebody should go down to the beach and keep a look-out, ready to give an early warning.'

'I'll go,' said Cyril, still buoyed up by excitement.

Adam said, 'It could be risky, Cyril. You come into the village with me. I'll get one of the men to go to the beach.'

Cyril said, 'That'd take time. I'm ready now. I can do it as well as anyone.' And to forestall argument he slipped out into the fading night. The Brigadier shouted after him, but he took no notice and sped away towards the sea. After a while he slowed to a walk. As he slowed, his exhilaration began to ebb, then to turn to apprehension. What was he letting himself in for? The deserted barracks loomed on his right; their very emptiness felt ominous. The Mother Country had pulled out in the face of these Santa Cruzians, and here was he walking on his own to the beach on which they would soon be landing. He must be crazy.

When he reached the shore it was almost light. Cyril peered out to sea. His heart bumped. A ship lay out there, a grey shape, a warship. At first nothing seemed to be happening. The ship was at the limit of his vision. He strained his eyes, thought he saw movement, decided he was wrong, peered again, seemed again to see something move, became confused and didn't know whether he was seeing or imagining. And then suddenly the image resolved itself and the dot on which his eyes were focused separated itself from the ship's outline. A craft of some kind had been launched and was approaching. It seemed to be growing bigger rather than moving, because it was coming towards him head-on. In reality it was travelling fast.

Cyril's heart was now beating rapidly. He slipped behind a boulder and watched. The vessel was a large landing-craft, sliding in now over the surf and crowded with figures. Before it grounded, men were leaping ashore and heading up the beach at a run. They were dressed in black and carrying automatic guns. They were purposeful, moving with practised speed; and they were a sinister sight. Cyril watched as they went swiftly past him up the gravelled road. The landing-craft moved away and the beach was deserted again.

He followed the landing party as closely as he dared, getting cover from the scattered boulders. They seemed to be surrounding the abandoned barracks and officers' quarters. Suddenly the quiet of dawn was split open by the sound of automatic fire. Men were kicking down the doors, breaking in through every entrance, smashing windows, hurling grenades, firing their automatics non-stop. In minutes most of them were inside. Bursts of fire and explosions went on for some time. Then came a lull, a last outbreak of firing and a final silence. The attackers began to pour back out of the building; it seemed to have become clear that there was no resistance. They were regrouping, gathering round a leader, moving away again.

The attack would have been murderous if anyone had been in the barracks. Cyril felt the deepest terror he had ever known; but with it, to his own astonishment, came a sense of inner resource, a kind of cold courage, and a knowledge that he wasn't going to go to pieces. It was daylight now, and, looking towards the village, he could see the Meeting-House, presiding over the huddle of cottages, with the Mother Country's flag still flying over it. Brigadier Culpepper would be sitting there, brave in his finery, a target for vicious attack. He couldn't have seen what happened at the barracks and probably didn't know what danger he was in. This ruthless mob would simply wipe him out. He must be warned to get away while he could.

At the moment Cyril had shelter from a boulder. Fifty yards beyond it was the beginning of an old drystone wall that had once marked out a field and led towards the village. He dropped flat on his belly and wriggled along, aware of his lack of cover. If his movement caught an invader's eye, no doubt there'd be a burst of fire and it would be the end of him.

But the burst of fire didn't come. He reached the wall and, bending forward, ran along it to the end near the village, where a fringe of outbuildings began. He slid from one building to another, gradually nearing the Meeting-House. Finally he darted across the last open space and in through the door. The Brigadier jumped up from his desk.

'Bloody idiot!' he said. 'Why didn't you go home?'

Cyril was white but determined.

'I came to tell you to get out of here. They've *pulverized* the barracks.'

The Brigadier said, 'I'm not deaf, I heard the din. I didn't think they made it by powdering their noses. Thank you, all the same. But this is my post and I stay at it.'

'Sir, you'll be murdered.'

'Maybe I will, maybe I won't. They'll see the sign outside: "Civil Administration". I expect the words are much the same in their own language. Anyway, I can take the chance. I'm an old fool of sixty-eight. It's young fools like you who need protecting. Get out if you can, and go home while the going's good.'

Cyril pushed the Meeting-House door a few inches open, glanced cautiously out, and saw that black-clad figures were closing in. He shut the door swiftly.

'The going's *not* good,' he said. 'They're surrounding us.'

'Then sit on that chair, look inconspicuous, say your prayers and hope for the best.'

Cyril sat down. Minutes went by. There was no action from outside. The Brigadier looked calm.

'They're there, but waiting,' he said. 'That's a good sign. If they were going to kill us first and ask questions afterwards, they'd have done it by now.'

Then, with a crash, the Meeting-House door was kicked open. Daylight streamed in.

The Brigadier motioned to Cyril not to move. They sat and looked at the empty doorway. More time passed. Then an automatic gun poked round the door, followed by a man who glanced swiftly round the room and signalled to another man to come in. The first man pointed his gun at the Brigadier; the other aimed at Cyril. Both were in black, with blackened faces and two or three days' growth of beard. The first man snapped out a phrase in a tongue which neither the Brigadier nor Cyril understood, and gestured violently.

The Brigadier said, 'He wants us to put our hands up. But I don't think we'll take the hint, do you?' He continued sitting with hands folded together on the desk in front of him.

The men exchanged looks. The first spoke to the other in his own language, then went out. The second man said, 'He go to find officer,' then added 'Don't move,' in an accent which suggested that he might have picked up the phrase from a film. He remained, gun still pointing at the Brigadier.

There was a hubbub of voices from outside, then a wait that seemed to last for hours. Then there were sounds of boots marching on gravel, of vehicles, of shouted orders, of more and more voices, more and more activity, but no more shooting. At last a youngish man, elegant in beautifully creased uniform, with Sam Browne belt and revolver, came in. He was handsome, with dark wavy hair, olive skin and small neat moustache. He waved the black-faced gunman aside.

'Good morning, Brigadier Culpepper,' he said.

The Brigadier bristled.

'Who the hell are you?' he asked. 'How do you know my name?'

'Come, come, Brigadier. I remember you so well, I should have thought you might remember me. Captain Montero-Garcia. Esteban Montero-Garcia. I was military attaché in your capital city two or three years ago.'

The Brigadier looked hard at him, then said, 'So you were. I've seen you in my wife's drawing-room.' He didn't seem impressed. 'If I remember correctly, you were something of a drawing-room soldier.'

Captain Montero-Garcia ignored the insult.

'Mrs Culpepper was kind enough to invite me once or twice,' he said. 'How *is* Mrs Culpepper, by the way? And your charming daughter, who must be quite grown up by now? They are not with you here, I suppose?'

The Brigadier made no answer, but countered with another question.

'What's your job now?' he demanded.

'I am aide-de-camp to the Governor. Major-General Rodriguez.'

'Governor? Governor of what?'

'Governor of Gomez Island.'

'And what the hell is Gomez Island?'

'Really, Brigadier. I should have thought you would have guessed. You are on Gomez Island now. It is an offshore island of the Republic of Santa Cruz. It has the honour of being named after our President.'

'Until my Government instructs me otherwise,' said the Brigadier, 'I shall suppose that I am on the soil of Halcyon, a Mother Country colony of which I am Commissioner.'

'I think you will find that your Mother Country will face facts. And no doubt you will face them yourself. At the moment, facts must be rather staring you in the face. We are landing troops as I speak. Not the Specials, who have done their excellent job already; just troops who will occupy our new colony and defend it against any attempt to recover it.'

Captain Montero-Garcia smiled.

'Not that I believe there will be any such attempt,' he went on. 'Your Mother Country put up a bluff—a rather expensive bluff—which failed. My forecast is that they will report the matter to the League of Nations, which will deliberate upon it until such time as the world gets bored with the issue. By then Gomez Island will be firmly established as part of Santa Cruz . . . I gather that in fact you have no defending force here at all?'

'I'm not here to give you information.'

'No, of course not. But we are finding out, and it is already my impression that the island is undefended. If I may say so, your Government made rather a neat job of pulling out its troops unnoticed. Well, it is a pleasure to see you again, Brigadier. I shall be back later with the new Governor, who will wish to make your acquaintance. I can promise you that you will be free to leave the island as soon as you wish, and in the meantime we shall do our best to make you comfortable. You will be allowed to remain in your house. I am sorry that for the moment we have to detain you in it, but that will not last, and if you care to co-operate with us I am sure it will be to our mutual advantage.'

Captain Montero-Garcia smiled again, bowed and withdrew. The man in black with the automatic gun stayed behind, expressionless, leaning on the doorpost.

In a couple of hours the population of Halcyon increased tenfold. Landing-craft arrived in relays; troops marched up the gravel road and were hooted to one side by overtaking armoured vehicles. There were no more special squads; the men who poured in now wore rough olive-green uniforms and steel helmets, and carried antiquated-looking rifles. Many seemed very young. The first arrivals fanned out through the village, where islanders stayed indoors as advised; others moved off towards the flatland, as if looking for resistance. The empty barracks and officers' quarters were quickly occupied, and a tented camp began almost at once to mushroom on the open land nearby; a strongpoint was set up on the way round the headland to Jonathan Wilde's house.

Islanders, peering apprehensively through their windows at very young men with guns, saw nothing of the wider picture; nor did the Brigadier and Cyril, confined to the Meeting-House. Around midday, Captain Montero-Garcia returned with a senior officer whose arrival caused the black-clad guard to spring to rigid attention. The Brigadier rose to his feet.

'Brigadier Culpepper,' Montero-Garcia said. 'I wish you to meet the Military Governor of Gomez Island. This is Major-General Rodriguez.'

The Major-General was a swarthy, heavily-built and formidable-looking man in his fifties. He smiled, though his eyes were cold. Behind him came a man with a camera. The General stalked forward and offered his hand to the Brigadier; the photographer positioned himself for a shot.

The Brigadier's hand remained at his side. For a long, long second, Major-General Rodriguez's hand remained extended and the camera poised. In that second the temperature in the room seemed to drop by several degrees. The Major-General's expression was one of surprise, followed by one of silent fury. He withdrew his own hand, turned on his heel, and stalked from the Meeting-House.

Captain Montero-Garcia said, 'That was a pity, Brigadier. General Rodriguez is a man of honour. In Santa Cruz, our honour is important to us. For one man to disdain to shake another's hand is an insult.'

The Brigadier said, 'I will not shake hands with the invader of a territory for which I am responsible. Nor will I have a picture of such an event going round the world.'

'I understand that, Brigadier. But the Major-General did not like it and he will not forget. As one who wishes you well, and hopes for good relations between us, I regret the incident. I do not suppose the Governor will change his mind about the privileges to be allowed to you. But this is a bad beginning. And now I must invite you to come outside and witness a little ceremony. In fact I must insist. Your young assistant must witness it too.'

The guard made a slight but explicit motion with his gun. The Brigadier and Cyril stepped outside.

There was a ring of Santa Cruzian officers, with a fringe of civilians who included a couple of men with notebooks and the photographer. The flag of the Mother Country was still flying from the Meeting-House mast-head. A young officer already held the cord that controlled it. At a signal, it began to descend.

The Brigadier turned his back.

Major-General Rodriguez saluted, and remained at the salute as the Mother Country flag came down and the scarlet and black of Santa Cruz went up in its place. The camera clicked several times. The ceremony over, the General shook hands with most of the bystanders, this time ignoring the Brigadier, before moving off accompanied by a group of subordinates.

The Brigadier said to Captain Montero-Garcia, 'I stayed

on this island in the hope of being of service to its people. That is still my aim.'

'It is an aim with which I sympathize. But you have done nothing as yet to forward it. Now, what about this young man?'

'Cyril lives in the village.'

'The village is Sergeant Jimenez's department. I see him over there. The man with the megaphone, standing by the truck. He'll make sure the boy gets safely home.'

A high open truck had been parked a few yards away from the Meeting-House, and a grizzled sergeant in dingy battle-dress stood beside it chatting to the driver. Captain Montero-Garcia beckoned to him imperiously. He came across, saluted, and was given a string of rapid instructions, of which the last was clearly to take charge of Cyril.

The Brigadier said, 'Goodbye for now, Cyril. Thank you for everything.'

Cyril had always been in awe of the Brigadier and addressed him as 'Sir,' but felt that their recent experience had changed the relationship. 'Cheers, Brig,' he said perkily. 'Maybe things aren't too bad. We're not corpses yet.'

Captain Montero-Garcia bore the Brigadier away. Sergeant Jimenez and Cyril looked each other up and down. The sergeant said, 'OK, kid. You just stick with me.'

Cyril said, 'You speak our language, then?'

'Do I speak your language? You bet I do. Like a native, kid. What was that you said? Native of where? Good question. You got a sense of humour. Like a native of *anywhere*, that's how I speak it. N'York, London, Sydney, you name it, I been there. On a merchant ship when I was your age. Ten years at sea, travelled the world. Then the Army. Goddam Santa Cruz Army. Don't tell 'em what I think of the Army. But I guess I get a chance to use my talent.'

'What talent is that?'

'*This* is my talent. Talking to you like I do. Most of our guys don't know any of your language, and how many of *you* know *ours*?'

163

'None, I reckon,' said Cyril.

'That's what I thought. I got a handout about this island. Guess your folk are mostly peasants, huh? Can't even read or write?'

'Well . . . I wouldn't call them peasants, exactly. Farmers and fishermen, I'd say.'

'Don't be embarrassed, kid. Our soldiers are mostly peasants, too. Or kids pulled out of the slums. Conscripts. I guess they can read and write, just. But ignorant . . . Now the officers, some of them speak your language real good. Like Montero-Garcia. But they got no time for common folk, no more than they got time for common soldiers. Wouldn't know how to talk to them. That's why they give this job to me. I got to get things through to the rank and file.'

'Is that what the megaphone's for?'

'Sure is. Maybe by tomorrow we'll have some kind of address system, but today I just shout at 'em, see? You can come round with me, and I'll drop you off at your own house.'

Sergeant Jimenez called something to the driver, who threw down his cigarette-butt and climbed into the cab. The sergeant hauled Cyril up beside him and picked up the megaphone. The truck crawled round the village, stopping half a dozen times while Sergeant Jimenez bawled out a list of instructions. Though his English was fluent, his accent was villainous, and the megaphone added its own distortion; but Cyril at least, after hearing it half a dozen times, was in possession of the message.

The island was now Gomez Island, and permanently part of Santa Cruz. Defacing the Santa Cruzian flag would be a crime. It was illegal to possess any kind of weapon, and islanders must stay indoors until all the cottages had been checked. Then they could go about their normal lives. They would not come to any harm so long as they obeyed orders. For the time being they would be allowed to use their own tongue, but a school would be opened at which they and their children could learn the language of their new Fatherland. The Army was their friend and the people of Santa Cruz were their brothers and sisters. Long live Marshal Gomez.

At Grandma Molly's house, Cyril was put down from the truck. He was relieved to see that Gerry had taken down the telltale wireless aerial. Sergeant Jimenez had bellowed out the orders in ferocious tones, but took an amiable farewell.

'What's your name, kid, by the way?'

'Cyril.'

'Hi, Cyril. It's good to know you. But Cyril, I got to give you a warning. I'm one of the good guys, see? The fellers you got to deal with are our sergeants and corporals. And, boy, some of them are tough. They get a real kick out of pushing folk around, and it don't stop at pushing. You tell your people that. Don't tangle with the noncoms or you'll come off worst.'

Chapter 17

LORENZO Juarez stumbled into line on the beach. The corporal was shouting at him. The corporal shouted at everyone. He stumped round the squad, pushing at some men, pulling at others, telling them they were the dregs of the gutter. Lorenzo hardly heard him. He was hungry and tired. He hadn't eaten since he embarked at Puerto San Jose the previous day. It was getting towards dusk and the wind was rising. His feet and legs had been soaked in coming ashore; he was still wet and his boots leaked. He'd been on this crowded beach for hours. He'd watched the landing-craft ply to and fro, the vehicles roll off and lumber up the road, the other squads move away. He might have known his would be last to go. He'd never had much luck . . .

The corporal had got his men into some kind of order. He stood, feet apart, and addressed them.

'Right, you sacks of crap,' he began, 'get ready to move off. And look sharp. You're on active service now. Do any of you know where you are?'

Most of them knew by now, but they waited for the corporal to make it official. When they went on board the night before, they hadn't been told anything. Most thought they were embarking for the southern tip of the Republic, where there was a training area. But overnight a rumour had spread around the ship. They were going to invade some island, it was said. An island they'd never heard of, with a strange foreign name. There might be fighting. This morning some of them had seen the special squad go ashore, and all of them had heard the firing. So the rumour was true.

Lorenzo had been in the Army for three weeks. He'd been conscripted in the shanty town in Gomez City, formerly San Marcos. His father had disappeared years ago, his mother had remarried but died of a fever, his stepfather had been arrested. He'd survived somehow until the Army picked him up. An ordinary story. He thought he was seventeen, but wasn't sure. They'd put his age as eighteen on the enlistment papers. Lorenzo had a gun but had never fired it. He didn't want to fight. At the moment, if he had any feeling beyond hunger and weariness, it was relief that he was ashore unharmed.

'We're on Gomez Island,' the corporal announced, 'which is Santa Cruz soil. Our lads captured it for the Fatherland this morning. Won some medals, I dare say. Smashed the resistance.'

The corporal didn't know whether there had been resistance or not. He was guessing. His superiors had not yet given him any information.

'Wish I'd been with them,' he declared, 'instead of nursemaiding you lot. But I suppose *somebody* has to train you, if you're ever to be any good. And an uphill job it is! Juarez! Stand up straight when I'm talking to you!'

Lorenzo forced himself upright, but felt himself sagging again almost at once.

'Now, we're moving off!' the corporal said. 'And you're the lucky lads. We've a patch of land allotted to us just outside the village here. Some squads are three times as far away, but I got a good pitch for us. Don't say I don't look after you. And listen, we don't go into any houses, see, or have anything to do with the people in them. And hands off the girls, that's orders. And when we get to the site we stay put, understand? There'll be food coming up later, if we're lucky. But there won't be tents—not till tomorrow. Tonight you'll be sleeping out. You'll roll yourselves up in your blankets and be thankful.'

'It's getting cold, Corporal,' one of the men complained.

'I can't help that, can I? I don't make the weather. At least it's not raining. Get into line and stop beefing. You'll be warmer on the march.'

Lorenzo slogged up the gravel road with the rest. The

corporal shouted at them from time to time, but they were weary and poorly trained, and kept falling out of step. He gave up; they straggled along somehow and arrived on the flatland at dusk. There was confusion over which squad was to go where, but it was sorted out in the end. A field kitchen had been set up; Lorenzo stood half an hour in line with his mess tin, and received some scraps of meat and a spoonful of rice. The men settled down, huddled together; it wasn't late but there was nothing to do.

Lorenzo slept. He woke some time later, chilled to the bone. In San Marcos—he hadn't got round to thinking of it as Gomez City—it never got cold like this. Several of his companions were awake; one or two had got to their feet, blankets still around them, and were stamping their feet and rubbing their hands together. The corporal was astir, too. He called two or three of them over.

'We'll have to make a fire,' he told them.

'What with?'

'*I* don't know. There must be wood around.'

'There was driftwood on the beach,' somebody said.

'Too far away, and you couldn't bring enough. Try the village. You go. And you and you and you. No, don't take your guns.'

Lorenzo was among the four men detailed. They were at the end of the village away from the Meeting-House. There was intermittent moonlight, but no lamp shone in any window. For some time they found nothing. Then they came on two or three feet of ancient, sagging fence that didn't seem to be serving any purpose. Two of the men wrenched it from the ground and made off with it towards where they were camped. Lorenzo and the other man separated, each of them prospecting on their own.

Lorenzo had no luck. He didn't want to go back and face the corporal empty-handed, so went on searching in a disorganized way. Close to one of the cottages was a shed. There might be wood in that; who knew? It was closed by a bar. Lorenzo lifted the bar and cautiously opened the door. There was a sudden burst of squawking and fluttering. Hens.

Lorenzo knew about hens. They were sold in the market of Gomez City. Hens were food. If his mates had made a fire, they could do something with a hen. Or hens. He put the bar back in place and considered. Rather than blunder round in the dark trying to catch one, he would report back to the corporal. The corporal could decide whether they were going to seize the hens, and if so, how.

He turned away from the door of the shed; and as he did so, somebody leaped upon him from behind, brought him to the ground, and held a lamp over him. It was a hefty male, who shouted at him in a language he didn't understand. He struggled to his feet. The attacker was stronger than he was. Lorenzo could only think of one thing to do. He ran. But his assailant—faster as well as stronger—caught and grabbed him, brought him down again, then pointed commandingly to the door of the nearby cottage.

All his life Lorenzo had been an underdog. Authority had the power. If authority told you to do something, you did it, or else something nasty happened to you. When you were at the bottom of the heap, authority meant almost anybody who chose to give you an order. Lorenzo did as he was told and went into the house.

Robert stared at his captive, who looked back at him apprehensively. Robert's mother and her new husband emerged from the sleeping-place and stared also.

'What were you doing?' Robert demanded. 'Trying to steal our hens, eh?'

The youngster he'd caught shook his head helplessly.

'He don't understand you,' said May wonderingly. 'Speaks a different language, I expect.' She addressed Lorenzo. 'No understand, eh?'

Lorenzo picked up the word 'No,' and repeated it hopefully.

'He's one of *them*!' May declared. 'A soldier!'

Isaac Reeves said to Robert, 'What happened?'

'Caught him breaking into the hen-house.'

The enormity of what her son had done was dawning on May.

'You laid hands on one of *them*?' she said incredulously. 'Then you can let him go at once, Robert Attwood! We don't know what might happen!'

But Robert wasn't attending. He was studying Lorenzo with interest. The lad was still cold, wet and shivering. His uniform was shoddy and ill-fitting and appeared to have been meant for a larger person. He wasn't wearing a cap, and even an islander, accustomed to cast-offs and reach-me-downs, would have rejected his boots.

Robert had heard from Cyril about the sinister, black-clad and black-faced special squad. It was hard to believe that this pathetic-looking boy was in the same army.

Lorenzo was well aware of what he appeared to have been doing. He wanted to indicate that he'd been looking for firewood, not chickens. But he had no words in which to say that or anything else.

He gestured towards the fire and mimed picking up sticks.

May Reeves misunderstood.

'He means he's cold!' she said. 'And he looks it.'

The boy was about Robert's age, and in her mind's eye a transformation took place. It might have been Robert who was standing there in that miserable condition.

'Come to the fire,' she said, 'and get warm.'

The words had no meaning for Lorenzo, but the gesture didn't need translating. He lumbered across the room. May pointed to the one broken-down armchair, and Lorenzo sat before the fire and stretched his boots towards it. Robert sat on a box close by, frowning. He wasn't sure that he approved of extending hospitality to an enemy, and, more important, an apparent thief.

May brought a cracked bowl from her shelf and tipped a little stew into it from the pot that stood as always on the fire. She offered the bowl to Lorenzo, who grabbed it eagerly and emptied it almost in a gulp. Isaac Reeves said in a warning tone, 'That's enough, May. There's the rest of the family to think of.'

Grandma Molly came in just as Lorenzo put the bowl down.

'Well!' she said, staring. 'A soldier! And one of theirs! What's he doing here, May?'

'Can't you see?' said Robert dourly. 'He's supping stew, that's what he's doing. And a minute ago he was robbing our hen-coop.'

Molly inspected Lorenzo with a bright, interested eye, and came swiftly to a conclusion about him.

'Poor lad!' she said. 'So you gave him some stew, May?'

'I did,' said May, adding defiantly, 'and I'd do it again.'

'Quite right,' said Molly. Then, 'It's you I came for, Robert. Gerry and Cyril have set up the receiver, now it's dark. They want you to go and help. They say the stuff they're picking up is so important that neither of them can leave it for long enough to fetch you. That's why I'm here.'

Robert looked dubious.

'Don't know that I ought to leave this fellow in the house,' he said.

'Now, now, lad,' said Molly. 'Have a bit of sense. Your mum and Isaac could handle *him* with their hands tied behind their backs. Anyway, he's not going to do nobody no hurt. It's written all over him. He's harmless.'

Gerry and Cyril were excited.

'We picked up the mainland,' Gerry said. 'Lots of news bulletins. They're all beginning with the invasion. Marshal Gomez claiming a great victory. The Mother Country keeping very quiet; says Halcyon belongs to it but rather than go to war it'll complain to the League of Nations. Gomez says he doesn't care two hoots for the League of Nations. The commentators all think he'll get away with it.'

'That's bad news,' said Robert. 'If we've got to have outsiders coming here, we might as well have them coming from the Mother Country and talking our language. Besides, I got to like the old Brig. He kept doing things wrong, but he meant well.'

This was a long speech for Robert. But the other two weren't listening.

Cyril said, 'That's not all. We know something the folks making the broadcasts don't. Tell him, Gerry.'

Gerry said, 'We can still pick up signals from the Commander-in-Chief, Southern Ocean. Not meant for us, of course. In Morse, and coded as well. But we still have our copy of the code book. Rawson can't have owned up yet to losing it. They'll soon find out, of course. Then they'll drop it like a stone. Can't use a compromised code book. But just for the moment . . . '

'Just for the moment,' said Cyril, 'we're getting it from the horse's mouth! Show him, Gerry!'

Gerry pushed across a piece of paper on which he'd pencilled a row of characters and a translation. Cyril read it out:

'STRATEGY 100 PER CENT SUCCESSFUL. LATEST OBSERVATIONS SHOW TROOPS STILL BEING DISEMBARKED. BELIEVED ALMOST 3,000 NOW IN TRAP.'

'You see?' Cyril said. 'It's a trap by the Mother Country. The Santa Cruzians are in it.'

'Yes,' said Robert. 'So are we.'

Chapter 18

*T*HE landings of Santa Cruzian soldiers continued for two more days. By the time they stopped coming there seemed no room for any more. A tented camp covered most of the flatland, and new arrivals had to bed down uncomfortably on the lower slopes of the Peak. There were no more crack troops; the reinforcements were raw and bewildered recruits like Lorenzo. They were set to work in shifts to construct defences of sandbags and trenches at all points where Mother Country troops might try to land. When not engaged in these operations, they were drilled, in the limited space available, by their NCOs.

At first the Santa Cruzians had little to do with the islanders. A few of them made themselves a mild nuisance when off duty by wandering round among the houses, peering in at cottage windows and doorways, and shouting the word 'Hallo,' which for most seemed to be the limit of their vocabulary. A few managed in spite of the language barrier to strike up some kind of relationship with an island family, and would sit in cottages in the evenings, silent but smiling. They had cigarettes, if nothing else, to offer to their hosts. Such friendships were prized by the Santa Cruzians; they meant warmth, company and sometimes a little food. Lorenzo was among the lucky ones, and often spent off-duty hours in Robert's house.

For the islanders themselves, life settled down to a degree of normality. The women worked in the vegetable patches and the men resumed fishing without interference, though the landing and distribution of the catch were always watched by rings of interested spectators.

Two or three weeks went past. The reconnaissance planes from the Mother Country's aircraft carrier flew over several times, attracting sporadic and ineffectual gunfire, but there was no other sign of activity on the part of the Mother Country. Gerry and Cyril could not intercept any more secret messages, for the codes had been changed. They heard news bulletins from the mainland, which told only of wrangles in the League of Nations. Gradually the Halcyon affair became less prominent in the bulletins until it barely figured at all.

But winter was approaching; the nights were cold, and strong winds added to the Santa Cruzian troops' discomfort. The sea-borne supply lines weren't equal to the task that had been set them; arrivals of food from Santa Cruz itself were irregular and insufficient. The men were bullied by their NCOs, underfed, hard-worked by day and cold at night, and their morale was low.

From the start, there were problems over firewood. It wasn't only a matter of keeping warm; the Santa Cruzian field kitchens were normally fuelled by wood, and none was arriving. Every bit of loose timber on Halcyon disappeared; fences vanished mysteriously overnight, and even wooden outbuildings were pulled down, sometimes by gangs of young soldiers against the resistance of the owners. The hen-hut that Robert had defended was seized, but Robert and Old Isaac had prudently moved the hens to a stone outbuilding, and they survived. Most island out-buildings in fact were of stone, for Halcyon was almost treeless and had always been short of timber. In the end, many of the Santa Cruzians learned of the uses of peat, and thefts were mostly from the islanders' peat stacks, which for a limited time could stand them.

Then thefts began from the vegetable patches. The little stone structures in which islanders stored their tools and lifted potatoes were raided first; then root crops were dug out of the ground. At this stage Adam complained to Sergeant Jimenez, who had a tiny cell of an office in a corner of the Meeting-House.

'Yeah, well, I know just how you feel, Adam,' said the sergeant amiably. 'It's how I'd feel myself. It's a lousy deal for you guys. I feel ashamed when you tell me about it, really ashamed. If there was something I could do, I'd do it like a shot. You know me, Adam. That's my sincere opinion, really sincere. Believe me, I'm on your side, Adam.'

'*Can't* you do anything, then?' Adam asked.

'Well, no, Adam, I guess not. It's their noncoms who have to discipline them, and you know what they're like. In fact the noncoms are often the ringleaders. I'm ashamed to admit it, Adam, sincerely ashamed, but there's nothing whatever I can do to help you. They'd just laugh at me.'

'Then can I see your commanding officer?'

''Fraid not, Adam. He's a busy man.'

'Surely I can see *some* officer?'

'I'll see what I can do, Adam.' The sergeant threw an arm round Adam's shoulders. 'I want to help you, pal, I really do. Trust me. Come back tomorrow.'

But Adam came back the following day and the one after, and got no further.

Brigadier Culpepper was as frustrated as Adam, though a good deal more comfortable. He was well aware that he was doing little or nothing to fulfil his self-imposed aim of looking after the islanders' interests under occupation. He was a closely guarded prisoner and had no communication with the village. He was not allowed outside except to walk in his garden, which was surrounded by a high wire fence.

Adam managed, with Cyril's help, to write a note which was delivered to him, opened, by Captain Montero-Garcia. It complained about the thefts. But Brigadier Culpepper got no more change out of the Captain than Adam had got out of the Sergeant.

'My dear Brigadier,' said Montero-Garcia, 'our NCOs are thugs and our privates are rabble, and there's nothing whatever to be done about it.' And he smiled his charming smile.

Adam did not consider it his business to give the

Brigadier news of Sonia. She had tried once to see her father, been turned away, and not tried again. Her conduct in living openly with Jamie was scandalizing the village. But Adam was no tell-tale. It was for Sonia and nobody else to tell the Brigadier what was going on.

Captain Montero-Garcia came in most days for a little conversation. The Brigadier had decided, on reflection, that he should seek out Major-General Rodriguez and explain that his refusal to shake hands was not meant as a personal insult but as a declaration of loyalty to his own Government. The aide-de-camp was happy to arrange it. The Major-General received the Brigadier, listened to him, and said coldly, 'I accept your explanation.' He added, with the satisfaction of one returning a snub, 'But you must excuse me, I have no time to talk to you. I am busy,' and turned away.

Captain Montero-Garcia remained friendly, and invited the Brigadier on several occasions to dine with him and a group of fellow-officers, though never when the Major-General was present. On these occasions the Brigadier was received courteously by the Santa Cruzians, who addressed him as 'Sir' and talked to him effortlessly in his own language. And the food and wine in the officers' mess were superb. One evening, in an atmosphere more mellow than usual, the Brigadier observed, 'Your Marshal Gomez is crazy.'

There were smiles all round. Captain Montero-Garcia put his finger to his lips in a mock appeal for caution, but nobody seemed to take offence.

'Of course he is crazy,' said one of the officers. 'How do you suppose he got to be where he is? To be crazy is a necessary qualification for running our country.'

'I mean,' said the Brigadier, 'that he is pouring in all these troops, spending all this money, and risking war with a Great Power, for a scrap of land that nobody wants.'

'It is of strategic value,' said Captain Montero-Garcia, 'perhaps. And in fifty or sixty years' time, when aeroplanes are a commonplace and ordinary people fly all over the world, it may be ripe for tourist development. Perhaps. But what the venture is about, my dear Brigadier, is prestige. If Gomez can humble a Great Power, he will capture its glory for himself. Still more important in his eyes, he will secure his position at home, where there are many plotting to topple him.'

'Our guest is right,' said a grizzled major. 'The man is crazy.'

'He is the son of a grocer,' said Montero-Garcia contemptuously. 'What do you expect?'

Captain Montero-Garcia, through the medium of Sergeant Jimenez, had assured the villagers that island women would be unharmed if they conducted themselves with discretion. Ferocious orders against molesting women had been issued to the troops; the slightest harassment would lead to severe punishment.

'But if I had womenfolk here, I'd tell them to be home by dark,' Sergeant Jimenez said to Adam. 'Orders are orders but guys are guys. Our boys are stuck here without any women, and I wouldn't advise tempting them.'

And it was a failure to be home by dark that led to catastrophe. Winter had come, and the days were short. On a wet afternoon, Sonia and Jamie slept in Jamie's cottage until dusk. Then the rain cleared away, and Sonia declared that she needed to breathe. Jamie set out with her for a walk along the slippery cliff path. There they met Corporals Felipe Lopez and Emilio Santos. What followed was a tragedy of incomprehension.

The Santa Cruzian NCOs, unlike the privates, had wine in their mess and in their institutes. It was pay-day. The two corporals were in a cheerful mood, neither sober nor totally drunk, when they met Jamie and Sonia. They were in fact among the less thuggish of the NCOs. Corporal Lopez had seen Sonia around before and admired her; naturally-blonde hair was rare in Santa Cruz, and Sonia's face would have been attractive anywhere. Like many of his fellow-soldiers, Felipe Lopez knew nothing of Sonia's language except a few phrases picked up from films. He greeted her with one of these.

'Hi there, beautiful,' he said.

Sonia smiled, partly at him, partly at the phrase, partly in sheer happiness.

Felipe, encouraged and acting on impulse, put both hands on her shoulders. He meant no harm. He had not the slightest intention of assaulting her. But Jamie wasn't the man to stand for it. He stepped toward Felipe, threateningly.

Felipe, floating pleasantly between drunkenness and sobriety, failed to recognize the movement as threatening. He took a hand from Sonia's shoulder and extended it to Jamie. He meant to shake Jamie's hand. Instead of shaking his hand, Jamie landed a fist in his face.

Felipe staggered backwards, shocked and dazed. Emilio Santos, less drunk than Felipe, shouted angrily at Jamie. Jamie had no idea what the words meant. He shouted back at Emilio that no dago bastard was going to lay hands on his girl, and that Emilio had better get his friend out of the way, fast. Emilio thought that Jamie was framing up to hit him; so he got in first and hit Jamie. Then they were brawling on the cliff path. Sonia tried in vain to come between them. Felipe, recovering, saw only that his friend was having a hard time and moved in to help him. Jamie turned, swung a wild fist at Felipe, and caught him off balance. He slithered on the wet path, and was over the edge.

Jamie and Emilio broke up instantly, went to the edge and peered down. The cliff was sheer. Far below were the rocks on which, six months earlier, Private William Boothroyd had met his death. Felipe Lopez was now meeting his.

Emilio, sobering rapidly, shouted to Jamie that he was under arrest. Jamie insisted loudly—but to Emilio incomprehensibly—that he hadn't meant to do that to the bastard. Emilio thought Jamie was resisting arrest, and in a moment they were at grips again. And then a little group of

Santa Cruzian privates came by, Emilio shouted to them, and they all weighed in. Jamie was overpowered and borne away, kicking and shouting, to the headquarters of the military police. Sonia, dazed and in shock, overwhelmed by the swiftness and horror of events, followed.

Captain Montero-Garcia arrived early at the Brigadier's house the following day, and he was not smiling.

'We have trouble with your people,' he said. 'A corporal of ours has been murdered.'

'By a Halcyon islander?' asked the Brigadier, startled.

'Yes. Our men picked him up. He doesn't deny it. A red-haired, wild looking fellow.'

'That'll be Jamie Campbell,' the Brigadier said. 'My God! What happened?'

'It seems the corporal expressed admiration of his girl; the fellow objected and there was a fight. The corporal fell and was killed on the rocks.'

'It may not exactly have been murder,' the Brigadier said.

'Under our martial law, there is little room for fine distinctions. The Major-General is incensed, and insists that an example be made. And, Brigadier, you must prepare for a shock. The girl is your daughter.'

'My daughter!'

'Your daughter, Sonia. It was a surprise to me. I was not aware that she was on the island.'

'Neither was I!' said the Brigadier.

'There is no doubt that it is she. She says so herself. And although she was still a child when I met her in your capital city, I recognized her at once.'

The Brigadier was shaken. He said, 'Excuse me while I collect my thoughts.' Then, after a pause, 'Yes, it must be Sonia. She must have found a way to return here. I didn't kr.ow about an affair with Campbell, though I must admit the possibility had crossed my mind.' He added heavily, 'Where is she now?'

'She is in the office of Sergeant Jimenez, who speaks your language. She is making a statement.'

'When she has finished, can she be sent to me?'

'Certainly. She has already asked to see you, but I was not prepared to authorize it until I had spoken with you.'

'What mental state is she in?'

'She is distressed, understandably, but composed.'

'And what will happen to the man?'

'I'm afraid there's no doubt about that. He will be tried later today. He will be found guilty and shot.'

'Sonia,' the Brigadier said. 'How *could* you?'

'How could I what? Live with Jamie?'

'I don't mean that. I mean, how could you do this to your mother? She'll have been going through hell. She can't know whether you're alive or dead. Compared to that, my feelings are a minor matter. I haven't been worrying about you. I thought you were safe in the Mother Country by now. But your mother . . . '

'She knows I'm a strong swimmer. And she knows I'm not mad. She knows I wouldn't have gone overboard if I couldn't make it to the shore.'

'I'll ask Montero-Garcia to get a message to her. There must be a way of doing it. He's an ex-diplomat. He'll know.'

'As for Jamie . . . ' said Sonia.

'As for Jamie . . . Yes, I do mind. You're not of age. Of course I mind that you were having an affair with a fisherman and concealing it from me. You could have ruined your life.'

'I'm not pregnant, if that's what you're afraid of.'

'Well, I suppose once we got you home nobody would know. Though you must realize, Sonia, that we're in a hot spot over here. It's a case of *if* we get home, not *when* we get home.'

'You make me angry, Father. I'm not going to leave Jamie and go home and be respectable. And you understand? You've got to get him off. I'll never forgive you if you don't.'

Major-General Rodriguez sat behind his desk. The Brigadier came in. He had been kept waiting for two and a half hours.

'I've come to ask for clemency for the man Campbell,' he said.

'I know what you have come for. You have come to plead with me on behalf of the lover of your daughter.'

'I am pleading on behalf of an inhabitant of this island. I have been told of the circumstances. I understand that Campbell thought your corporal was assaulting my daughter.'

'I am aware of the facts. But Campbell struck the first blow, and it was a blow from him that sent Lopez over the edge. Gomez Island is under martial law, and he could have been summarily executed for attacking a member of our forces. Nevertheless, I chose to hear what he had to say. His guilt is beyond doubt. He did not deny what he had done. Even if there had been provocation, it could not have exonerated him.'

'There is the matter of intention. He didn't *mean* to kill.'

'Brigadier Culpepper, do you not think it impudent to appeal, for the sake of a man with whom you are connected, to an officer whose hand you disdained to shake?'

'I find it humiliating,' said the Brigadier. 'But I am doing it.'

'You are doing it in vain,' said Major-General Rodriguez. He signalled to an aide and gave him a brief instruction in his own language. The man went out.

'Wait for a moment,' the Major-General said.

The Brigadier sat for a minute. There was silence in the room. Everyone was listening. Then from outside a fusillade made the windows rattle.

'That is my answer,' said Major-General Rodriguez.

181

Chapter 19

*T*HE Brigadier was not a stranger to death or to grief. He had lost many comrades in the Great War, and had not ceased to grieve for them. But he had never grieved as a lover, and Sonia's desolation left him at a loss. For two or three days she wandered round the bungalow silent and stunned while the passion welled up inside her. Then it burst out; she wept and stormed, blamed herself and her father, blamed the Mother Country and the Santa Cruzian commander, blamed God and fate, blamed herself again, wept and wept.

At times she shouted to her father to go away when he came near her; at other times she sought him out and threw herself into his arms. Once she cried pathetically 'Oh, Mummy, Mummy!', though she had not been close to her mother for years and not addressed her as 'Mummy' since the age of seven. And then, after a week, came calm, and apparent acceptance. Sonia smiled, made small jokes, and announced that she was going into the village to find Tilda.

Tilda had been brought up under the moral code of the island, and had shared the islanders' sense of shock at what they saw as shameless behaviour by Sonia and Jamie. Yet at the same time she had felt that a window—opened a crack when she wrestled with Robert in the Dell and slept in his arms on Kingfisher—was opened further by her awareness of the joy that Jamie and Sonia were so obviously sharing. Pleasure in love was not among the listed ingredients of life on Halcyon, but could it really be bad? Perhaps it was something one should hope to experience. She hugged and comforted Sonia, and wept a little for Jamie on her own account.

Grandma Molly hugged Sonia, too, and had down-to-earth comfort to offer.

'You're young,' she said. 'You'll get over it. There'll be another man in your life before long.'

'There won't be another like Jamie,' said Sonia.

'No, of course not. He'll be like himself.'

Captain Montero-Garcia came to the bungalow and suggested that by way of a change Sonia should join her father as a guest in the Mess. Sonia went, appeared to enjoy herself, flirted a little with the younger officers, returned home, and wept again.

On the following day, the captain looked grim and for once seemed hostile. All these weeks, he said, the Mother Country had done nothing about the seizure of the island except argue in the League of Nations. Now, suddenly, a Mother Country warship had attacked a Santa Cruzian cruiser and sent it to the bottom. Two hundred men had been drowned; another two hundred had been picked up by a Santa Cruzian vessel and were at this moment on their way to the island. It was an attack without warning and without declaration of war.

'But your invasion of Halcyon was without warning and without declaration of war,' objected the Brigadier.

'That was merely occupying what belonged to us. And it was not done without warning. We repeatedly said we would do it. It is not our fault if you chose not to believe us.'

'*I* think,' said the Brigadier, 'that sauce for the goose is sauce for the gander.'

'In my opinion,' said Captain Montero-Garcia, 'what your country has done now is *not cricket*. I can think of no stronger condemnation than that.'

The day after that, troops and islanders were awakened before dawn by the sounds of bombardment. For a brief while, as the ground shook beneath their homes, islanders thought of earthquake or volcanic eruption. But it was shelling at close range from a Mother Country warship. It continued for an hour, and was mercilessly accurate. A few of the first shells landed on the flatland or hillside, or fell into the sea, but then the guns found their range.

Shell after shell hit the primary target, which was obviously the complex of buildings put up during the brief occupation by the Mother Country. The barracks and officers' quarters were destroyed, and men in them killed, wounded or trapped. Whether by design or accident, the Brigadier's bungalow half a mile away was untouched, but the Meeting-House was reduced to debris. Gaps were torn in the defences the Santa Cruzians had built along the beach. The village itself was almost unharmed, but a stray shell destroyed the cottage of Ben and Alice Jonas, killing Ben outright and half burying Alice.

With daylight the shelling stopped as suddenly as it had begun; there was only dust in the air, an occasional clatter of falling rubble, the shouts and cries of rescuers and rescued. The flatland was a scene of crowded confusion. Troops were rushed up to meet an expected invasion and make hurried repairs to the defences. Others worked rapidly through demolished buildings, dragging out dead and injured. The Santa Cruzian field hospital, which had been standing idle since the day of the invasion, went into hectic action.

While the Jonases' neighbours George Wilde and Jack Reeves dug Alice out of the wreckage of her cottage, Marge Kane ran to fetch Adam and then Grandma Molly, who had long been the island's healer and bonesetter. But Alice's injuries were beyond the power of Molly to treat.

'We must get her to hospital!' Adam said; and Alice was carried, half conscious and unaware of Ben's death, to the marquee in which the Santa Cruzians were struggling with the crisis. The scene was chaotic. Scores of soldiers were injured, some desperately; there were not enough doctors or trained support staff, and the orderlies were inexperienced and mostly incompetent. There were no women on the strength.

184

Grandma Molly was shocked.

'These fellows supposed to be looking after hurt people?' she enquired. 'They ain't got no idea what they're doing. It takes women for a job like that. Adam, go and get Lizzie Oakes. And my Tilda. They're needed.'

The hospital commandant had no knowledge of Grandma Molly's language, or she of his, but it didn't matter. He was run off his feet in all directions, attempting to cope with a disaster beyond his resources. He looked blank when confronted, and turned away to deal with urgent and conflicting appeals. Molly and the other two rolled up their sleeves and got on with caring for the wounded.

It was a task for strong nerves and strong stomachs. Men lay on the ground untended, some naked and bleeding, some still in bloodsoaked uniforms that had to be agonizingly cut off, some with limbs mangled or missing, one with half a face, another with the back of his head blown off. Two surgeons operated hastily and drastically. There were not enough painkillers.

Molly, and Lizzie who was the island's midwife, used such skills as they had, and some they didn't know they had. But often they and Tilda could do little for sufferers but cradle them, murmur to them, touch them gently, smile when the urge was to weep. A boy of Lorenzo's age, hideously injured and half-conscious, looked up as Molly approached him, murmured 'Mama', and died. A man with both legs shot away, a crushed hip and a great gaping wound in the stomach was still alive. One of the surgeons, a young man in his twenties, looked at him in desperation, went for a revolver, and shot him dead, then dropped the gun and stood back, shaking. Lizzie Oakes took the surgeon in her arms, held him to her and kissed him; she had never before in her life kissed a man other than her husband.

It went on for three days. Molly, Lizzie and Tilda ate when they could, slept when they could, never left the field unit. They had no time to worry about the possibility of more shelling. Gradually the situation came under control;

makeshift beds were devised, surviving patients were made comfortable, surgery became less heroic, cases of lesser urgency received treatment. Late on the third day, Captain Montero-Garcia arrived and took Grandma Molly aside.

'We are grateful to you ladies,' he said, 'but the Commandant feels it inappropriate that enemy nationals should be attached to his staff. He wishes you to return to your homes.'

To the sufferers, the three were heroines already. There were painful leavetakings. Molly, Lizzie and Tilda left in tears, went home and slept the clock round. Alice Jonas, her wounds treated and bandaged, also went home, to learn of her husband's death.

Tilda told her mother as best she could what it had been like, but there was much that she couldn't put into words, and there were sights of which she could hardly face the memory, though she would carry it with her for the rest of her life.

'Remember telling me,' she asked Annie, 'the day Robert took his oar, that I was a woman? Well, I wasn't. But I am now.'

The expected invasion did not come, and there was no more shelling. But a few days later a Santa Cruzian ship bringing food and supplies to the island was sunk by the Mother Country navy, and soon afterwards another one. In the news bulletins broadcast from the Mainland Colony, Halcyon emerged once more as a leading item. One night Cyril and Gerry, listening in as usual, heard that the Mother Country had declared a blockade of Halcyon. It would continue, the announcement went on, until the Santa Cruzians decided to surrender.

Next day came the response from Marshal Gomez, recorded and re-broadcast from the Mainland Colony. Santa Cruzians, he said, would never surrender. Gomez Island was part of their homeland and they would defend it to the last drop of blood. Victory would be theirs. The broadcast ended with martial music.

Two supply ships got through in the next month, but two more were seized or sunk and a Santa Cruzian destroyer was sent to the bottom. The soldiers were cold and hungry already, and now it was the depth of winter.

At first, the Santa Cruzian officers and the islanders themselves suffered least. The army had always been run on the principle that the officers were a class apart and had the best of everything. The senior officers moved into the Brigadier's bungalow, the Brigadier and Sonia being moved to small rooms at the back; an emergency mess and sleeping quarters for junior officers were run up alongside, and the officers' mess had first claim on such food and drink as did arrive. Non-commissioned officers had the best of the rest.

The unlucky conscripts, who made up most of the rank and file, were soon on starvation rations. The officers did not feel any pangs of conscience at living comfortably when the soldiers' conditions were miserable. They were used to being surrounded by poor people in poor conditions. That was the way things were.

The islanders had known hardship before, and were used to it. And they had extra lines of defence. For a while, there were the cans and packets and dry goods that they'd inherited from the stores. Then there were the supplies concealed in the motor car; a party went round the headland one night and picked them up from the cave, bringing them home in heavily-loaded backpacks. The fishing continued; islanders had their sheep and their hens and what was left of their vegetable produce.

But the hens and the vegetables went, stolen by hungry soldiers. The sheep dwindled in number; and few of them were killed and eaten by their rightful owners. Then the day came when *Petrel*, landing with its catch, found a mob of soldiers, led by a sergeant and a corporal, waiting for it. In almost no time, the catch vanished; the fishermen who tried to defend it were defeated by force of numbers. The boat itself was seized, but did the soldiers no good, for a scratch crew soon ran it on a rock; the boat was wrecked and all but one of the men drowned. The wreckage, when washed up, was immediately used as firewood.

The winter gales grew fiercer. They were nothing new to islanders. The gales came every year, and the cottages were built to withstand them. Stone walls were two feet thick; thatched roofs were weighted down with heavy boulders. But the men in their tented camp had little protection, and the weather was merciless. Tents were anchored down with all the ingenuity that their wretched occupants could devise; but even so, many were torn or blown away. Soldiers appealed to islanders for floor space in the cottages and were usually given it. Any food they and the cottagers could lay their hands on was shared.

Blinding rain and spray drove over the flatland, slashing like icy knives at all who had to move in the open. More and more men reported sick, and there was little the sick bay could do for them.

Then, by way of the mainland wireless bulletins, the news came through to Cyril and Gerry that the Mother Country had become aware of the islanders' plight. It was Daphne Culpepper, now back home, who brought it to light. A letter to a leading newspaper pointed out that when the Mother Country troops withdrew, the islanders had been left to the mercy of the invaders. Mrs Culpepper said that her husband the Commissioner and their daughter had insisted on staying, and she had just heard that they were both alive, but there was no other information on how the islanders were faring. And the Mother Country's blockade must be hitting them equally with the Santa Cruzians.

The press—said the wireless bulletin—had taken up the story. Thousands of people who had never heard of Halcyon were suddenly concerned for the welfare of its people. There were demands on all sides for a Mother Country force to go in and rescue them. But the Government resisted all such demands. So far, hardly a drop of Mother Country blood had been spilled, and that was how matters should remain. All that was required was a Santa Cruzian surrender.

Marshal Gomez had been given the opportunity of a propaganda victory. He announced, to much trumpeting by his own administration, that he would release any islanders who wished to leave.

One morning Sergeant Jimenez arrived at May Reeves's cottage.

'Hi, there,' he said.

Robert was down on the shore beyond Potato Beach, looking for shellfish and seaweed. There wasn't much of the former to be found. The weed he was collecting was of a kind known to the islanders as 'famine weed'. As a last resort it could be boiled and eaten. It was stringy and unpleasant in taste, and there wasn't much nourishment in it, but it was something to put in empty bellies.

May and Polly looked at the sergeant and said nothing. Polly had long since lost her usual bounce; May was depressed and lethargic.

'It's you I want, kid,' said the sergeant to Polly.

This approach roused May's flagging spirit.

'You keep your hands off her!' she told him.

'Calm down, Momma. I don't mean the kid no harm. Polly, isn't it? Look, Polly, I got something for you!' He drew from his pocket a wrapped bonbon.

Polly seemed dazed. She hesitated. The sergeant unwrapped it and popped it into her mouth.

'There!' he said. 'Good, eh? That's a present. You know who it's from? It's from the big white chief. The Major-General himself. How d'you like that, huh? The Major-General thought of you. He said, "Sergeant, take this candy and give it to Polly. And tell her there's more where it came from." He wants to see you, Polly. You gotta come along of me and say hallo.'

'Oh no, she won't!' said May fiercely.

'I told ya, don't worry, Momma. It don't mean nothing bad. The General likes to talk to kids, that's all. You can come with me and see for yourself.'

'I certainly will!' said May grimly.

Major-General Rodriguez had a new office, in a temporary building rapidly run up since the shelling. The sergeant showed May and Polly into it. A moment later the photographer who had recorded the raising of the Santa Cruzian flag appeared. An aide thrust a bouquet into Polly's hands. Polly held it, not knowing what she was supposed to do. The Major-General leaned down to her, smiling. The camera clicked. The Major-General relieved her of the bouquet, and the camera clicked again.

Someone lifted her on to his knee, for which she was a little too big to be comfortable. Her mother started forward, but was held back by the sergeant. The smile was still fixed firmly to the General's face. The camera clicked again. Polly said, 'I don't like you.'

The General kissed Polly. Click. The photographer said something which appeared to be a request for another shot. The General tried to kiss Polly again, but she turned her face away. The General made an impatient remark and allowed her to get down. He bowed briefly to May and gestured for them to be taken away. Outside the office, the sergeant said, 'That was great. You'll get your picture in lots of newspapers, Polly. Now, you can find your way home, can't you? 'Bye, sweetie. 'Bye, Momma. And by the way, the General forgot to give you this.' He pressed a very small bag of candy into Polly's hand.

Captain Montero-Garcia's hostility had only been temporary. Discussing with the Brigadier the Gomez offer to release the islanders, he remarked apologetically, 'I am afraid that does not apply to you, my dear Brigadier, or to your charming daughter. You are too valuable. However, the natives can go. Knowing your concern for them, I am sure you will be relieved.'

'The offer may be rejected,' said the Brigadier. 'The Mother Country may not be keen to have Halcyon islanders on its doorstep. The further away and the less they are heard of, the better, so far as the Colonial Administration is concerned. And perhaps my Government thinks you will soon have to surrender anyway.'

'If it thinks that it is mistaken. The winter will not last for ever. And we have our intelligence. Your Government lacks determination. It does not want to fight a war. When it realizes it cannot eject us without bloodshed, it will back off. You will see.'

'I don't think you believe what you are saying,' said the Brigadier.

The Brigadier seemed to be right in thinking that the Mother Country would not jump at the Gomez offer. Days went by without any response. Another supply ship was seized.

Then the picture of Polly and the Major-General appeared. The photographer who covered the occasion had been from an international agency, and his pictures had found their way around the world. The shots that showed Polly apparently presenting a bouquet and that showed the General kissing her, appeared in the newspapers of Santa Cruz and countries sympathetic to it. But the one that was printed very large on the main news page of every paper in the Mother Country was the one in which the General was trying in vain to plant a kiss while Polly turned away in rejection.

There was something in her posture, in her expression of mingled fear and contempt, in the hideous smirk on the General's face, that struck a chord in everyone who saw the picture. There were instant demands that Polly and the other islanders should be saved; that the Mother Country should not leave its own loyal subjects to face the same fate as the Santa Cruzians. There were indeed some who felt that to starve the occupying force into submission was itself unethical, but many more who insisted that it was better than bloodshed.

Two days later, through diplomatic channels, Marshal Gomez's offer was accepted, and arrangements made to remove the islanders to the Mainland Colony.

As Captain Montero-Garcia had foretold, the offer was not extended to the Brigadier or to Sonia. Nor was the Brigadier allowed to confer with the islanders. Adam, however, called a meeting at which he asked all islanders whether they wished to go.

Hardly any of them had a positive wish to go to the Mainland. They were deeply rooted, and their fear of the Outside World had not been reduced by the events of recent months.

'I was born here,' said old Noah Attwood, 'and I've lived here 88 years, if not more. I got a right to die here undisturbed.'

'You been disturbed already, Noah,' Johnny Oakes pointed out. 'You'll have to die wherever you can.'

May Reeves mentioned the rumblings underground—of which there had been several lately—and the smoke that Robert had seen rising from the Cracks. Perhaps, she said, they would all be safer away from the island. This did not in itself make much impression; islanders had lived with such indications for centuries and nothing had happened. In the end the argument that won the day was the argument from hunger. There had been hardship and even near-starvation before, but never anything like this. It would be madness to stay on in these conditions; and the children and old people would be the first to go to the wall. Adam took a vote, and a big majority was in favour of leaving.

Adam had put forward the argument that prevailed. He had felt it his duty to do so. But after the vote he announced that he himself would stay whatever happened. He had been chosen as Reader out of respect for his grandfather, the first Adam Goodall, he said; and everybody knew what the original Adam had replied when invited to leave: 'The day I became Reader, I took this island as I took a wife, and that's for the rest of my time.'

Argument broke loose. There were others, mostly young, who wanted to remain with Adam. Adam's wife, Ellen, was one of these, but was dissuaded; she was six months pregnant. Gerry Baines, the former wireless operator, said he wouldn't go back to be court-martialled. Cyril said Halcyon was a dreadful place but he'd kind of got to like it and he would stay with Gerry and the wireless set. Grandma Molly said she wasn't moving for anybody at her time of life and anyway Cyril and Gerry needed looking after. Tilda said she was staying with Molly, and Robert said he was staying with Cyril and Gerry; everyone supposed, rightly or wrongly, that they were staying for each other's sake. A parental appeal to both of them to think better of it was firmly rejected; and the authority of parents no longer held.

A couple of days later, the launches which had removed the Mother Country soldiers returned, manned by the same Marine NCOs as before, to take the Halcyon islanders on the first stage of their journey to the mainland. A little band of six remained behind to wave them on their way: Adam, Robert, Gerry, Cyril, Tilda and Grandma Molly.

They soon became a family. All six shared Molly's cottage. Old ideas of propriety survived to the extent that the four males slept in one room and the two females in the other. The remaining cottages in the village were promptly occupied by Santa Cruzian sergeants and corporals; the privates were left half-starved and shivering in their tents.

Survival was a full-time occupation for the six. The rations, such as they were, that were doled out to the Santa Cruzians did not come the islanders' way. But they still had a few resources. Molly's goat was concealed in a hollow among the bracken and tussock-grass on a lower slope at the far side of the Peak, and still gave a little milk. On the far side of the island, too, thoughtful islanders had sown a few vegetables during the colonial administration, and so far the Santa Cruzians had not discovered them. Sea birds could be shot with illicitly-retained guns, though most made poor eating. There were shellfish and famine weed to be gathered. On the rare occasions when the gales moderated, the remaining boat, *Shearwater*, could be secretly rowed out after dark, between rocks that were dangerous enough in daylight, returning with luck before dawn with a catch of fish. Then the six feasted.

Nightly after supper, they listened briefly to the Mainland Colony radio; but Cyril had no hope of getting fresh batteries, so listening time was sternly rationed. One night, after a day on which battering gales had kept them at home with little food and nothing to do, the news bulletin was followed by the start of a dance music programme.

'Remember how we danced in the old Meeting-House?' Cyril said to Tilda.

Tilda nodded. She felt a sudden yearning for the past. The Meeting-House didn't even exist any more.

Grandma Molly could read her expression.

'Let's have a bit of music for once,' she said. 'We all need cheering up.'

The radio band played a foxtrot. Tilda's feet tapped; Cyril stood up and gestured to her, and they danced, almost on the spot, in the tiny space in the middle of Molly's living-room while the others sat around. Robert scowled. Cyril thanked Tilda as he relinquished her hand and went to switch off the set.

'One day I really will teach you the tango,' he told her.

Tilda grinned wryly. 'I'll believe that when it happens,' she said.

Sometimes Lorenzo, the private caught by Robert in the hen-house, joined them; and one evening towards mid-winter he brought a friend, Ramon Ortega, who knew enough of their language to give them news from the tents. Hunger was getting worse. Even the officers were rumoured at last to be on short rations. Off-duty soldiers had hunted and shot wild dogs until there were none left on the island; even rats were said to have been killed and eaten. It was rumoured that the body of a man who died had been eaten by his comrades, though Ramon did not believe this.

The privates were still drilled and bullied by their NCOs, though they had barely strength to march, and their resentment was mounting. Most, according to both Lorenzo and Ramon, had no interest in keeping Gomez Island for Santa Cruz; all they wanted was to go home, where they could be warm and dry and, if not well fed, at any rate better fed than here. They would—he added, with the air of one uttering a dangerous heresy—be glad to surrender. But surrender was not the way of Major-General Rodriguez and it was still less the way of Marshal Gomez.

The night after this visit, Gerry and Cyril picked up the mainland radio as usual, and found there was a new story to lead the news bulletin. Brigadier Culpepper and his daughter, it was announced, had been declared by the Santa Cruzian Government to be hostages. If the Mother Country's blockade was not called off in the next seven days, they would be shot.

The Brigadier, who did not have access to a radio, was given the news by Captain Montero-Garcia.

'I am sorry about this, Brigadier,' the captain said. 'It does not please me. It is not the way civilized societies should behave. But I do not need to tell you the predicament my Government is in. This is a desperate measure.'

'So you've changed your tune,' the Brigadier said. 'You admit that your position is desperate. Well, I can tell you at once that the Mother Country won't give up the blockade for the sake of two lives. Nor should it. If your Government means what it says, it has passed a death sentence for no purpose.'

'I'm afraid there is no doubt that Marshal Gomez means what he says. He doesn't place a high price on the lives of individuals.'

'For myself,' said the Brigadier, 'it doesn't matter. I'm an old man, I've had a good life. But Sonia . . . surely he doesn't need to make a hostage of Sonia?'

'I have said, I am deeply sorry.'

'Oh, I don't care,' said Sonia. 'Why should I? They shot Jamie, they may as well shoot *me*.'

The Brigadier was shocked.

'That's a dreadful thing for a young person to say. However fond you were of Jamie, you have to go on living.'

'Doesn't look as if I'll get the chance, does it? If they kill me, I just hope it'll be quick, that's all.'

Chapter 20

FOUR edgy days followed. Each night, the little family in Grandma Molly's cottage gathered round the wireless set to listen to the news bulletin—frequently half-drowned by interference—from the Mainland Colony. Day by day the Mother Country Government declared afresh that it would not be blackmailed. Sections of the press, it seemed, were calling for an immediate invasion of Halcyon, or for the sending of a highly trained special squad to rescue the Brigadier and his daughter from under the noses of the Santa Cruzians. But the Mother Country Government insisted that its strategy was working; moreover, it said, any invasion or rescue attempt would certainly have as its first consequence the immediate execution of the hostages. Meanwhile the League of Nations passed more resolutions calling on both sides to negotiate. Neither took any notice.

The world was, for the moment, aware of Halcyon's existence. But the island itself seemed ominously quiet, apart from some underground rumblings from the volcano. There had been more of these in the past few weeks than for some time past, but the islanders themselves took little notice and the occupying troops had other things on their minds.

Early on the fifth day there was a louder and more prolonged rumble; the ground shook under Grandma Molly's cottage and a couple of pans clattered down from the shelf. Cyril started up in alarm.

'Old Smoky's got a bellyache again,' said Molly. 'It's a bad 'un this time.'

'Might it be going to erupt?' Cyril asked. 'I mean, *really* blow its top?'

'Some day it will. That's what a clever chap said that

came here in the last missionary's time and reckoned to know about such things. Said it might come next year or next century, or maybe not for hundreds of years. We've heard it like this before. It grumbles for a while and then it dies down. Though I must say, I've never heard it as bad as this in all my born days.'

Adam looked thoughtful, but said nothing. Robert said, 'Me and Cyril's going over to Black Bay to collect famine weed today. We'll go past the Cracks.'

This called for an uphill walk from the village and past a secondary crater of the Peak. Robert and Cyril stood looking at the Cracks. They'd become larger since Robert was there with Peter Willett and Sonia, and the wisp of smoke was thicker. There was old lava all around them from minor eruptions of the past, but there was also a spill of lava that looked recently cooled, and the vegetation around was scorched. As they peered, a sound like the clearing of a huge throat came from below, and was followed by a belch of hot smoke and steam, with an overpowering stench. Some small stones and grit flew into the air. Robert and Cyril ran choking down the hill. They heard but didn't see a gurgling spew of fresh lava. Then everything subsided; the smoke cloud drifted away and there was just the wisp as before.

Robert said, 'It's nothing. Often happens.' But Cyril was shaken.

'What if it's going to be the big one next?' he asked.

'It won't be. We know Old Smoky. Makes a lot of fuss, but that's all.'

Cyril said hopefully, 'I expect the Cracks are a kind of safety-valve, and it'd be more dangerous if the stuff was all bottled up.'

'Maybe,' said Robert.

'We should tell Adam what we've seen.'

'All right. But come on, we want to get to Black Bay and back by dinner.'

They were back at Grandma Molly's cottage around midday, with sacks of the barely-edible seaweed. But what they saw and heard in the village put thoughts of Old Smoky out of their minds. From the front of the house, Adam, Molly and the others were watching a great hustling and shoving of men in the familiar dirty olive-green Santa Cruzian uniforms. A crowd of soldiers was flowing down from the village and out of the tented camp, and coalescing in the space before the new makeshift officers' quarters. There was angry shouting; there were cries of pain and protest as more and more men pushed forward from behind and those in front were trapped for lack of space. The shouts rose to a roar. Then somebody, apparently an officer, was addressing the men from behind a shield. They were howling him down. Stones were thrown. The crowd surged forward.

And then the shooting, the rattle of submachine guns, the falling bodies in front, the mass of the crowd turning tail, fleeing. The cottages filling with men, forcing their way in, getting out of the line of fire; others darting behind houses, others again running away towards the vegetable patches or round the mountainside. And then the only sounds the shouting of orders and the groans of wounded men.

Grandma Molly said grimly to Tilda, 'Come on, love. They need us again.'

But they were turned back at once. The Santa Cruzian authorities had no intention of letting outsiders see the deaths and injuries inflicted on their own men. Lorenzo and Ramon came to the cottage during the evening, unhurt but angry and depressed, and offered a guess that twenty had been killed and about fifty injured. Ramon added sourly, 'A great victory for the officers and NCOs.'

'What was it?' Adam asked. 'A mutiny?'

Ramon shook his head. 'Not mutiny. The men hungry, they want food. An officer tell them, no food. They say, officers have food. The officer say, not true, officers hungry also. Then some men at front of crowd shout,

"Surrender island, let us go home." And others push forward, officers think they are attacking, give orders to fire.'

'And what happens now?' Adam asked. 'Will the men try again?'

'No. What good? They kill more of us, that's all. No, I tell you what happen, Adam. One of three things. Your country lift blockade. Or we surrender. Or we all die of starvation.'

The Brigadier heard the shots and the shouting.

'What was all that about?' he asked Captain Montero-Garcia, when the captain came to see him that evening.

'It was nothing. A little minor difficulty with trouble-making elements. One comes across them from time to time.'

'It sounded like a lot of noise for a little minor difficulty.'

The captain let this pass.

'Brigadier,' he said, 'I have a proposal to put to you. It comes from Major-General Rodriguez himself. He points out that it will be to your advantage to respond favourably.'

The Brigadier was on his guard at once.

'Go on,' he said warily.

'General Rodriguez wishes you to make a broadcast.'

'A broadcast? To whom?'

'To the world, Brigadier, no less. He would like the world to hear your words. He wishes you to appeal to your own Government to lift the blockade, and thus save the lives of yourself and Miss Culpepper.'

'Absolutely not,' said the Brigadier. 'I'm surprised you even bother to ask me. I shall do no such thing. Nor would there be any benefit to you if I did. I can tell you at once that my Government would ignore such an appeal. The Mother Country doesn't give in to blackmail.'

'So it keeps telling us. But there would be a considerable impact on world opinion. General Rodriguez believes that the callousness of your Government would be clear to all.'

'I've told you,' said the Brigadier. 'The answer is No. There is no point in discussing the matter.'

'Please hear me out,' said Montero-Garcia. 'I told you it would be to your advantage to respond favourably. You see, my dear Brigadier, if you would agree to record such a broadcast—the General has it in mind to transmit it tomorrow night—we would release your daughter at once. Unconditionally, without regard to whether the broadcast had the desired effect or not, Miss Culpepper would go free. There is a little group of your compatriots still in the village, and we would have her escorted to join them. Your Government could arrange for her to leave the island with a safe conduct should she wish to do so; it would be for her to decide.'

The Brigadier was on the point of exploding in anger. Then, as the meaning of the captain's words sank in, he controlled himself.

'You mean,' he said in a slow, level tone, 'I can save my daughter's life by consenting to make this appeal?'

'Precisely.'

'It's a filthy tactic.'

'To be frank, Brigadier, it does not appeal to me. But we are at war, and war is a filthy business. Some would say that starving us out is itself a filthy tactic.'

'I wouldn't dream of making such a broadcast to save my own life,' the Brigadier said.

'Of course not. That is the attitude we would expect from a man of your calibre. But to save your daughter's life, sir—is not that a different matter?'

The Brigadier said, 'Even if I were willing to agree to your proposal, how could I trust your General to honour it?'

'The General gives you his word, sir. The word of an officer and a gentleman. You have my own word also. Is that acceptable to you?'

The Brigadier had formed a view of General Rodriguez, as he had of Captain Montero-Garcia. He did not like the

General and was wary of the captain, but he did not think their cherished honour would allow them to break a word given in such circumstances.

'Yes,' he said reluctantly, 'that is acceptable, damn you. But your proposal sticks in my throat.'

'You have my sympathy,' said the captain. 'It is a difficult decision. I am glad I do not have to make it myself. I suggest you take a walk in the garden and consider it. I'm afraid I cannot give you long. I will come back later for your answer.'

'You will have your answer within the hour,' said the Brigadier.

'You gotta leave here, honey,' Sergeant Jimenez told Sonia Culpepper. 'And no, you can't see your pop before you go. He don't want to see you.'

'He doesn't want to see me?' said Sonia. 'That's ridiculous. He *always* wants to see me.'

'Not this time he don't. I don't know why. It's his own choice. He says he won't see you.'

'And they're releasing me but not him? Why?'

'I tell you, I don't know. Nobody don't tell me nothing. All I know is, you're to go free, and you can have a safe conduct to leave. Let me know about it when you've talked to your folks on the island. If I was you I'd be off like a shot. Anyway, I gotta deliver you to the end cottage, where Grandma Molly lives . . . Gee, that Grandma Molly is some lady. The boys all think she's the greatest. Pity they sent her home from the hospital. It's the brass hats again. Those guys don't know when they got a good thing . . . And that goes for you, too, sweetie. You and me should get together some time.'

'Oh, bugger off!' said Sonia.

Brigadier Culpepper sat in his room in the bungalow. A guard lounged in the doorway. After an hour's anguish, the

Brigadier had given his answer to Captain Montero-Garcia, who had received it without a word. He had recorded a broadcast. It was as toneless and impersonal as he could make it, but there had been no disguising its content. It was an appeal to the Mother Country Government to lift the blockade of Halcyon and, in effect, relinquish the colony. Now he was alone with his thoughts.

I couldn't face Sonia after doing that. And I couldn't have asked her before I did it. She'd never have let me make such a deal. But if I'd refused we'd both have been shot. Now it's only me. I shall lose maybe ten years of life. That's nothing. She'd have lost fifty or sixty. She'd have paid the price for my conscience.

But to do such a thing to my country . . . to be a puppet for such as Marshal Gomez. The contempt they will have for me back home; and, even worse, the sorrow. The friends and colleagues of years who will say to each other, 'I wouldn't have thought it of old Culpepper' or, 'Henry was a brave man in the War, but now . . . ' The anguish it will cause to Daphne.

And it will cost the Mother Country something. They won't turn aside, of course, but the days are gone when they didn't have to care what the world thought. They care about world opinion now. And the world will find them heartless. The world has tears to shed for an old man and a pretty girl. More perhaps than for a few thousand wretched Santa Cruzian conscripts.

I owe the Mother Country everything. Born and brought up there, married there, a soldier in her Army, an administrator in a dozen Colonies. Loyalty to her has been the guiding principle of my life. And now I do this to her.

I put my daughter before my country, that's the plain truth. And I would do it again. Tomorrow night the appeal I recorded will go out. I may be forgiven by the Government, by my wife, by my old friends. They will say they understand. But I shall die disgraced.

Chapter 21

WHEN Sonia arrived at the cottage, Molly and Tilda were still complaining about being sent away from the scene of the massacre.

'They say we're the enemy!' said Tilda crossly. 'But we went there to save folk, not to kill them.'

'And those poor lads!' said Molly. She was in a high state of indignation. 'Not much more than children, some of them. If their mothers could see what's happening to them here . . . It makes my heart bleed.'

Sonia's arrival was a diversion. Molly and Tilda embraced her. Sonia told them of her release.

'They say I can leave the island,' she said. 'But I'm not going until I know what's happened to my father.' She was distressed. 'I don't know why they've let me go or anything. I feel there's something nasty somewhere.'

'You look thinner, love,' said Molly.

Sonia looked around the group.

'*Everyone* looks thinner,' she said. 'What did you have for supper?'

'Seaweed soup,' said Cyril.

'Golly! . . . Was it nice?'

'No, it was horrible.'

'What did *you* have, Sonia?' Adam asked.

'Paella, in the officers' mess. Not too good and not much of it. But better than your soup, I should think.'

'Some of those poor lads out there been eating *rats*!' said Molly.

'It's nearly time for the news,' Cyril said.

He tuned the wireless. Through the crackles came the bulletin from the Mainland Colony. Halcyon had slipped from top place. There were rumours of unrest among the

Santa Cruzian troops, said the bulletin, but these were not taken seriously. Meanwhile, there was worldwide disapproval of the death threat hanging over Brigadier Culpepper, but there were no new developments, and it looked as if he faced execution in two days' time.

Cyril turned off the set as soon as the item was over. When the present battery was finished, he would have no more.

'We got to do something about the poor old Brig,' he said.

There was a long roll of sound from under their feet. The cottage windows rattled. Molly and Adam looked at each other.

'There's been too many of those lately,' said Molly grimly. 'And I never knew one like that before. I can feel in my bones, something's going to happen one of these days.'

'I hate to say it,' Adam said, 'but I think we should get out of here.'

Everyone stared.

'You've always said you wouldn't leave for anyone or anything,' Cyril reminded him.

'That's right. But I'm not crazy. We're no good to anyone dead. If we don't get killed by the other side, we'll be starved to death by our own. And I'm getting scared by Old Smoky. What if this time it really does blow up? It's my view as Reader that we should withdraw as soon as possible. Maybe with luck we'll be able to come back and start again later.'

'Withdraw?' Cyril said. 'Where to?'

Molly, Tilda and Robert all knew.

'Kingfisher!' said Tilda and Robert simultaneously.

'That's it. We still have one boat. The weather's calm—well, fairly calm—and it looks set for a while. We can make it. Seven of us can last through the winter on Kingfisher.'

'Seven?' said Sonia. 'You're counting me?'

'Of course. If you want to come.'

'And abandon my father?'

There was a pause.

'He'll be dead in a few days' time, most like,' said Robert tactlessly.

Adam said, 'I wish there was something we could do about him. I got quite fond of the old boy, even if he did get everything wrong, begging your pardon, Sonia.'

'I know he got things wrong,' said Sonia, 'but *I'm* fond of the old boy, too, seeing he's my dad. But we were both under guard twenty-four hours a day, and I expect he still is. The Santa Cruzians won't listen to us. What can we do?'

Cyril had gone to the window.

'There's a crack running from the corner of this window,' he said. 'I reckon it's from the shaking we just had.' And then, 'Somebody's coming. It's that fellow Montero-Whatnot. What does *he* want?'

Adam opened the door. Montero-Garcia was immaculate as ever in well-pressed uniform with shining shoes and polished Sam Browne belt; but for the first time there was something nervous about his expression.

'Miss Culpepper is there?' he enquired.

'Yes.' Adam turned to Sonia. 'Do you want to see him?'

'Of course I do. Tell him to come in.'

Montero-Garcia bowed and clicked his heels.

'Never mind that nonsense,' Sonia said roughly. 'Tell me about my father.'

'Your father is well. He has recorded a broadcast appeal to your Government to lift the blockade. He did so to save your life. We said we would release you, and we have done so. For a reason which will emerge in a moment, I reserved it to myself to inform you.'

Sonia said slowly, 'It won't work, you know.'

Montero-Garcia said, 'Of course it will not. I told Rodriguez so, and he told Marshal Gomez, but they insisted. The episode distressed me deeply. Essentially it is a propaganda exercise. It did, however, serve one useful purpose. You, at least, Miss Culpepper, are free.'

'I seem to be a survivor,' said Sonia bitterly.

'It is a great thing to be a survivor. Many of us Santa

Cruzians have been asking ourselves how *we* can survive. The truth is that on this island we have no hope. Your Government will not call off the blockade. No supplies are now getting through. Either they will starve us out or they will soften us up and then *wipe* us out. The fool Gomez has bitten off more than he can chew, and we are paying for it.'

'Do you expect me to sympathize?' Sonia asked.

'No, but I hope you will listen. I respect and admire your father. I think with your help it may be possible to rescue him.'

There was a startled silence.

'You mean *you* want to rescue the Brig?' asked Cyril incredulously.

'I mean precisely that.'

Adam said, 'What about your loyalty to your own side?'

'My loyalty is to my country. I no longer have loyalty to Gomez; he has forfeited it. It is in the interest of Santa Cruz for him to fail.' Montero-Garcia smiled. 'And I am not entirely without self-interest. It would not be unwelcome to me to earn the gratitude of your country. A senior diplomatic post in your capital has long been my dream. Sooner or later there will be a new regime in Santa Cruz, and my dream could be realized.'

'And you really think you could rescue the Brigadier?' Adam asked.

'I think so. I am in charge of him. Those who guard him are my subordinates. If I choose my time, towards the end of the night shift, I can send the guard off duty and take over myself until the arrival of his replacement. Then, with luck, I can walk straight out of the bungalow with the Brigadier. A greater difficulty is to get him off the island. You are not, I suppose, in contact with your country's forces in the southern ocean?'

'No,' said Adam. 'When we rejected the offer to leave, they left us to our own devices. We haven't a wireless transmitter. But . . . ' He hesitated a moment, uncertain whether Montero-Garcia was to be trusted, then decided to risk it. 'We have a boat. And I was saying only a few minutes ago that I think it's time for us to go.'

'Where is your boat?'

'It's at the other side of the island. Five miles away across country, with no road and a steep climb down when you get there. And it's a dangerous coast.'

'Could it be brought round to this side? Somewhere near the Brigadier's house?'

'Last time we brought boats round, four men were drowned. And we'd have to do it at night, which is riskier still. You're asking a lot of us. I suppose with luck we could manage it. But we couldn't bring the boat to Home Beach, because of the invasion defences. Your people guard that beach all the time.'

Robert said, 'Billygoat Gulch is the nearest safe landing. Three miles from the village, round the headland and past the wireless station.'

'I can't get the Brigadier as far as that,' said Montero-Garcia. 'There won't be time.'

'The motor car!' said Cyril. 'What about the motor car?'

'Yes, the motor car!' said Robert, suddenly excited. 'The Brig and me hid it in a cave just under the cliff, not far from his house.'

'And I can drive!' said Cyril. 'If he can get down the cliff to the car, I'll *drive* him to the boat!'

'Trouble is,' Robert said, 'the Brig nearly killed himself getting up that cliff, and getting down's much worse. He'd never make it.'

There was silence for a while. Then Robert remembered.

'The blowhole!' he said. 'It's in the next cave, almost. If we could get him to the top of it . . .'

Grandma Molly said, 'I remember when the sea used to shoot up through that blowhole every high tide, as tall as a tree. It was before your time, Adam. When the pressure came off, it never blew again. But it was still a dangerous place. Your grandad had a boulder rolled over it.'

'The boulder can be moved,' Robert said. 'Me and some lads done it once, larking about. We got down into the cave below quite easy. I reckon with a bit of help the Brig could do it.'

'Then have we not the makings of a plan?' asked Montero-Garcia.

Adam said cautiously, 'Suppose for a moment we could get the boat to the right place and the Brigadier into it, the fact is that *Shearwater* is a leaky old tub. There are seven of us, and with you and the Brigadier there'd be nine. A full load. If the weather turned nasty we'd be in trouble. And what if a Santa Cruzian vessel came after us?'

'The seas round here are bristling with your country's ships,' said Montero-Garcia, 'as we know to our cost. It is far more likely that one of *them* would pick us up.'

'We'll be making for Kingfisher,' said Adam, 'if we decide to go ahead. Who's in favour of trying it?'

Every hand went up.

'Excellent,' said Montero-Garcia. 'Then we must work out a detailed plan. The timing will be like that of a military operation. I hope you have watches.'

'We have three among the six of us,' Adam said.

'That will be just enough. Now, let us all put our heads together.'

As Montero-Garcia spoke, there was another prolonged rumble underground.

'I don't know which is a bigger threat to Halcyon,' said Adam, 'the war or the volcano. But for the moment our job is to survive.'

It was a couple of hours until dawn: an overcast sky, as dark as you ever saw on Halcyon. The four who were to crew the boat moved toward the west coast along sheep-tracks between rough grass and scrub: Adam leading, then Robert, then Gerry, then Tilda. The sea could be heard long before they reached the clifftop. It was always rough here: waves crashed against a coast of black jagged rock, and the prevailing westerlies were behind them. No one but an islander would have thought it possible to bring in a boat anywhere along here, or, having done so, to get it out again. But *Shearwater* was there, far below them, upturned above the water-line in a small stony bay.

Gerry didn't say a word, but Tilda could sense that he was afraid of the descent. She pressed his hand reassuringly, then went down alongside him, helping him find handholds and footholds. Near the bottom he became more confident and began to manage by himself; and this led almost to disaster, for he lost his grip and fell the last few feet to land with jarring impact on the shelf of flat stones that lined the sea's edge. He picked himself up, apparently unhurt, and joined the others; they turned the boat over and pushed it across slabby rocks to the water.

The tide was on the ebb. Beside the sea it was never quite dark, and the size of incoming waves could be gauged. The four were poised ready, and when Adam shouted 'Now!' they leaped aboard and were away, rowing fiercely. They had to be off the rocky shelf before the next big wave came in. At once they were drenched in spray; but Adam had judged the launch well. The lull between waves lasted long enough, and the next one, though carrying them back towards the rocks, left them clear. They rowed on at full stretch, unable to ease up until at last, with the ebb-tide in their favour, they were a safe distance from the coast and could head south and round the uninhabited end of the island.

'You all right, Gerry?' Tilda called.

'Yes, fine,' Gerry answered. 'I'll have some spectacular bruises by tomorrow, that's all.'

They passed headland after headland, gulch after gulch, with Gerry clearly weakening and Tilda having to ease up to match him at the other side; Adam and Robert pulled strongly and steadily away. And they were round South Point and heading north along the eastern coast of Halcyon. It was another succession of headlands and gulches, and in the dark it wasn't easy to tell one from another; but Adam and Robert knew them all. Eventually Adam shouted, 'Billygoat next!' and they were pulling inshore, beaching the boat in a safe, sandy inlet. Adam looked at his watch and said, 'Our timing's right. Keep your fingers crossed.'

Molly, Sonia, and Cyril were waiting for them. Adam said, 'Right. You know what happens now. Robert and Cyril and I walk to Skull Cave and get the car ready, Molly and Sonia join the boat crew. Three women in a crew of four . . .'

Molly said, 'What you worrying about, Adam? Think we can't manage it?'

Adam looked at Molly, tough and muscular for all her seventy years, and at Tilda, tough and muscular and young as well, and was reassured. A crew that included them would cope.

Molly, assuming command of the boat, said, 'Seawater out, drinking water in'; and while two of the crew baled out the boat the other two put cans and bottles of water aboard. They put such food as they had on board, too. It was pathetically little. Adam, Robert and Cyril set out on foot across the sand.

The Brigadier had slept poorly for several nights. He had often been under fire in the Great War and had seen many men die; but it was easier to face a risk, however great, than a death sentence, and he now knew fear as he had not known it before. Additionally, he worried about the futures of his wife and daughter. But he was uneasily asleep when Captain Montero-Garcia came into his room and gently shook his shoulder.

'Who is it?' he demanded.

'It is I. Montero-Garcia.'

'What do you want now? At this time of night?' The Brigadier's tone was hostile; then an obvious thought occurred to him and he couldn't keep the note of hope from his voice. 'Don't say I'm getting a reprieve?'

'I'm afraid not. Your Government has done nothing to prevent your execution.'

'Then why are you here?'

'Please keep your voice down, Brigadier. Your daughter is free. Would you like to join her?'

'What do you mean?'

'I may be able to achieve what your Government cannot.'

'I don't understand you.'

'I am about to try to help you escape.'

'*You*? I don't believe it.'

'It's true.'

'But why?'

'Because, Brigadier, I like and admire you. My admiration has grown during your imprisonment. It is perhaps a kind of love. You had better believe me. And we must move fast.'

'This is some sort of trick.'

'I assure you it isn't. I have got rid of the guard, but we shall not have long. Get yourself dressed, quickly, and come with me. When I tell you, you must run for it. With luck we shall get away. Without luck we shall be killed. Come.'

Montero-Garcia had a bunch of keys. He unlocked the door of the room, then the side door of the bungalow, looked out cautiously, and signalled to the Brigadier to follow. They crossed the garden; with another key Montero-Garcia opened the gate. There was no sign of activity.

'Now!' he said. 'Run for your life!' He raced ahead of the Brigadier towards the cliff, then veered a little to the right. There was a figure ahead in the gloom. Robert. And there was the boulder.

'We moved it!' Robert hissed.

Where the boulder had stood was a hole. Montero-Garcia halted, motioned to Culpepper to go first. The Brigadier hesitated for a moment on the brink. From below someone grabbed his ankles, and down he went, feet first. The sky disappeared. He was sliding in the dark down an earthy slope. He came to a stop, on his back, half-suffocated. Then he was sliding again, then dropping, then being caught in someone's arms. He was in a cave. There was a little light from a lamp. There were people. Adam and Cyril. They were holding him up. He was shaken, almost collapsing. He managed with an effort to stand on his own feet. Robert landed beside him in a shower of earth, and a moment later came Montero-Garcia.

'Magnificent!' Montero-Garcia said. 'Now, on our way! Swiftly!'

The Brigadier, shaken, didn't know where he was or what was happening. They were hurrying him in near-darkness through a rough natural tunnel: now over ridges of pebbles, now through patches of shallow water, now round obstructions. At last there was a half-circle of grey outdoor light ahead. There was a sound, a loud continuous sound that echoed from a roof and walls all round. The light was increasing. The sound came from a machine. The motor car, canvas hood rolled back, was waiting, with engine running. Cyril leaped into the driving-seat. The Brigadier was bundled in beside Cyril; Adam, Robert and Montero jumped in behind. The motor car was speeding away along the beach, over dry black sand, through pools, round rocks.

The sky was lighter now. The sea looked mercifully calm. Kingfisher could be seen, a small dark shape on a dawn-pink horizon. Then from the cliff came bursts of automatic fire, aimed at them. Bullets made little spurts of black sand. But the car was a moving target and the light poor; there were no hits. Foot hard down, Cyril was pressing on, skirting obstacles, taking risk after risk, getting away with it.

Round the headland, waiting for them, was *Shearwater*: crazy, unseaworthy, nailed together from ancient wreckage, patched and patched and patched again. The boat was afloat now, with water between it and the shore, the three women and Gerry at the oars. Cyril drove the car straight towards it, deeper into the water until the engine died and the occupants were struggling out, wading knee-high then thigh-high, then dragged over the gunwales; the boat almost capsizing but righting itself, low in the water. Adam and Robert were grabbing the fifth and sixth oars, the Brigadier dazed in the stern, Cyril crawling to the bow and picking up in his arms, miraculously dry and unharmed, the wireless set.

Chapter 22

As the islanders rowed away, there was an ear-shattering explosion behind them that might have been the crack of doom. It was followed by a long roll as of thunder. The lower side of the Peak, overhanging the village, peeled away, hung briefly in the air intact, then crashed down in a torrent of boulders and rubble. From behind it, chunks of rock and red-hot cinder were thrown up, hurled over land and hissing sea. Two rocks fell alarmingly close. The sky was suddenly dark again, but it was a darkness lit by a red glow and an occasional flaring of fire. There were the intermittent long-drawn-out roars of further landslides. A series of waves tossed the rickety old boat around, and water poured in over precariously low gunwales. Cyril and Montero baled furiously as the rowers pulled away; and *Shearwater* stayed afloat.

A motor launch with searchlight came racing out from Home Beach and seemed to cast about in search of the island boat. But the beam never picked it up, and the launch soon disappeared from view.

There was argument over what had happened to it. Adam thought the Santa Cruzians had run it on a rock; Robert suggested that it had been holed by a flying boulder; the Brigadier thought it had given up the search and returned to what must now be a scene of devastation. With no further sign of pursuit, Adam decided to risk raising a sail; but the heavily loaded boat still had to be helped along by muscle-power.

An hour or two later, when *Shearwater* was far offshore, the Cracks burst open and magma spewed out to form a new cone on the slope of the Peak. Its fire coloured luridly the undersides of clouds of smoke; great showers of red-hot fragments were thrown into the air and glowing lava flowed towards the village and beaches. A final, tidal wave lifted the boat high, threatened to swamp it instantly, then passed beneath it and rolled on.

Later still, exhausted and soaked to the skin, the boat crew saw that the growing, still-glowing cone had put a new jagged edge to the profile of the Peak, while above it hung a great mushroom-cloud of smoke.

Chapter 23

*T*HE escaping party never reached Kingfisher. A Mother Country destroyer picked them up and landed them a few days later in the Mainland Colony.

The day after the eruption, with the new cone still throwing up rocks and spilling lava, and an unknown number of lives already lost, the Santa Cruzian commander surrendered. The day after that, Marshal Gomez was overthrown, and executed by a firing squad. Major-General Rodriguez shot himself. The Mother Country blockade turned overnight into a rescue action.

Halcyon made front-page headlines for another week. The Brigadier, his daughter and Captain Montero-Garcia were flown by stages to the Mother Country and featured in all the newspapers: it was one of the world's great real-life escape stories, they said. The islanders' part in it interested them less than those of the Great War hero, the pretty daughter and the handsome captain. Then came news of a famine in Asia, a diplomatic crisis in Europe, an air crash in America, a great international fraud; and there were royal families, sex scandals, sporting triumphs, crimes and disputes and disasters and all the routine astonishments that caught the attention of the world. Interest in Halcyon waned as quickly as it had grown.

Esteban Montero-Garcia resigned his commission and became Santa Cruzian Ambassador to the Mother Country. No one ever knew whether he was a self-seeking traitor or a man of conscience who had served a higher cause than patriotism. Probably he himself didn't know.

Most of the islanders were found homes and jobs in the Mainland Colony and were fêted and made much of until they ceased to be a novelty. Then they became a nuisance.

They wanted to go home. They asked again and again. They saved up their earnings and put them in a pooled bank account to buy what they'd need when they returned.

The Department for the Colonies resisted. It didn't want them to go home. It had had enough of Halcyon, and would have preferred to write it off. The Mother Country had withdrawn its forces from the region. Though the volcano had subsided, the island was said to be devastated and uninhabitable. But two or three ships sent boats ashore and reported that it was as habitable as it had ever been, if one didn't mind taking the risk of further eruptions.

Brigadier Culpepper's appeal for an end to the blockade had never been transmitted, and no one ever knew about it. The recording disappeared; sometimes he had nightmares in which it came to light. His conscience remained uneasy, and he was also unhappy about the mistakes he felt he'd made as Commissioner for Halcyon. But he went on living; there was work for him to do. Back in the Mother Country, he campaigned untiringly for the islanders' right to return. In this he was helped by his wife, his daughter, and his daughter's fiancé, Lieutenant Peter Willett.

In the end it was agreed that an advance party of islanders should go to Halcyon to decide for themselves, and if they found survival would be possible the Mother Country would help them by providing breeding livestock and materials for repairing houses and building new boats. After that it would wash its hands of them, which was what they wanted. The Brigadier resigned his post as Commissioner and successfully recommended an unpaid Commissioner to succeed him: Mr Adam Goodall. As this would not cost anything, the Colonial Administration had no objection.

Fifteen months after the eruption, the advance party landed on Halcyon from a naval frigate. Adam led it. With him went Johnny and Lizzie Oakes, George Wilde and Tilda, Robert and Cyril and Gerry, and (on her own emphatic insistence) Grandma Molly. It was spring. They had a dinghy with oars and sail, some tools and timber, spades and forks and seed potatoes, and food for a month. They found the Home Beach strewn with rocks, lumps of hardened lava, and torn and spilling sandbags from the Santa Cruzian defences. A little smoke still rose from the new crater. But the Halcyon breeze blew fresh, bearing smells of sea and seaweed rather than sulphur. The flatland was green again, and the cliffs as thick as ever with nesting sea birds.

The lava had stopped at the edge of the village. In one of the cottages there were people living: three Santa Cruzian deserters, who had stayed behind and survived mainly by scavenging. One of them was Ramon, whom they knew already and who spoke some of their language. Was there —Ramon asked—room for them in the community?

Adam thought there was. Ever since the loss of *Kittiwake*, three years before the invasions, there'd been a shortage of men. 'And it's the way we live,' he told them, 'absorbing incomers. They come here, and sometimes they like it. Then they stay, like Cyril and Gerry. And you. So it goes on. I guess it always will.'

The village wasn't in as bad a state as they'd feared. A couple of houses were cracked open or leaning at crazy angles, but the rest could be repaired without too much trouble, though volcanic dust lay over everything. Only the Meeting-House, destroyed by a shell during the bombardment, was totally beyond rescue.

The advance party worked hard. Tilda was joyful at being back, opening heart and lungs to Halcyon, drinking the fresh island breeze, loving to see the sea birds dip and wheel above, knowing it was where she belonged. No one, man or woman, claimed any privileges. When the sea was calm there was fishing from the dinghy, which was what they all liked best to do; and all took their turn. All climbed on the cliffs to gather eggs, except Cyril, who suffered from vertigo and got a temporary job as language teacher to the Santa Cruzians. Women and men alike laboured with their hands, repairing cottages, clearing the overgrown vegetable patches, digging, planting potatoes for when the others came.

There was little they could do about the Meeting-House. They were too few in number and had not the materials. When the main body of islanders arrived, they would build a new Meeting-House. Shortly before the others were due, the little party got together to clear the dust and debris that lay thickly over the site. The floor was pitted and scarred, but not as bad as it might have been. In a corner, crushed beyond repair, they found the gramophone, surrounded by fragments of broken record. They all looked at it ruefully.

'We'll buy a new one on the mainland with some of the money we've saved,' Adam said. 'And a wireless set, or two or three. And maybe a couple of bicycles, who knows?'

Everyone was awed. Gramophones, wireless sets, bicycles: the century was catching up with them. They liked the century quite well, at a distance.

Cyril was looking at the newly-brushed floor.

'Come on!' he said to Tilda. 'We can do without the gramophone.'

He sang, in a light tenor, a popular song of the year before. In the roofless ruin, with sky above them, and stepping clear of the worst bits of floor, they danced a foxtrot. When he finished singing the lyric, Cyril began again, softly, his voice close to her ear. Tilda felt she could dance as well as she could climb, as she could sail a boat or swim or milk a goat or do anything she wanted to do; she was full of strength and confidence; she was happy, happy, happy.

Robert watched her, a thoughtful look on his face.

'That's enough for now!' said Adam. 'There's work to be done!'

Cyril said to Tilda, 'One of these days I'll teach you the tango.'

Tilda laughed until she cried. Then they all went on working.

Later, after supper, Robert took Tilda to walk in the Dell. She was a little sleepy, but not unwilling.

'I been thinking,' Robert said. 'I been thinking. I know we're intended, but if you don't really want me you don't have to have me. I can take a trip to the mainland some time and find a girl there.'

'I expect you can,' Tilda said. 'I seen one or two of them looking interested.'

'Not that I wouldn't rather have you. I would. But if it's *him* you really want, you can have him.'

'Robert,' said Tilda, 'being intended wouldn't make me marry you, whatever anyone said. You know it wouldn't.'

'Yes, I know,' said Robert glumly.

'But it wouldn't stop me, either. Now see if you can make a better job of kissing me than you did before.'

Robert took his time and made a better job of it.

Tilda said appreciatively, 'That was good. You know, I really do like you, Robert. I *might* wed you. In fact I dare say I *will*, in time. But whatever happens, whether I marry you or not . . . '

A pause.

'Well, what?'

'I'll make sure Cyril teaches me the tango.'